A CROWN OF IMP
AND BONE

IMP SERIES
BOOK 12

DEBRA DUNBAR

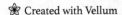 Created with Vellum

1

I stood in front of an interdimensional rift, using my hands to show its outline to Gregory. It was the fifth one we'd closed today, and I would bet my Corvette that it would be back in place within the next twenty-four hours.

"All we're doing is inconveniencing these motherfuckers," I said as the angel stepped forward.

"Are you suggesting we just do nothing?" Gregory snapped.

He was grumpy. The fae were coming through passages and snatching up humans. Even the elves hadn't been this brazen in their kidnappings. And the handful of angels Gregory sent to guard these gateways and thwart them were either missing or found dead—which was why he'd decided the two of us needed to close the gateways. Ourselves. Every two days for probably the rest of our lives.

It sucked. Especially since my Epic Wedding was in three months. Would we be teleporting around with this archangel to close fae portals on our wedding day? On our honeymoon? I bristled at the thought. These fae were fucking with my wedding plans, which pissed me off far more than them snatching humans.

"What I'm suggesting is that we take an army through one of the gates and teach these dickwads a lesson," I grumbled. "And that we do it soon. I need this resolved in the next ninety days."

Ninety days. *Before* our wedding.

Nyalla was distraught about the humans being kidnapped by the fae, though, which meant I at least had to appear sympathetic toward their plight and not just focused on my nuptials. Nyalla had spent the first eighteen years of her life as a changeling slave to the elves in Hel. Now she was not only the human advisor to the Ruling Council on affairs pertaining to humans, but she also headed the committee that was in charge of the elven integration into the human world.

She was upset about the fae swooping in from Aerie and kidnapping humans. And she'd insisted that I should be upset as well. It was another reason for us to attack these motherfuckers. Temporarily closing these gateways wouldn't be enough to even slow down the tide of human kidnappings, we needed to do more—a whole lot more.

I liked to pretend I didn't care, but when Nyalla was unhappy, I was unhappy. She was like a daughter to me. All it took was an expression of disappointment in those blue eyes of hers and I was off to move heaven and earth. Or in this case, kill fairies.

"Our strength and abilities would be severely hindered in Aerie," Gregory informed me. "Most of the angelic host is just beginning to adapt to their corporeal forms, asking them to fight in a physical realm where they would need to rely on physical weapons wouldn't deliver the result you're hoping for, Cockroach."

"Well, we have to do something," I snapped, just as grumpy as he was. "Just closing their portals isn't enough. If we can't send an army of angels to teach them the error of their ways, then we need to...I don't know, send an army of demons who are used to fighting in corporeal form."

"They will have little more than human fighting skills," Gregory reminded me as he closed the fae gateway. "Most of their demonic abilities will be lessened or non-existent in Aerie while the fae will have their full magical powers."

"We can't just close their portals for all eternity," I huffed.

"It takes a lot of power for them to create six gateways every two days—so much power that I'm sure they'll eventually give up," he said, a tinge of doubt in his voice.

With a flash of light and a spin of vertigo that was still a bit disorienting, we'd left Denmark and were in the south of Spain.

Once I'd regained my balance, I turned around to look for the gateway. It was a quarter mile away from where it had been located two days ago. The portals were always in the same general areas in Ireland, Denmark, Wales, Scotland, Spain, and Finland, and there were always six of them. If I'd been the fae in charge of this, I would have randomized their terminus here in the human world, ensuring it would take weeks or even months for us to find them, but the fae were either not so creative, or they lacked the ability to put the portals anywhere but in these six general spots.

"That fairy from Alaska said all this is because of a broken contract, and that it's only going to get worse," I said as I walked toward the interdimensional rift glowing in the distance.

"It is. And it probably will," he grumbled, following me.

I winced, because this broken contract had to do with

some jewelry my adoptive son had innocently stolen from Aerie. Lux had misunderstood his role as a ring-bearer in Amber and Irix's wedding and had amassed quite the collection of pilfered rings—many of them belonging to powerful magical beings. I'd returned most of them, but had held on to a few. And I was undecided about taking this particular one back. If a stolen ring had broken a ten-thousand-year-old contract between the fae and the angels, then it might not be wise to give it back without some sort of negotiation first.

As for the other two rings...well, the one on my left hand was my engagement ring, and the witchy hag it belonged to was sort of leasing it to me. The other one belonged in Aaru. I had no way of returning that one since we were all presently banished.

No one besides a select few on the Ruling Council knew I was responsible for the angels being banished from Aaru, and no one but me, Gregory, and Nyalla knew Lux was responsible for this current mess.

"What were the details of this contract?" I asked, thinking that if I was in a bargaining position, I could maybe reinstate the terms in return for the ring.

The archangel sighed, running a hand through his chestnut-colored curls. "We haven't been at peace with the fae since we assisted the elves in leaving Aerie. Two and a half million years ago, before the war that split the angelic host, we decided that the humans would be the ones to receive the angelic gifts and be ushered into a holy evolution. The fae discovered this and sometime after the war in Aaru, they began to subvert our efforts. At first we thought the demons were responsible, but as the fae began to increase their stealing of humans, we realized they were to blame."

I grumbled and glared at Gregory. Of course they'd thought it was us. We were the snake in the Garden of Eden, the temptation on the Mount, the ones who got blamed for everything.

Okay, demons were responsible for a lot of that shit, but not *everything*.

"We eventually went to war with the fae, and after twenty thousand years, they called a truce and negotiated the contract," Gregory continued.

"Wait," I interrupted. "You went to war with them? And were winning enough that they agreed to peace talks? How, when you said the angels are at a terrible disadvantage in Aerie?"

"I honestly don't know," he confessed. "We *are* at a terrible disadvantage in Aerie—us attempting to fight there is the reason I know this. And while the Gregori had been in the physical realm long enough to hold their own against the fae here among the humans, we weren't exactly winning the fight. Something happened that made both fairy kingdoms eager to negotiate, and I never could discover what that was."

Damn. Because if we could figure that out, we could replicate those attacks or actions and force the fae into compliance once more.

"The contract between us stipulated that no angels were to enter Aerie," the archangel continued. "The fae were only allowed three gateways into this world, and they could only take humans who had agreed to go with them as part of a good-faith bargain."

My eyebrows shot up, because I knew from the elves what these "good-faith bargains" were like. If the fae were anything like their tricky-bastard cousins, these deals were far from being in "good-faith."

He sighed and shot me a knowing look. "Indeed, it was what the humans would have called a 'devil's bargain,' my Cockroach. The agreement with the human would be in exchange for something desired from the fae, but there were loopholes and trickery. Still, it kept the fairy-folk from running off with entire villages of humans against their will."

I halted, jamming my fists on my hips and glaring at him. "Devil's bargain? Really? When will we be free from these hurtful stereotypes? I might need to bring this issue up before the Ruling Council. Demons have rights too, you know."

Gregory's slow smile warmed my heart along with the rest of my body. He stepped into me, wrapping his arms around my waist and pulling me against his rock-hard chest. "There are good reasons for those stereotypes, Cockroach. Demons are wily, sneaky psychopaths, and their Iblis embodies all of those traits. It's why I love her so much."

I rested my head against him, feeling his intense heat scorching through me. "I love you too, you prudish, inflexible asshole."

His spirit-self pushed into mine, merging around the edges. I swear my eyes nearly rolled into the back of my head. I'd never get tired of how it felt to have him merge with me. I teased him with my own spirit-being, pulling back, then brushing against him, merging then disengaging. It was a dance that was bringing me tantalizingly close to orgasm.

"We have one more gateway to close," he whispered in my ear.

Just as his words registered in my brain and I realize they weren't dirty talk, he'd pulled away from me, spun me around, and pushed me forward.

Jerk.

"One more gateway, and then we can fuck, right?" I asked.

He chuckled. "One more and I promise I'll satisfy your every need."

"Every?" When we'd first become intimate, Gregory only wanted to join our spirit-selves. But now he was happy to give me the physical pleasure my corporeal form desired. And on a very rare occasion, he'd allow me to do the same to him.

I got the feeling no one was supposed to know about that, though. So mum's the word.

"What are the fae doing with all of these humans?" I wondered. If they were being feted, and life was one endless party in Aerie, we could stop endlessly closing gates and just let the fae have the whole damned lot of them.

"Some humans are used as servants. Others are used for breeding as a form of unwilling surrogacy. Others are used for hunting, torture, and other entertainment."

So, not feted and partying it up then. Damn.

Gregory glanced over at me. "Don't tell Nyalla. She's upset enough about this."

I had no intention of telling Nyalla. "Maybe we should set traps for the fae as they come through the gates. Kill them off until they decide staying home is safer."

"None of the traps I've devised to date have worked," he admitted. "And they've become better at their glamour. Not only can they appear as humans or animals, they are able to escape detection when they are this side of the gateways. Even their energy signature is masked."

I snorted, because I could do that as well. Gregory, the most powerful of the archangels, hadn't detected me when we'd been in the same room together once. He'd always complimented my ability to bury my spirit-self deep within my physical form to escape notice.

I might be the Iblis, but I was still a lowly Imp. If *I* could manage that, then it wasn't a surprise that these fae could as well.

But I could ponder this fae problem later. We had one more gate to close and then some filthy dirty sex to have.

"Here's the portal." I outlined it with my hands, then shrieked as something burst through the gateway and plowed into me, knocking me to the ground.

Not something, *someone*.

2

I shoved the stinking heap of rags off me and scrambled to my feet, staring down at a human. He had a weird drapey thing on that had seen better days, and smelled like he'd been wearing it twenty-four-seven for months.

"Help me!" He looked back and forth between Gregory and me while scooting on his butt away from the gateway. "They'll kill me if they catch me. Help!"

I hesitated for a second, confused about this guy's circumstances and how he'd managed to escape. Then I realized immediate action was necessary.

"Close the gate," I shouted to Gregory as I ran to show him once more where it was. In my rush to outline the portal for him, I accidentally brushed my fingers through the outline of the gateway.

A burning heat turned my fingers red and sparks flew from the opening. Before I had a chance to do more than yelp, shadowy figures slipped through the passage. I jumped back, tripping over a rock and falling once more on my ass. That probably saved me since one shadow swooped through the space where I'd stood half a second ago. A tendril of the creature brushed the top of my head and I felt that same burning in a streak along my scalp.

The human screamed, scrambling backwards as the creatures floated toward him. Gregory roared and dove forward through the things before I had a chance to warn him. Scooping me up in his arms, he threw me.

As I tumbled through the air, I realize that angels had serious throwing arms. Gregory should be playing Major League baseball. Or tossing cabers at one of those Scottish festivals. I flew so fast that I was afraid to reveal my wings in case they were ripped clean off my body. It felt like ages before I finally hit the ground, and once I'd landed I wished I hadn't. My face plowed a row through the soil, small rocks slicing through my skin.

Once I stood, I took a quick inventory, making sure all my various corporeal parts were working. The finger that had brushed through the gateway was still numb, but no longer looked like I'd shoved it into a campfire. Looking back, I realized the angel had managed to toss me a good quarter-mile. And from what I could see, he was taking on *all* of the shadow creatures. None were flitting through the sky or across the landscape, or attacking the human. No, they were all huddled in a lump of gray around a tall, buff angel, ignoring the filthy man who was cowering behind a patch of weeds.

The angel vanished for an instant under the shadow creatures' onslaught. I didn't hesitate to reveal my wings and take to the sky, streaking toward where he fought the shadows. I drew my sword as I dove, slashing through the shadowy creatures.

Their insubstantial bodies separated with a sizzle of sparks, as I cleaved a path to my beloved who was somehow grappling with the creatures. He looked up at me, his eyes widening in alarm.

"Cockroach! Get back!" he shouted.

I paid no attention, even as the shadows I'd split combined again into whole, lethal forms. Swinging the sword wildly, I kept slicing and dicing, figuring that even if I wasn't killing them, I was at least keeping them from attacking my angel.

"Cockroach, go," Gregory insisted.

"I'm not leaving you here to fight these fuckers by yourself," I shouted back. Even though he seemed to be holding his own, the angel was striped with burned flesh. Given his ability to regenerate and heal, that was pretty fucking alarming.

Spinning around, I tried to keep the shadows away from me, but they were reforming faster from their injuries, and a few of them managed to swipe me before I could cut them apart again. This strategy wasn't going to work long-term, or even short-term it seemed. And the fact that my sentient, kills-everything weapon didn't have more of an effect on these creatures worried me. Still swinging, I shot a few with lightning and my energy, dismayed to see those did even less damage than the sword. With nothing to lose, I shoved my hand into one and tried to devour it.

Devouring was my icky superpower. Demons and angels both found it disgusting and perverted, but it had saved my life countless times, and this was getting close to one of those save-my-life emergencies. I felt the shadow creature's shock and alarm as I spooled its life force into myself. Then it vanished. I'd killed it, but I felt a wave of nausea roll through me that I'd never experienced when I'd previously devoured someone or something.

I really didn't relish the idea of devouring any more of

these things, but killing one wasn't going to get us out of this mess so I reached out and spooled another one of them into me.

This time I did puke, vomiting up lunch, breakfast, and what felt like most of my lower intestines. The violence of my physical reaction broke my focus and my sword arm dropped. Two of the shadows latched on to me, searing clear through flesh and bone with their heat. I felt the burn down to my spirit being, and screamed in between gagging and retching.

"Cockroach!" Gregory shouted. I got the impression he was just as angry with me as he was with the shadow creatures. His alarm kind of pissed me off. I appreciated that he loved me and didn't want me to die, but I wasn't the sort of demon/angel who wanted to be tossed a quarter of a mile away to safety while someone I cared deeply about fought the enemy single-handedly. Don't get me wrong, I was all for running away when I was overwhelmed by numbers, or someone stronger than I was, but I wouldn't abandon someone I loved.

And yes, that was a huge change from the imp I'd been a few short years ago.

"I got this," I told him as I tried to devour another one of the shadow creatures. I only got about halfway through him before I started puking again. It didn't kill the thing, but it was enough that it pulled away from me, listing to the side as another shadow dove in to take its place.

"Cockroach," Gregory growled.

I felt him grab my shoulder and pull me against him, spinning me around. My sword vanished and I found myself plastered against his chest, looking up into his furious dark eyes. Out of the corner of my vision I saw half a dozen of the shadows prone on the ground, like a gray gauzy film over the grass and dirt. Huh. I guess Gregory *was* doing pretty well on his own, even if he did look like an incinerated zombie right now.

One of the shadows grabbed his shoulder, blistering the skin and turning his flesh a sickening charcoal shade. I felt its poison sinking through him into his spirit being and snarled, furious that something would dare to harm my beloved asshole, even if he didn't act as though he were affected by the attack at all.

"Hold on," Gregory said.

His voice had a timbre that sent warmth through me to the tips of my toes. I held on, not just physically but with my spirit-being since I knew that's what he'd meant. The black of his irises bled through the whites of his eyes, and time slowed as he enveloped me with both his arms and his angel essence. The shadow beings continued to grab us, but all I saw was him. All I knew was his warmth, and the eternity reflected in his dark eyes.

In that moment, he was *my* eternity. He was an embodiment of whatever was here at the beginning of time, through to the very end.

The end. I'd be at his side, because I was the Ha-Satan, the devourer. I'd bring about the apocalypse and together we'd sweep the floors of the universe, put the chairs on the tables, and lock the doors behind us.

And then with a burst of energy, life would begin again.

As if he'd read my mind, Gregory exploded in a blast of light and power that rivaled the sun. I burned with him, nestling myself into his spirit-being where I was safe without a corporeal form. In theory, I should be able to manifest as any form of matter, or energy, in this world, but I was still a little shaky on the execution when it came to things like this.

Gregory was a master. The angel contained his nuclear event to a ten-foot radius, destroying the remaining smoke creatures with his light and heat. When he pulled the energy back and manifested a more human corporeal form, none of our foes remained. Just as important, no radiation remained. I assumed my own human form, then pulled slightly away from him to look around. We were in the center of a blackened blast radius that had created a hole in the ground so deep that I could barely peek over the edge. Everything was dead within the circle aside from us, but outside of our giant divot, grass and flowers grew, birds sang, and insects chirped.

"That's pretty fucking impressive," I told the angel.

His arms tightened around me and I felt the seductive brush of his spirit self. "That's because *I'm* pretty fucking impressive."

I laughed, not just at his rare use of profanity, but at his ego. The sin of pride might have been what humans blamed for the fall of the original Satan, but I'd discovered this archangel of mine also had his share of that sin.

Then I realized we'd forgotten about the human. Looking around, I didn't see him or his charred body.

"Did you accidentally cook that fugitive dude?" I asked. "Or did he freak out and run away while we were fighting?"

"I transported him away. Somewhere he'd be safe," the angel told me.

"Where?" I was pretty sure I knew where, but asked anyway.

"Your house." He shrugged. "You take in all the misfits and refugees. Besides, I wanted to question him, and we planned on going to your house after we were done here."

"To fuck," I reminded him. "We were going to my house to fuck. Which I guess isn't going to happen now since I have an unexpected houseguest that we need to question, and I probably will need to feed."

"I'll need a precipitation-ticket on the sensory sexual activity," he informed me. "This human may have important information for us."

It took me a second to realize he meant "raincheck."

"You do realize that there might not be a living human to question when we get back?" I asked. "Nyalla is home today, and she has a violent streak. Finding a strange man suddenly in our living room might trigger an impulse action like decapitating him with an axe."

He nodded. "Good point. I hadn't expected you to have an axe in your living room, though. And I'd assumed Nyalla would be sympathetic toward a dirty human dressed in rags crying for help."

The axes were because Lux and I had been engaged in a throwing competition last night. The drywall had been pretty torn up, but Lux had repaired it all before bedtime. If the kid ever wanted a side-gig, home renovation was definitely an option. And Nyalla *would* be sympathetic—but possibly *after* she'd decapitated him.

"What *were* those things?" I eased free of his arms and looked around the blackened circle. "I'd expected fairies to look kind of like the elves."

"I have no idea what those things were," he told me. "The fairies we've battled in the past look similar in appearance to elves, although I've been told they were actually wearing a glamour."

It wasn't like either of us were in our natural forms either. We were beings of spirit, needing to house ourselves in a corporeal form to survive here. And demons loved changing up their appearances. It meant I wasn't one to throw stones at the fae wanting to use glamour.

"So light and heat kills them?" I asked, climbing out of the dead-zone hole he'd created. "Or is it just light? They were pretty fucking hot themselves, so I'm guessing it wasn't the temperature part of the attack that killed them."

He shrugged. "I don't know. My sword wasn't very effective on them, so I took a guess based on their attacks and defenses, and their reactions to my own attacks and defenses."

"You took a guess..." Shit. This guy was just as crazy as I was. Which was probably one of the reasons I loved him so.

He laughed. "You are a terrible influence on me, Cockroach. My vibration pattern is far from center. I act on impulse and intuition instead of logic and knowledge. I sacrificed all I have held dear just to be by your side, to experience the joy of your merging with me."

"I don't think that's an unholy thing," I informed him. "The corporeal sex probably is, but not the angel sex. Although that thing you do with your mouth and those teeth of yours? Hot damn, that's better than heaven."

I'd been to heaven—Aaru—and it had kind of sucked. But I knew he loved the place, so I felt like it was a good comparison.

He grinned, then his expression turned serious as he jumped out of the dead-zone hole. "We should close that gateway before more of those things come through."

I held up my hands. "Dude, there's nothing to close. You blew it up with your super-nova thingie."

He frowned, turning around slowly as if he didn't believe me.

"I promise you it's gone," I assured him. "You fried the crap out of it. Hell, you might have cooked everything on the other side as well."

He shook his head. "I kept the light, heat, and radiation

contained to minimize the damage. Also, the way interdimensional gateways are structured limits heat and radiation transference as well as other things. A burst of light might have gotten through before the gate was destroyed, but I doubt that would have done much damage."

I snorted, thinking of all the times Gregory had fried my retinas with a burst of light. Even though I was sure the fae could fix the damage as well as or better than I could, it was still amusing to think of a bunch of blind fairies stumbling around the forest.

Had the light been what destroyed the shadow creatures? Or the heat? Or the radiation? Or some combination of the three? That might be good to know in case they came through other gates before we'd managed to close them. We could instruct the humans to carry high wattage halogen lights with them, or flame throwers, but didn't know what we could do about them using radiation as a weapon. Humans randomly releasing radioactive isotopes every time they saw a shadow they thought might be a deadly creature wouldn't be good.

"Shall we go back to your house and interrogate your newest houseguest? Assuming that Nyalla hasn't killed him, that is," Gregory added.

I kind of hoped he wasn't dead. This guy might have knowledge about the fae that could help us. I was already making a mental list of ideas to conduct my own sort of impish warfare, but suggestions from a human who'd been their captive would be welcome.

"Interrogation first. Then we have sex," I reminded the angel.

He smiled, then planted a soft kiss on my forehead. "Then we have sex. I promise."

3

Nyalla had not killed the refugee. Instead we arrived back home to find him clean, wrapped in a sheet, and eating a bowl of chicken noddle soup. Now that I was able to finally get a decent look at the guy, I realized he was younger than I'd originally thought. The man appeared to be in his twenties, with shoulder-length dark brown hair and blue eyes. He was pale and clean-shaven, and I remembered that he hadn't had a beard or anything when he'd run through the gateway and flattened me.

"You're safe here," Nyalla told the man. "Sam will protect you. She's Satan, and no one messes with her."

Everyone messed with me, but I didn't bother to correct her. Instead I went into the kitchen, and grabbed a beer from the fridge. Nyalla followed me, getting a beer for herself.

"His name is Joe Paskin," she told me. "And that's all I know other than that he had escaped the fairies, and that you saved him. He was pretty panicked when he arrived, but I wasn't sure if that was from the teleportation or whatever he was running from."

"Probably both," I said. "Thanks for getting him cleaned up, fed, and calmed down."

I glanced through the doorway into the dining room to see Gregory sitting across from the human. The air was thick with blue, letting me know that the angel was using his persuasive powers to further calm the guy and gain his trust. I didn't want the interrogation to start without me, so I brought my beer into the dining room and sat next to Gregory. Nyalla followed me in, but stood just outside the kitchen, leaning against a wall and biting her lip.

How many bad memories had Joe's presence brought up? She'd been taken from her crib by the elves as a changeling, so she wouldn't remember her actual kidnapping, but she certainly remembered all the years of slavery and abuse. I gave her a reassuring smile. "You can go upstairs if you want, Nyalla. Or out by the pool."

She shook her head, putting her shoulders back. "I'm okay. Really."

I hoped so, because Joe's experience might be terribly close to what she'd gone through herself.

"So...we've got some questions, Joe." I took a quick swig of my beer and set it down on the table.

"But first, please tell us your story," Gregory said. "When were you kidnapped by the fae and how did you escape?"

The man pushed his empty soup bowl away and hunched forward on his elbows. "I'm not sure how long ago I was taken by the fae. It felt like I was there for years. I remember that I went to bed like usual. It was a Friday night in April. Something woke me in the middle of the night and I found myself out in the middle of this field in my underwear. I thought I'd been sleepwalking, but I didn't recognize the field. Plus, I'd been living in an apartment in Glasgow as part of a work-study program with the University, so it's not like I was walking distance to the countryside."

I'd just assumed the fae took whatever humans were nearest the gateways they'd opened, but the portals were always in a specific geographic area. Now that I thought back on the spreadsheets Nyalla was keeping of reported kidnappings that may or may not have been perpetrated by the fae, the missing people hadn't always been close to the gateways.

How *were* the fae selecting their victims? And how were they transporting them from their initial locations to the portals?

"Did you see anyone else near you when you awoke?" Gregory asked. "Other humans? Animals?"

He shook his head. "Not at first. I was disoriented, then I started to panic, wondering where I was and how the heck I was going to get back to my apartment when I had no phone or wallet and was dressed only in my underwear. Then I saw an old woman."

"An old woman?" I asked. "In the middle of a field in the middle of the night? Where did she come from?"

"I don't know where she came from. She was just there, about twenty feet away and coming toward me. I was a little embarrassed because I was in my underwear, but I was also relieved to see someone who might possibly get me back home. I called out to her and asked her if she could help me, but she didn't answer. When she got closer, she looked up at me, and she changed from an old woman into a beautiful woman of golden light. That's all I remember."

"What do you mean 'that's all you remember'?" Gregory asked. "What happened to you in Aerie?"

"I have vague memories here and there. It's really all a blur," he said. "But I remember overhearing something about me being sold, and I knew I needed to try to snap out of whatever they were doing to me and get away."

Nyalla sucked in a breath at his words. "Did they lock you in your room at night? Were they drugging you or using some sort of spell to make you compliant?"

"I think it was a spell because my more lucid moments were when I was alone," he said, pivoting to face Nyalla. "I wasn't locked in my room, but after the first few nights, I realized I had nowhere to go. The place I was staying in...it was like a maze that kept circling back on itself. If I left my room, no matter where I went I always found myself back there."

Gregory frowned. "How did you manage to escape?"

"I must have eventually been sold because I was led away, transported by some other fae who must not have been quite as good at the magic that made my memory and awareness blurry," he explained. "We came to an area where I saw other humans being brought through a glowing light and led away. I knew it was my only chance, so I just ran for it."

Nyalla made a sympathetic noise, her arms wrapping around her chest. Gregory nodded at Joe's story. Me? I wasn't sure what to think. This whole tale was full of well-timed coincidences, and while my life seemed to hinge on well-timed coincidences, I was kinda calling bullshit on this. The guy wasn't lying that I could tell, but I got the impression he wasn't telling the complete truth either.

There might be a completely innocent reason for that. He didn't know us, and while we'd saved him from those shadow fae, he had no idea what our motivations might be. Powerful beings who'd battled powerful fae and been able to teleport him to another continent? I didn't blame him for not completely trusting us. Or not trusting us at all.

"What about those shadowy fuckers that chased you through the gateway?" I asked. "Were they escorting the newly captured humans? Were they with the group taking you to your new owners' residence? Do they just lurk around somewhere, ready to spring into action and apprehend fugitives?"

He shuddered. "I don't know. The moment I ran for it, they appeared and began to chase me. If the portal hadn't been so close, I don't think I would have made it through."

"What about the other fae?" Gregory asked. "The ones leading the humans as well as the ones escorting you. Did they do anything when you ran for the portal?"

Joe frowned in thought. "I think they tried to cast some sort of compliance spell on me because things got a little fuzzy, but I was so close to the portal it probably didn't have time to fully take effect. And it abruptly cut off as soon as I went through."

I glanced over at Gregory, trying to read his stoic expression. The only fae I'd ever met was that windbag Gwylla. She had some pretty amazing powers when it came to manipulating the environment, but beyond that, I didn't know squat about her. Or squat about what other fae might have as far as skills and abilities. According to Gregory, they'd held their own with the angels in the war between them, which wasn't any small feat. But I knew that the angels kind of sucked when it came to fights in the physical realm. They were awkward in their corporeal forms, and weren't used to battling here in this plane of existence. They were a far more formidable foe in Aaru than they were here, in the human realm.

Those shadow fae had been pretty fucking intimidating. Real fairies? Powerful fairies? This guy was lucky to have escaped—really lucky. And he was doubly lucky because we'd been on the other side of the gateway. If he'd run through ten minutes earlier, then those shadow fae would have caught and killed him. And ten minutes later? Well, we would have closed the gateway and his opportunity for escape would have vanished before his eyes.

"Are you done with questions?" Nyalla stepped forward. "Joe has to be exhausted after all he's gone through today. Maybe he can retire to the guest room, get some sleep, and be available for further questions tomorrow? I should have the online delivery of his clothes by then too."

Oh yeah. Guess the guy couldn't wear a sheet for the rest of his life, like he was at a never-ending college-frat toga party.

"I think we're done for now." Gregory nodded at Joe. "Sleep. You will be well taken care of here—and safe, as Nyalla said. As for future questions, I'd appreciate if you tell us about Aerie and the fae. Their powers, their social structure, and their weaknesses."

Joe nodded, his shoulders slumping. The guy did look exhausted. And no wonder. He'd been fleeing for his life, and he probably had known his chances of making it out alive were slim to none. But he'd beaten the odds, and now he was walking with Nyalla up the stairs to my guest room where he'd sleep knowing he was free once more, and back on this side of the portal.

I waited until he was in his room and Nyalla was downstairs before motioning for her to sit and turning to Gregory.

"What do you think?" I asked.

"He isn't being completely truthful," the angel said. "He definitely was kidnapped and enslaved by the fae in Aerie, but the story of his escape is...I believe you would call it sketchy."

I almost applauded at the correct word usage.

"He definitely wasn't faking his fear and confusion when he arrived here," Nyalla said. "The poor guy was shaking. And under those rags he was so thin."

"That's what bothers me," I spoke up. "He'd just been sold. He was being escorted to new owners. Why was he dirty and wearing rags? Why was he undernourished? When he came through the gateway and knocked me over, I'd assumed he was some homeless dude who'd been wandering around for months on his own."

Nyalla glared at me. "Maybe the fae don't treat their humans well. Some elves did the same, especially those humans who didn't have any magical ability."

I winced, remembering that Nyalla had been one of those humans.

"You were treated poorly, but the elves would never have allowed you to go unbathed to the point that you stank like that man. Or had you wearing filthy, smelly rags," I countered.

Her mouth tightened, and her shrug was a terse movement. "Perhaps the fae do not have the olfactory senses that the rest of us have. Or maybe he was assigned to manual labor outside with livestock, and living in a stable area where no one cared that he bathed or had clean clothing."

It was a valid point. And I hated that this conversation was bringing up memories that were hurting Nyalla.

"I have never encountered those shadow fae before," Gregory said, breaking the heavy sadness of the moment. "They were not part of the fae offensive back when we were battling. With Joe's story, I believe they might be some sort of hunter force used to track down escaped fugitives or used for another purpose within Aerie."

"The elves would often tell stories about the fairy-folk," Nyalla mentioned. "Those stories were farcical and derogatory, but occasionally they would talk about the brutality and cruelty of the fairies toward their foes. One story I overheard had to do with the Shades. They were insubstantial fae that were neither of the dark or the light court. They lived in the absence of light, but were creatures of heat—so they combined qualities of both courts. Prey were anything living. They'd decimate forests, leaving barren wastelands behind, but they preferred to eat humans and humanoid beings, burning and turning them to a liquid they could digest. It was supposedly a slow and excruciating process. Only the most powerful fae could keep them in check and use them to their purposes. Other fae and elves were just as much at risk of being eaten as humans."

I stared at her, not sure if this was a boogeyman tale that the elves had exaggerated for dramatic effect or true. The shadow fae had burned the areas they'd touched, clear through my flesh to my spirit being. But I'd devoured them. They'd tasted like shit and I'd barfed, but I'd still managed to devour two and a half of them. So they might be powerful, but they weren't indestructible.

"I would not put it past the fae to send these shades into the human realm," Gregory said with a frown. "They're taking humans without bargaining first. The next step might be outright attacks."

Nyalla's eyes widened, and I put a reassuring hand on her shoulder. "That's not going to happen, because we're going to go on the offensive. Forget shutting down gateways every two days. We need to go through the portals and attack these motherfuckers where they live."

Gregory sighed. "We discussed this, Cockroach. We angels cannot win against the fae by entering Aerie."

Fine. The angels might not be able to win by entering Aerie, but I might be able to. Gregory might be okay with staying this end of the gateways, closing portals and playing defense, but I was done with that shit.

I was going on the offensive.

4

I was brooding over the situation throughout the night and the next morning.

Gregory had made good on his promise of epic sex, but in the middle of the night he'd vanished to take care of something. I'd gone downstairs for a snack and found Nyalla crying on the sofa, Boomer curled up next to her with his chin on her lap. I made us both bowls of ice cream, and we'd chatted. She'd cried a little more on my shoulder while I'd felt the ache of shared pain that always seemed so strange for a demon.

And then we'd both gone to bed, Boomer following Nyalla into her room in case she needed additional comfort or protection from bad dreams, and me to my room where I slept like the fucking dead, waking to the smell of coffee.

By midmorning, Joe was wearing more than a sheet thanks to a quick online order delivery. He'd gotten some coffee and a bagel, then went back upstairs saying that he wanted to spend most of the day catching up on sleep. Around noon I left him a note about the food in the fridge and went outside to chill by the pool with Nyalla. While she listened to music on her headphones, I couldn't stop thinking about the disaster I'd made of everything.

The demon territory on the western part of the continent was a total shit-show and Doriel was not performing as I'd expected. Elven-trained sorcerers and mages were flooding the markets with magical devices—some of which evened the playing field, and others that did nothing but allow paranoid, unstable humans to kill innocent supernatural beings. A few groups of elves had jumped into positions of political power and were being dicks. A few angels, realizing that they weren't going back to Aaru anytime soon, had banded together and seized several countries on the Asian continent.

They'd tried to grab Australia, but had been quickly routed. I wasn't sure if it was the spunky humans, the deadly animals, or governmental bureaucracy that rivaled anything the Ruling Council could put together that caused their exodus, but they'd left the country, and declared none of them would willingly go back.

The angels weren't my problem, and neither were the elves anymore, but the demons out west? I needed to do something about that situation. As soon as I dealt with these fucking fae...and had the most amazing wedding ever.

The fae seemed to be kidnapping between twenty and sixty with every portal they opened. How many fucking slaves did they need? Or was it more about pissing off the angels than a steady supply of human slaves?

And Joe... Nyalla had scolded me for doubting his story. What reason would he have to lie, after all? He'd clearly come through the gateway. He was obviously human. Those nasty-ass shadow fae had come after him. True, there had been a lot of coincidences aligning in his escape, but as I'd said, it wasn't like I hadn't had my share of perfectly-aligned coincidences in my life either. Chaos worked that way some-times, and there was no saying it hadn't all come together for this poor human.

How many had tried to escape and failed? Ended up dead in Aerie in some forest or village? Maybe Joe was just the lucky one.

"How did things go yesterday with the fae portals?" Nyalla pushed her sunglasses up on her head and pulled out her earbuds. "With getting Joe settled, I forgot to ask."

"They're closed. Again," I grumbled as I pushed my own sunglasses up. "For now. We'll need to do it all again tomor-row. They're reconstructing them as quickly as we take them down."

Nyalla made a sympathetic noise. "There needs to be a long-term solution."

"There is, but it's war," I told her. "Evidently there was a war before and the angels weren't exactly coming out on top when the fae inexplicably offered peace talks. It would be even harder to rally them for this sort of thing now, with the angelic host divided and kicked out of Aaru."

"Well, we have to do *something*," Nyalla replied. "If the angels can't take decisive action, then maybe the humans need to do so."

I snorted. "What, like launch missiles through the gate-ways? We don't know what works against these fae."

Nyalla shrugged. "They're kind of related to the elves, right? So our iron and steel might be a weakness for them. Or we can attack with weapons they're unfamiliar with. The elves were really thrown by technology when they came here thinking they'd overthrow humans and rule. How many were taken out by buses and cars in that first week? Or farmers with shotguns?"

"I'm not sure if that's a smart strategy for the humans

right now. I'd hate for an army to go through the portals, only to find out that shotguns and buses don't work the same way in Aerie or on the fae," I told her

Nyalla made a frustrated noise. "Sam, what is happening? The elves, the angels, and now the fae? I expected some turmoil with everything that's been going on, but I hadn't expected things to go on this long, or to keep getting worse."

Yeah. Me too. Chaos was a transition. It was *not* meant to be an endless state.

"This issue with the fae is a top priority—at least as far as I'm concerned," she continued. "The humans under Elven control seem fairly happy with their fate, and the angels aren't killing any humans. But the fae...they're taking people. Are the humans enslaved, like what the elves did? Or do they face a worse fate."

I winced, remembering what Gregory said. That wasn't anything I wanted to share with Nyalla though. It would just upset her, and there wasn't anything she could do to help the situation.

No, it seemed that this fae problem had landed in my lap. Just like everything else.

"I'm worried, Sam." Nyalla shifted on her lounger to face me. "I feel for all these humans. People are innocently going for walks, gardening, sleeping, or cooking dinner and they're being snatched away. We can't just allow this to continue."

She was right. I was going to take action. I just wasn't sure exactly what that action was going to be.

"Tell me about this war between the angels and the fae," Nyalla said. "Was it over the elves? I know the angels supported them when they left Aerie."

"I don't know much about it beyond what Gregory told me yesterday." I told her what I knew, about the elves and the war and the sudden peace talks as well as the details of the contract.

Nyalla gasped. "Wait. Lux. Oh no. The contract stipulated no angels were to be in Aerie, but he went there to steal that ring. So this isn't *just* about the ring like Gwylla had said. It's also about Lux entering Aerie. He broke the contract, didn't he?"

That was exactly what I feared, but I didn't want to jump to conclusions. "I'm not positive. There's a chance they didn't know he was there. Lux is pretty stealthy, and he's a little guy. I get the feeling he was in and out as soon as he grabbed the ring."

Nyalla sat up and faced me. "Gwylla said that eventually their queen will invade our world and try to take over."

Gwylla was a bore who talked endlessly about culture and customs and stuff I didn't give a rat's ass about. She was also dramatic. I took whatever I'd managed to pay attention to in her endless speeches with an ocean of salt.

"I don't think this queen is going to cross the gates unless she's sure she'll win the fight," I assured Nyalla. "By now her guerilla-style kidnappers would have told her this world has changed. Grabbing humans when they're not expecting it is different than having to face guns and anti-tank missiles. That's not even considering the shifters, the sorcerers, and the angels. Or the elves who won't appreciate their cousins trying to butt in on their turf. No, I think they'll keep to what they're doing and hope that the angels bring the fight to Aerie, where the fae would have even more of an advantage."

"Maybe." Nyalla's voice was hesitant. "But the angels won't go to Aerie. And in the meantime, the fae are taking humans."

"I wonder if returning the ring would *really* help?" I mused.

Maybe returning the ring wouldn't make a difference, but I should at least to see if I could negotiate something in exchange for it. It's not like I wanted the thing, pretty as it was. Right now it was just hanging out in a dresser drawer with my underwear and socks.

I had forbidden Lux from going back to Aerie to return it, and even though the contract appeared to have already been broken, I didn't want to risk sending him back there. But me? I wasn't *really* an angel. That particular war had happened after the Angels of Chaos had been banished, so any contract wouldn't have included them. Nor would it have included demons.

And it definitely wouldn't have included me, who'd only been formed less than a thousand years ago.

I was exempt from whatever agreement the angels had made. And if these fae were anything like we were, then loopholes in contracts were a way of life.

"Gwylla claims the ring's return would lessen any retaliation by the fae," Nyalla told me. "Evidently the ring is very important to their queen. According to her, this queen absolutely will want it back."

I frowned, thinking that if the queen wanted it back so bad, then it really would be a solid bargaining point in negotiations. I couldn't help the niggling feeling that I should keep the ring, and instead leave a note that I had it and was willing to negotiate terms for its return.

Not that Gwylla would like that. She had been insisting I return the ring for over a month now.

"Call Gwylla and tell her I'll take the ring back," I said to Nyalla. "Get her to set something up, and I'll take it from there. I've also got a few ideas that might force the fae into peace talks, even if this ring doesn't do the job."

There was a noise behind me, and we both turned to see Joe standing at one of the sliding glass doors. He was wearing the gray sweatpants and white T-shirt Nyalla had ordered for him, and had a coffee mug in one hand.

"Sorry, I didn't mean to interrupt. I just wanted to let you both know I'm up and in the dining room, eating leftover pizza." He smiled. "And thanks again for letting me stay here. I'm pretty sure my landlord has rented out my apartment by now, so it might take me a while to find a place."

"It's no problem at all," Nyalla told him. "I got you a prepaid phone to call your friends and family and let them know what happened. It's on the kitchen counter."

"Thanks." He nodded, then slid the door closed and walked back into the kitchen.

"That poor man," Nyalla said. "I'm sure his loved ones are desperate over his disappearance. They'll be so excited to know he's alive and safe."

Safe. I thought of the shadow fae chasing him through the portal, and wondered just how safe he really was. Maybe it was a good thing he was staying here for a while and not immediately flying back to his family and friends.

"You still have that elven net?" I asked Nyalla.

She nodded. "And the spelled bullets, and the wand, and the scroll. And if that doesn't protect against the fae, I'll just shoot them or whack them on the head with a shovel and run over them with the brush hog."

"That's my girl," I told her as I settled back into my lounge chair. "Now, let's talk about something more exciting —my upcoming wedding."

"Wedding planning is on schedule." Nyalla smiled. "I've

got all your guests set up with rooms at the hotel. And there are auditions from three more Elvis impersonators for you to review. You're going to need to make a decision soon, before the one you want gets booked for something else that day."

"About Elvis..." I squirmed, knowing how Nyalla felt about last-minute changes.

She sighed. "You're not thinking of raising the real Elvis from the dead again, are you? I don't trust that necromancer Dar found, and Gregory told you that Elvis has been dead too long. You'll end up with a skeleton wearing mildewed silk and rhinestones who can't speak, let alone sing."

I pouted, still annoyed that my archangel fiancé had vetoed Zombie Elvis officiating our wedding.

Gregory had agreed to a human-style wedding. Once he'd slipped one of the stolen rings on my finger, I'd totally cut him out of the party planning, telling the archangel that his only job was to show up in a tux with his selected best-men similarly attired. I knew Raphael was planning some sort of bachelor party for them, and Gregory had come up with a honeymoon plan that he absolutely refused to even give me the slightest hint about, but that was it. When he'd put his foot down on Zombie Elvis, I knew there would be no swaying him. But as good as the impersonators I'd auditioned had been, none of them had that "wow" factor I was really looking for.

If Zombie Elvis was out, then I needed to come up with a new idea, something better than an Elvis impersonator and something that wouldn't be so outrageous that Gregory put his foot down once more.

"I've decided that Dolly Parton is going to officiate at our wedding," I told Nyalla.

She burst out laughing, stopping and turning to me after a few seconds. "You're not serious?"

"Yes, I'm serious. Dolly is fucking amazing. She's got a great voice. She's funny. She's a snazzy dresser and has some damned fine boobs. And she's alive."

That last one was especially important, I'd discovered.

Nyalla frowned. "She's agreed to do this? I mean, I don't know much about the woman, but I get the idea she might not be a fan of Satan—either the historical one or the one currently holding the title."

"She hasn't agreed yet," I told her.

I was hoping the fact that I was marrying the Archangel Michael might sway her mind, but just in case, I probably needed to put a kidnapping plan together. I couldn't take the risk that she'd turn me down this close to the date. Hopefully once I had her hog-tied in my basement, I could convince her to officiate in our wedding.

After all, it was better to beg forgiveness than ask permission.

BEFORE BEDTIME HARPER had brought Lux home, pumped up with sugar and excited from his sleep-over with his best-buddy Austin. He went out with me to take care of the horses and Boomer, then we curled up on the sofa together to watch a movie.

Lux was a movie-talker, so I was subjected to a running commentary about both the socio-economic and racial themes in Avatar, as well as a thought-provoking discussion about farts. He'd started to settle down after an hour, and by the time the credits were rolling, the little guy was ready for bed.

I scooped him up in my arms, dismayed to see his eyes pop open as I lifted him.

"Time to sleep," I told him as I headed for the stairs.

He squirmed. "Taking the ring back? The fairy ring?"

Lux couldn't read *everything* that went through my mind, but I wasn't used to censoring or hiding my thoughts around him like I sometimes did around Gregory. And while he'd been lecturing me about colonialism themes in the movie, I'd been mentally trying to plan my trip to Aerie.

"Yes, sweetie. I'm going to take the ring back." Eventually, once the fae had agreed to a few things. I had some plans up my sleeve, and I'd decide which one to do when I was actually standing in Aerie

The little angel frowned. "I messed up. Wasn't supposed to go to Aerie. Not supposed to take rings."

Whether he'd been the catalyst for this or not, it wasn't his fault. He was a little angel who was growing up outside of Aaru, and it wasn't like any of us had a handbook for that sort of thing.

"No, but you didn't know you weren't supposed to go to Aerie. I didn't know either. And I've stolen plenty of shit in my life. There's no shame in that." I leaned down and planted a kiss on Lux's forehead, thinking that for an Angel of Order, he had a whole lot of Chaos going on.

5

Gwylla waved her hands, saying something about court ceremony and the importance of lineage.

It was a struggle to pay attention to her, with her boring and long-winded speeches. I secretly thought she might be related to Gabriel the way she went on and on about etiquette and rules and the fae's convoluted hierarchy of titles.

There was no reason I needed to know all this shit.

"Why did the fae agree to negotiate with the angels ten thousand years ago?" I interrupted. "It sounds like the war was kind of a stalemate and that the fae were determined to fight it out to the very end. Why the sudden change of heart? What made them decide to negotiate for peace?"

Gwylla blinked at me, her abnormally huge eyes downright alien-looking in their shape and size. "I do not know. I was not privy to that information. At the time I was equally surprised about the peace negotiations and the terms of the contract we were told the king and queen agreed to."

"How did they react to the contract terms after thousands of years of scooping up humans by the truckload?" I asked.

The fairy glanced over at Nyalla and squirmed. "There was a lot of unrest. Even the lower caste households relied on human labor. And..."

Her voice trailed off. I didn't push her to continue. I didn't want Nyalla to know what else the fae were doing with their human captives.

"Perhaps it was an internal conflict that brought them to the negotiating table? Some warring factions in Aerie or unrest?" Nyalla suggested.

Gwylla laughed, the sound disturbingly like wind-chimes. "There are always warring factions in Aerie. The Seelie and Unseelie are forever trying to take each other's territory. I cannot recall a day when the Kingdom of the Sun and the Kingdom of the Moon have not been in conflict. That would not keep the queen or the king from continuing the war they'd waged upon the angels. But perhaps an insurrection from within the kingdom would. I was in Aerie at that time, though, and I do not recall any particular threat from inside the kingdom. The queen at that time was well liked. She had four children of her blood that stood in line to inherit, but none of them were old enough to stage a coup attempt."

I'd had some vague idea of provoking rebellion within the kingdom or pitting the fae against each other, but I wasn't sure how that would play out. I'd keep that idea in my back pocket, but I still should come up with more as backup plans.

Gwylla shrugged. "I was exiled a very long time ago and have not been in contact with anyone from Aerie since. Things may have changed since I was there. I would have no way of knowing."

I narrowed my eyes. "Then what's going to happen when you open up a gateway to Aerie? I'm assuming any sort of non-fae created gateway would set off an alarm, but wouldn't one from an exile of the court trigger those same alarms?"

She squirmed. "Probably. So you'll need to hurry. Return the ring to its rightful place, then get back as quickly as possible. They won't be expecting me to be in Aerie after all this time, so I don't think they'll initially notice, but if I have to hold the portal in place for a long time, they might notice and investigate."

Great. She didn't *think* they'd notice? And how long was too long? An hour? A day? A week? Even if she put me smack dab in the middle of the queen's dressing room it would probably take me more than an hour just to find the right jewelry chest and the right drawer.

"Do you think if she returns the ring, it will stop the fae from kidnapping humans?" Nyalla asked the fae woman.

"It might, but it might not. As you mentioned, this could be just as much about the contract with the angels as the theft of the ring. The contract would have been breached the moment an angel entered Aerie," Gwylla said. "As small and sneaky as the child angel is, I don't know if he went unnoticed. But returning the ring should keep the queen from crossing into this world with an army. I don't know the exact powers of the ring, or its provenance, but it *is* a royal artifact, and she will be desperate to get it back."

"Okay. So I'll return the ring and hope for the best," I told her, although I was planning something much different. Yes, I had the ring in my pocket, but I also had a note telling the fae queen that I was willing to give back her ring, but only in return for something from her.

And just to be on the safe side, I'd written the note in

Elvish. That way they'd be to blame for the theft instead of Lux.

I also had plans for the fae gateways, but if I could manage to get some concessions in exchange for this ring, it would be worth the trip.

That's what I decided Plan A was. Employ a combination of annoyance along with a carrot to tempt them. Hopefully the annoyance alone would make the fae desperate to cut a deal with us, but if not, I was hoping the promise of the ring would sway them.

Gwylla shot me a sideways look. "The queen might also demand to punish the thief who stole her ring."

I bristled, because there was no way I'd hand my son over to some fae bitch. He hadn't known what he was doing was wrong, and I would not let him pay the price for his mistake.

Hopefully she'd blame it on the Elves: if not, I'd include a no-punishment line in my bargain. And if that didn't work, then I'd stand in for Lux.

"I'll say that I stole the ring. If she wants to punish me, then I'll face her myself."

And I'd try my best to kill her, even devouring her if I needed to. Although given how ill those shadow fae had made me, trying to devour a powerful queen would probably kill me and leave her with little more than a hangnail.

"Sam..." Nyalla's voice was soft and full of worry. "You're not invincible. Even cockroaches sometimes die."

Gwylla sucked in a breath at what should have been an insult, but to me it wasn't—not anymore. Gregory called me Cockroach, and that had become a name I'd accepted and embraced. It was a term of endearment from him, and I'd grown to admire the insects that lurked unnoticed and seemed damned impossible to kill. They survived extreme temperatures, radiation, lack of oxygen.

But a well-placed boot would end their life, and that was something I needed to remember.

"I'm not sure the fae will truly know what to do with you." The fairy tilted her head. "Your energy signature is not the same as the angels who signed the contract. While your presence in Aerie would be seen as a trespass, it wouldn't violate any bargain or agreement that I'm aware of."

Well, at least *that* was something that worked in my favor.

"If the contract is already seen as null and void because a baby angel crossed into Aerie, then what does it matter if angels do?" I asked. "The fae are coming here, killing angels and snatching up humans right and left. Angels crossing into Aerie shouldn't be making things worse than they are."

Gwylla wiggled her hand back and forth in a very human gesture. "The best course of action would be for you to get the contract reinstated. Return the ring. If that doesn't work, then go on to negotiate some restitution or punishment for the theft. Then claim that any injuries have been redressed. If they insist the trespass is the issue, well, that's going to be another matter you'll need to account for in any negotiations."

I hated that her advice was to basically roll over and beg the fae for peace. With demons, that sort of approach would never work. We were brought to peace through fear—fear that we might lose, that we might get killed, that we'd suffer enough losses that our own household would turn against us. Giving this queen the ring and offering restitution meant I was weak, that all of us were weak.

We weren't weak. We were tricky motherfuckers. I'd been underpowered by comparison before and still came out on top. This might be the one time I failed, but I'd rather go down fighting than begging.

"What about all the humans who have been taken?" Nyalla demanded. "This queen gets her ring back, and gets restitution, but we humans get nothing? This whole issue is between the angels and the fae, not the humans and the fae."

Gwylla sighed. "The fae view humans as little more than animals, where the angels are seen as slightly less than equals. Without the contract in place, they don't even have the need to bargain with humans to take them into servitude. They'd just take what they wanted."

"That's not making me feel any better about this," Nyalla snapped. "Humans are no longer what we were ten thousand years ago. We deserve restitution. If a nuclear bomb took out an angel gateway to Hel, then the same thing can happen to the fae portals. Or we can just lob bombs through them and turn Aerie into a radioactive wasteland."

I grinned, my heart swelling with pride. Nyalla was truly *my* girl.

The fae woman, on the other hand, sucked in a breath, clearly uncomfortable with Nyalla's threats. "You would destroy an entire realm?"

Nyalla snorted. "We've been willing to destroy our *own* planet over all sorts of petty stuff. Fae invasion? Humans won't hesitate to attack once they know what's going on. Right now they think the missing people are due to human crime. They've put up with demons, elves, and angels and they're at the end of their patience. Fae snatching up random humans is going to push mankind over the edge."

Gwylla looked over at me, her brow furrowed.

"Totally true," I told her. "Humans are a lot like demons.

We all love to blow shit up, and have some hair triggers when it comes to a fight."

Nyalla's threats got me to wondering. Maybe all we needed was to advise every human to carry an iron railroad spike around with them for self-defense in case some fae tried to haul them off to Aerie. Or use bullets with a high iron content. Everyone in the States had a dozen guns, and most people had no problem stuffing them in the waistband of their jeans when going to Walmart or Starbucks, or even heading down to the mailbox. Sadly, a lot of cosplayers might die in a case of mistaken identity, but there were always friendly fire mishaps in war.

"Let us all hope the situation doesn't come to that," Gwylla said, breaking me out of a daydream where gun-toting, cowboy-hat-wearing humans shot down dozens of those shadow fae. "If you can convince the fae to return to the terms of the contract between them and the angels, the fae will only take humans as part of a bargain. Once that occurs, the humans can attempt to negotiate for...restitutions."

Yeah. I was pretty sure how that would end. Still, the humans were a lot smarter and stronger than others gave them credit for. The fae might end up begging to pay restitutions to keep from being shot up with iron bullets or stabbed with railroad stakes.

Or nuked.

"Just to clarify something," I said, an idea forming in my mind. "The contract was between the angels and the fae, so I assume that means the contract was with Angels of Order? Angels of Chaos would *not* be bound by this contract? Or demons? So if I'd taken an army of demons into Aerie, it wouldn't have violated the bargain?"

Gwylla nodded. "Normally you would all be considered

one race of angels and equally bound by the agreement, but since the war and exile of your kind happened over two million years before the war between the angels and the fae, you are no longer considered to be 'of one.' You and your brethren are not bound by the terms of the contract."

It was as I suspected. Demons and Angels of Chaos were not bound by the agreement. Which meant we were free to fuck shit up.

Loopholes. It was all about loopholes with angels, demons, and evidently with fae.

"Here's my plan," I told Gwylla. "I'm going to dash in, leave the ring"—actually leave the note—"dash out, and then see what happens."

"I am considered banished and no longer in contact with the Seelie or any of the fae in Aerie," Gwylla reminded me. "All I can do is advise you based on what I know of the court structure and laws when I was there. Returning the ring to its rightful place might be enough to satisfy the queen. If not, she will send a message that she wants the thief as well."

Over my dead body.

Annoy the fae. Ring negotiation. Take the blame, if necessary. I preferred the third to be: beat the ever-loving shit out of these fairies and have them begging to reinstate the former contract.

"Why risk opening a gateway yourself when I could go through one of *their* gateways?" I shuddered, thinking of the shadow fae. "Or maybe that's not the best idea."

"It's not at all a good idea," the fairy agreed. "Do not under any circumstances go through a fae-created gateway. They are most likely guarded or trapped. I will create one for you that should place you in the south wing of the Seelie queen's palace, close to the royal dressing chambers. The divination spell I cast told me that the ring belongs in the sixth drawer of the third jewelry box from the left."

This was bullshit. Sneaking through a castle and leaving a note in a jewelry box? This had to be the most anticlimactic quest ever. It would be far more entertaining if returning the ring involved chucking it in a lake of molten lava at Doom Mountain. I could even bite off some diminutive fae's finger first, just to stay reasonably true to cannon. That would be so much cooler than putting a note in a jewelry box in some foppish dressing chamber, then negotiating for the ring's return.

Gwylla went on another long spiel about the exact placement of the ring, then began reciting a list of the queen's other magnificent jewelry. Sighing, I tried to compose my expression into some semblance of interest while I ignored her and turned my thoughts to a more interesting topic—my upcoming wedding.

Should I have lions at the ceremony? Lions with diamond collars and silk leashes? If they escaped their handlers and ate a few of the guests, then all the better. And Dolly Parton...yes, I totally needed Dolly Parton to officiate. I'd have the Elvis impersonator sing at the reception, and maybe even do a duet with Dolly, but she absolutely needed to perform the ceremony. This was going to be the wedding humans and angels talked about through the ages.

Losing myself in daydreams of gauzy dresses, "Jolene," big hair, and lion-mauling, I was startled to hear Nyalla calling my name.

"Sam? You'll be ready, right? Day after tomorrow at noon?"

"Absolutely," I replied.

Nyalla sighed then turned to Gwylla. "I'll make sure she's there on time."

6

"What are you doing?" Gregory asked as I dragged the industrial-strength crate across a field in southern Wales.

"I'm doing what I do best—fuck some shit up." I plopped the crate down and the contents snarled and slammed against the sides. The door bent a bit and I winced, thinking maybe these crates weren't as sturdy as the manufacturers claimed. But then again, the box was sold to contain dogs, not Durfts.

The archangel sighed. "You plan to throw those animals through the gateway prior to our closing it, I assume?"

"Damn straight, I am." I glanced down at the crate that now had a second dent in the side. "Think you could work your mojo on these guys until I've got them in to Aerie?"

Durfts hated everyone, but they seemed to hate humans and angels a bit less. With humans, it was an individual thing, although I had no idea what the Durfts' criteria were for tolerance versus murderous rage. With angels, some had the ability to calm the creatures as a sort of enchantment. I'd seen this enchantment slip and backfire before with hilarious results, but Gregory never seemed to have that problem.

"No." He smirked. "They won't attack me, and watching you get mauled as you try to stuff them through the gateway will be very entertaining."

Asshole. Although I should have expected his response. My beloved could be insanely protective if I was truly in danger, but he really enjoyed watching me lose a fight.

"Fine. But if one decides to bite you, you're on your own." It was unlikely to happen, but it made me feel better to let my intentions be known.

Scooting the crate closer to the portal, I tried to figure out the best way to get this done. I could lob them through, but I didn't know how long this gateway was, and having them trapped inside a corridor wouldn't serve my purpose. Plus there was a chance they'd come racing back out. Not only would they chew me up if that happened, they'd also run off to fuck knows where. Gregory would then tell the Ruling Council, and they'd make me go round the Durfts up, claiming some shit about invasive species. No, I was going to have to take these monsters through myself if I really wanted them to cause havoc among the fae.

Good thing Gwylla had assured me that my presence in Aerie wouldn't further violate the contract.

Taking a deep breath, I opened the crate, and grabbed a Durft in each hand by the scruff of its neck. Holding my arms out as far as I could, I managed to make it into the portal without more than a few deep scratches from their claws.

Gregory shouted, but I was through before I heard more than "Cockroach!"

Thankfully the gateway was only a few steps between the two worlds. I didn't even pause to look around once I'd gotten to the other side, just threw the Durfts, turned around, and dashed back through the portal.

Gregory was still shouting when I appeared. "—idiotic, stupid, insane things to do…"

"Close it! Close it!" I framed it with my hands, hoping that the Durfts didn't come running back through.

The archangel might have been pissed at me, but he understood the urgency of the situation. With a burst of light, he closed the gate. Then he continued to shout at me. I waited his tirade out, because there was no sense in arguing when he was like this. Besides, I'd always found Gregory to be irresistible when he was furious. Although I doubted any sexual overtures, physical or non-corporeal, would be welcome at this moment.

There was a lot of ranting on how a group of shadow fae could have killed me, or any number of lethal creatures could have killed me, or how a fairy could have taken me prisoner, thus forcing Gregory to either capitulate to their demands, or create a portal, storm through it, and leave a trail of dead in his wake to free me.

The latter scenario appealed, but I kept my mouth shut.

When he'd finally calmed down, I spoke my piece.

"Just closing portals isn't going to convince the fae to back off, but you know how annoying I can be. I intend to bring chaos to these fae, to show them what the Ha-Satan, what an Imp is truly capable of."

He stared at me for a moment, then his lips twitched. "I'm not happy about you risking yourself like this, but the idea *is* clever. You do realize this is a long game you're playing, though? These Durfts will harass woodland creatures and the locals, but the royalty won't be bothered."

I shrugged. "My plan involves more than Durfts. Disrupt their food chain. Hit them where they will hurt the most by destroying both their decorative gardens and the ecological balance in Aerie. And yes, annoy the locals. The powerful stay in power because they are satisfying the needs of the populace. Either they're happy because their lives are awesome, or they're content and not willing to attempt a coup because of inertia and complacency."

"Or the powerful rule through force and fear," Gregory reminded me.

I shrugged again. "Maybe, but they'll have limitations on their resources. Fighting the other kingdom, constantly recreating portals and snatching humans, plus an internal rebellion? That's not going to be sustainable—at least not for long."

He shook his head. "Cockroach, you know better than that. I never thought I'd accuse you of unfounded optimism, but here I am. If they're keeping their populace at the edge of starvation, those fairies will not have the resources or the strength to attempt rebellion. Their only focus will be on survival."

He was right, but I had a feeling that wasn't the case in Aerie. Fae cared too much about beauty to have starving, disease-ridden commoners ruining their bucolic country-side. Yes, they could hide some away out of sight, but not the entirety of the masses. I had a gut feeling about this. I'd spent my life following my instincts, and that's what I intended to do here.

Three gateways in, I'd run out of Durfts, so I improvised. Drop bears were sent through the gateway in Ireland and two hippos through the one in Scotland. Through it all, Gregory looked on, amused.

Amused, and ready to haul my ass out of danger if I needed help.

Thankfully, there was nothing on the other side of the

portals besides weird twisty forests, orchards with fruit-laden branches, rolling fields of green and blue, and rocky terrain. Luckily the hippos had gone into a forest and a field, and not the mountainside. I would have hated to go to all that trouble to grab them if they'd promptly fallen off a cliff to their deaths.

When the portals were all closed, we headed back and I gave my household instructions for when we had to do it all again in two days. More Durfts were needed, as well as other creatures. I sent Snip to bargain with a plague demon for me, and ask Dar to see if he could lean on a certain corporation who was courting his political favor with large campaign donations.

I didn't need the cash, but I'd hoped this corporation could make a different sort of donation—one I was sure would absolutely enrage the fae.

7

The next day at noon Nyalla and I were freezing our asses off in the middle of Ireland, next to a large mound of dirt. I'd been to Ireland before and had seen adorable thatch-roofed cottages, turbulent cliff-faced seashores, and mossy-banked rivers. I'd never seen a heap of dirt like this before though.

"What is this thing?" I asked, gesturing at the dirt.

Gwylla said something unpronounceable. At my blank look, she informed me it was a sacred magical burial mound.

The fae woman stood beside us, her silver dress some magical middle place between liquid and solid. As she gave us her final instructions, I couldn't resist poking at the fabric. My finger sank through and came back wet and slippery, like I'd touched an oil slick. The dress rebounded to fill in the hole my finger had caused, rippling around the fae woman's arm.

It was really cool, and I found myself wanting to try something similar. Maybe I could ditch the gauzy dress I'd picked out for the wedding and do something like this instead. Gregory had taught me to hold water together in spheres a few years back. It couldn't be that much more difficult to form the water around my body in a kind of dress. Married in a dress of water? It would be amazing. And if my concentration slipped during the vows, I'd be naked. Which was also a winning scenario.

"Do you have the ring?" Gwylla asked.

I pulled it out of my pocket and waved it at her. She recoiled, then motioned for me to put it back. I assumed it was something to do with the magic that disturbed her, and not the artistic qualities of the ring itself. I couldn't feel any magic at all off the thing, but had to admit that it was rather pretty. The elves I'd known in Hel had always been skilled at creating these delicate, intricate things, and judging by this piece of jewelry, I was guessing their fae cousins had similar talents.

It was a wide band of an unfamiliar silvery metal with tiny inlaid faceted gems. There was an inscription inside the band that wasn't in Elvish or any language I knew.

Gwylla repeated her instructions again about how many lefts and rights I was to go and which cabinet and drawer I was to put the ring in. Then she waved her hands and sang a song in a voice so high-pitched that I feared she might summon every dog in a five mile radius. Once she was done with the tune, a sparkling gateway appeared in the side of the dirt mound.

"You can't open a gateway in the air?" I complained. "Do I really have to go through a pile of corpse-filled dirt to get to your homeland?"

"This is the only way," she replied.

I was calling bullshit on that. Wild interdimensional gateways were in the air, and I was sure some of them went to Aerie. Plus, the elves had originally come from there and I couldn't see any of them crawling through dirt holes.

Taking a few steps forward I squinted, unable to see through the gateway to the other side. Which kind of sucked. Without a clear view I couldn't time my entrance, and with my luck, there was a good chance I'd burst into Aerie standing on top of a banquet table in the middle of a huge feast, or during a fairy orgy or something.

"Hurry," Gwylla told me. "I can only hold this passageway open for so long."

Great. That meant if I was delayed, I'd have to wander around looking for one of the naturally occurring rifts that led me back home. Or wait for Gregory to come rescue me. Normally neither of those options would bother me, but I still had a good bit of wedding planning to do with the date rapidly approaching and didn't have the time to waste hanging out with a bunch of fairies.

"I hope there's an orgy," I told Nyalla as I walked through the gateway.

I didn't walk into an orgy or a feast. Instead I bounced off of something hard and damp and fell onto the soft mossy ground. For a few seconds, I thought the fae woman had pranked me and I was in fact inside a dirt grave. It took a while for my eyes adjust to the relative darkness and realize that I wasn't in a grave, *or* a palace. I was in a thick forest, my only illumination coming from the moonlight filtering through the canopy of leaves and branches.

Clearly Gwylla had grossly overstated her skills, because there wasn't a castle in sight. I stood, brushing off my pants and wondering if I should just go back. But I'd come this far and really wanted to leave my note somewhere it would be found before I returned. And my note wasn't likely to be found in the middle of a forest, especially a forest of moving trees.

Yep. They'd moved. Not branches-moved, but actually moved.

A few of the trees lit up with an eerie phosphorescent glow, giving me an even better view of the forest. Three of the larger trees twisted, turned, and shuffled a few feet closer. Their leaves whispered and rustled without a hint of wind, giving me the impression that they were talking.

"Hello!" I shouted at them. "I'm looking for a Seelie royal castle with a whole lot of jewelry boxes. Can one of you trees escort me, or at least point me in the right direction?"

The trees rustled and parted. I took a few tentative steps forward, not sure if they were helpfully giving me directions, or guiding me into quicksand. Hearing a crashing noise, I quickly retreated, cursing that Gwylla had gotten her coordinates so wrong.

A deer the size of a large pony burst into the clearing and abruptly stopped, staring at me.

I was doing some staring of my own. The thing had antlers that were a good ten feet from tip to tip, and was a solid pearlescent white with eyes that glowed bright blue. Around its neck was a dainty gold chain with a ruby the size of a quarter hanging from it. The hunters back home would have shit their drawers in excitement because this stag looked to be a fifty point buck. I was guessing a bit there because it was hard to count since the deer was stamping, snorting, and tossing its head at me.

Hadn't Gwylla said something about the flora and fauna being deadly here? I seemed to have remembered that and the creepy trees were totally supporting that idea. The only dangers I'd figured on were deadly traps in the palace and accidentally running into a guard before I'd stuffed my note into the jewelry box and gotten the hell out of here. I *hadn't* expected the possibility of being killed by a giant albino deer within six seconds of arriving in Aerie, though.

Which was better, being engulfed by a giant moving forest, or trampled by a giant stag? And where the fuck was this damned castle, anyway?

The buck pawed and snorted again. I held up my hands, trying to think what might appease a deer. Were they like horses? I didn't have any sweet-feed or peppermints, but I dug in my pockets and came up with a package of Skittles. They were Lux's current favorite snack, and if a young angel liked them, maybe a freakishly huge deer would too.

"Hey there Mr. Stag." I tried for a soothing tone of voice as I ripped the top off the Skittles pack, tossing the paper to the ground. Yeah, I was littering, but I figured that was the least of my worries right now. "What color is your favorite? Lux likes the red ones best. I like green because green candy is supposed to make you horny." I took a quick glance at the deer's undercarriage but didn't see anything there indicating gender or that this beast even had sexual organs at all. "How about yellow?"

I picked a couple of yellow candies from the bag and held my hand out flat, just like I did when giving treats to my horses. Whether feeding equines or monstrous deer, it was probably equally important to ensure they didn't have the opportunity to bite off your fingers along with the carrot or peppermint—or in this case yellow Skittles.

The stag walked forward, still snorting and pawing. I kept still with my hand out, trying not to make eye contact with the thing. I felt hot breath blowing against my fingers, then soft velvety lips taking the candies from my hand. The buck crunched them, then nudged my hand for more.

"You like these?" I asked as I poured more of the candies

into my palm. "I'll let you have them all as long as you don't kill me. Deal?"

The deer snorted. I was taking that as a "yes," so I continued to feed him the candies three or four at a time. I had no idea what my end game was here other than not being gored by this guy's antlers. I doubted he'd lead me to the castle, but I doubted the trees would either.

"Say, you wouldn't happen to know the way to the palace, would you? Specifically the dressing room for the queen?" He ignored me, so I continued to feed him candies as I looked around. The damned trees were so tall and close together that the castle could be twenty feet or twenty miles away and I wouldn't know the difference. I was going to have to wander around for a bit to see if I could find it, although I was worried if I lost sight of Gwylla's portal, I'd never find it again.

Not that I blamed the fairy overmuch for overshooting her intended mark by probably a few hundred miles. It had been a long time since she'd been in Aerie, and I got the feeling that stuff here moved around on its own. Which definitely meant it wasn't a good idea to wander far away from the gate. With my luck, the trees would shift around and I'd wind up lost in this forest forever.

"You look like the stag on the Jägermeister bottle. Only more jacked-up with bigger antlers," I told the deer. "I don't believe they could have managed to fit your image on the bottle, so they probably downsized your impressive rack."

He nodded, eying my empty palm expectantly.

Pouring the last of the candies into my hand, I tossed the empty package and let my new friend eat Skittles while I looked around. The trees hadn't advanced since the stag had entered the clearing, so that was a plus. Of course, there was no telling what they'd do if the stag left after the Skittles were gone. I stroked the deer's head, still debating whether to wander the forest in search of the castle, or to go back until Gwylla was a little more accurate with her portal location.

"Nice bling you got here, buddy," I said as I lifted the ruby pendant from the deer's neck. "Not the sort of thing I'd expect a woodland creature to wear, but I guess if you've got fifty feet of antler rack, a gemstone necklace completes the look. Have you thought about earrings? Bracelets around your hooves? You could get a dozen more of these and drape them over your antlers. Go all out, you know, rapper-style."

The stag snorted again, making me wonder if he understood me. Then he froze, swinging his head to the side and nearly clocking me with his antlers.

I let go of the necklace, ducked to avoid impact, then stepping to the side and standing upright again, wondered what the deer heard.

In the distance I heard a faint sound, like someone blowing a trumpet. The stag trembled, turning those blue eyes back to me. His gaze met mine, and I saw his fear. The horn sounded again, this time closer and the deer bolted, nearly knocking me over in his haste to get away. I spun around, not sure how he would get through the forest with that huge spread of antlers, but the trees quickly parted before him, and the stag vanished in a blur of white.

This time the trumpet noise sounded practically on top of me. Before I could scramble out of the way, a dozen dudes on horseback blew through the clearing, knocking me to the ground and trampling me with their hooves.

8

I lay on the ground and groaned, listening to the riders thundering off through the forest. I was bruised and filthy, my hair and clothes thick with mud. Standing up, I swiped a hand across my face and realized that it wasn't just mud coating my skin, but horse poop.

Fuckers.

Yeah, it was dark, but anyone who galloped through the forest on a nighttime hunt probably could see well enough to know there was someone *standing right in their path*. I was pissed, and in my anger, I forgot all about the note, as well as my concerns about potentially being lost and trapped in this weird-ass forest forever.

Revealing my wings, I shot upward to fly just above the tree line. The trees had parted to make a clear path for the stag and his pursuers, and I could see both from this vantage point. The stag was a white blur. The horsemen who followed him were less visible, but the moonlight glinted off their unsheathed weapons, and the dust cloud kicked up in the wake of the horse's hooves was unmistakable.

I swooped lower and picked up speed, eyeing the horsemen's weapons. The only animals humans hunted on horseback nowadays were foxes and coyotes, and that seemed to be mostly for the joy of the chase and the love of hounds. Humans hunted deer from a stand or a blind, using guns or bows. It seemed weird that the fae were chasing down this stag on horseback with big-ass swords and spears.

Elves back home had allergic reactions to iron and iron alloys, so either the fae didn't have this issue or these blades and tips were bronze, or some other metal native to this world. I thought about diving down and snatching one so I could better assess the molecular structure of the blade, but they were gaining on the deer and I was pretty sure what would happen to it if they got within spear-throwing range.

"Run, Jägermeister," I shouted as the woods began to move together in front of the deer. The stag reared, pawing as the trees closed ranks. The hunters slowed, one of the spearmen taking aim. I dove down as he released it, snatching the spear mid-flight and landing in front of the horsemen.

"He's mine," I shouted, flexing my wings. That usually worked in the human world, and had actually been working in Hel since I'd proven how lethal I truly was. These fae clearly hadn't gotten the message though, and my street cred meant nothing here.

Another rider threw a spear, and I dropped the one I had, jumping upward to grab it before landing back on the ground with my wings outspread. "Stop that shit," I scolded. "No killing this deer. No. Bad fairies. Bad."

The horses shuffled aside to let a leggy black horse through. The rider appeared male with waist-length flowing black hair, ivory cheekbones sharp enough to slice deli meat, and pointed ears. He extended a sword my direction and said something in a language that sounded like Elvish if the elf was singing and had his testicles in a vise.

I didn't understand any of it, but I was pretty sure he was commanding me to move so they could stab Jägermeister.

"Not happening." I twirled the spear to reverse it, then bopped the horse on the nose with the blunt end.

Trust me, I didn't hit it hard because I like horses. I would have preferred to whack the fae guy on the head with the spear end, but it didn't reach that far. Either way, I startled his horse enough that it reared up, pawing the air.

Just like the damned elves in Hel, this guy had a seat like Velcro and didn't fall off. His companions roared in anger, and I realized that one demon/angel with a spear probably couldn't do much against a bunch of mounted, armed fae. This wasn't like facing a bunch of humans on horseback. I had paranormal abilities, but so did they.

And according to Gregory, my paranormal abilities were probably not going to work here, so I was even more screwed.

They charged. I quickly backed up, yelling profanity as I threw the spear—which did nothing besides splat on the ground, quickly broken by the horses' hooves.

The stag raced back and forth at the line of closely packed trees. I ran forward to grab it, thinking I'd teleport somewhere in the forest with the deer, but before I could get to him, the trees parted and the stag bolted.

I spread my arms and my wings wide, trying to impede the hunters, but again they just plowed over me. It hurt the first time, but this was worse since my very sensitive wings were exposed. Instinctively I hid them before they were seriously damaged, but I still felt the ache of horses plowing into the appendages and bending them ways they should not have been bent.

Feeling completely inept, I jumped up once the horses were past me and revealed my wings again, once more taking to the skies. My wings ached. My body ached. My head ached. But I wasn't going to let these assholes skewer the deer that I'd just been feeding Skittles to, so I flew as fast as I could, passing the hunters and diving down once I was over top of the stag.

I landed on the thing and wrapped my arms around his neck, expecting him to panic. I wasn't disappointed. Horses bucking? I was used to that, but deer bucked differently and I felt myself flop around on his back, sliding partway off his side. I wasn't sure how much longer I could stay on, so I tried to teleport us somewhere, anywhere but here.

And I failed.

Fear spiked through me. Gregory and I had once gone through an interdimensional rift where none of our powers had worked, and he'd found himself rooted deeply into corporeal sensations. I didn't get the same sensation from this place, but clearly there was something different here.

We weren't in Kansas anymore, Toto. And I couldn't fucking teleport.

I managed to pull myself onto the stag's back and tried to stay balanced while he ran. The good news was he seemed to have found renewed vigor and energy, even with the added weight of my body on top of him. The bad news was a couple of spears nearly hit us, one tearing through the sleeve of my T-shirt before stabbing into a tree with a "thunk."

I'd been concerned about the forest turning against us, but the assault of one of their own by the fae must have made a difference. A path opened up before us, and branches closed behind us, slowing down our pursuers. The stag's sides heaved with effort, and he took a sharp right through the forest. I went to grab mane, only to realize that deer didn't have manes. Instead my hand snagged on the necklace around his neck.

Holding on, I made it around the corner before the chain gave way. I wrapped an arm around the deer's neck, dropping the necklace onto the forest floor. The stag sucked in a breath, and suddenly we were no longer in a forest. Instead we were in a hallway, with the deer slipping and sliding as it tried to get traction running across marble mosaic floors.

Fae screamed, throwing folded cloth and trays of food as they got out of the way. I screamed as well, not sure what the fuck was happening, since *I* hadn't been the one who'd teleported us here.

Then we vanished to appear somewhere else. Now we were running through what appeared to be a throne room. A larger group of fae were screaming and running, hands waving above their heads. Even though I was still in danger of falling off, I focused on the amusement of the whole situation. This stag was totally a kindred spirit. And there was no way I was going to let some fairy assholes kill him.

The stag raced around the assembly, snorting and pawing and causing all sorts of chaos. We rounded a corner, and his insanely large antlers caught on one of the wall tapestries, tearing it from the rod. He shook his head, and the fabric whipped around us, covering my head. I scrambled, trying to get it off while trying to stay on the deer. Remaining on was my priority, because I had no idea where I was, and without the ability to teleport, I could be stuck wherever I fell for months or even years.

Not that I had any hope of getting back anytime soon. Even if I continued to ride the stag, I could end up thousands of miles from Gwylla's gateway, wandering the woods on deer-back.

My head finally came free from the tapestry. It trailed along either side of us like Superman's cape. Fae still were screaming and scattering. The deer's big-as-fuck antlers caught various fabric and metal bling as we tore through the throne room. He tossed his antlers and snorted, running in random directions. Guards had swarmed the hall and were throwing spears at the deer, a group of them advancing with swords drawn. Just as one of the guards raced forward to swing at the stag, we vanished again and appeared in a large room—thankfully one with nobody else inside.

The tapestry was still wrapped around us like an ornate cloak, and shit still dangled from the deer's antlers. Jäger-meister snorted, pawing at the brightly colored rug on the marble floor. I looked around, suddenly remembering the ring and the note offering both threats and negotiation that I intended on leaving in the ring's place. Was this the dressing room that Gwylla was supposed to port me to? Was there a line of jewelry cabinets nearby? I didn't really want to get off the stag to search, just in case he vanished on me and left me a gazillion miles from the portal, so I nudged him with my leg, moving him around the perimeters of the room in search of a jewelry closet.

There were a few doors that I managed to push open while still seated on the stag. The first two held veritable tunnels of clothing. The third was a square room with tall narrow dressers. I urged the deer inside, leaning over to pull open a few of the drawers. They were filled with gold chains, gemstone pendants, cuff bracelets, and earrings.

I had no idea if this was the queen's jewelry cabinet or that of some other rich bitch in the fae world, but I figured it might be wise to drop the note here. I pushed the reluctant

stag forward, counting the cabinets until I reached the one
Gwylla had specified. Pulling the note from my pocket, I
leaned down to open the drawer. That's when I heard a
scream from behind me.

Instantly we were in the forest again, me perched
halfway off the side of the deer as he crashed through the
trees. I heard the squawk of a horn, and Jägermeister picked
up speed. I managed to right myself again, my priorities
shifting. I'd dropped the note when the fairy screamed. It
might not be in inside the jewelry cabinet in the spot where
the ring was supposed to be, but it was close enough. Plus it
was probably more likely to be found where I'd left it. Either
way, my job was kind of done. Right now I needed to get the
hell out of here before I was killed, *and* before this stag was
killed.

We tore through the woods, me trusting the deer to
guide our way. The hunters were drawing nearer, and I
thought about telling Jägermeister to teleport. Then I saw a
clearing and a solid stripe of green, with a glowing jagged
line behind it.

The portal.

I dug my heels into the deer's side, slapping his neck to
guide him toward the gateway. He obliged, tearing through
brush and dodging trees with his giant fucking antlers as he
headed to the clearing. A spear whistled past us, sinking
into the ground. I bent lower over Jager's neck, clenching my
legs and urging him onward. He put on a burst of speed,
heading right toward the glowing gateway.

We ran through, nearly knocking Nyalla and Gwylla
down as we plowed through the portal.

"Close it! Close it!" I screamed as the stag whirled
around, trying to buck me off.

Gwylla shot me a panicked look then closed the portal

just as the hoofbeats sounded near the entrance. I blew out a breath, thankful that the huntsmen hadn't followed us into the human world.

"Sam! What happened?" Nyalla stared at the whirling stag, wide-eyed.

The deer shook his head, flinging metal and fabric across the ground. I held on to the tapestry around its neck, but slid sideways onto the animal's side. The brocade tapestry ripped and I slid even further. The stag side-stepped, and that was all I needed to fall onto the ground, the tapestry piled on top of me. By the time I pushed it off my head, the stag was gone and both Nyalla and Gwylla were staring at me.

"Did you return the ring?" The fae woman asked.

I staggered to my feet, the tapestry hanging off one shoulder. "Are you fucking kidding me? No, I didn't return the ring. Your gateway put me smack in the middle of a forest, not in the queen's dressing room."

Of course, I hadn't planned to return the ring anyway, but she didn't need to know that. She also didn't need to know that I'd left a note that would probably piss the Seelie queen off even more than she already was. Nope. Gwylla could take the blame for this one with her shitty location skills, buying me some extra time and maybe an extra visit to the fae realm to cause more mayhem.

Gwylla frowned, tapping her chin. "The palace and surrounding forest move. Everything in Aerie moves, but I thought I had calculated the timing and location correctly. Either way, the castle should have been within walking distance."

"Walking distance." I glared at her. "The trees felt like they wanted to kill me. That stag would have killed me too if I hadn't fed him candy. Even if I'd managed to find the palace and make it there alive, I'm pretty sure some fairy would have noticed me and killed me before I got through the gates."

"Hmm, true," the fae woman said, looking unconcerned about the threats I'd just encountered in her homeland.

"Then there were the huntsmen," I added. "They didn't even apologize for mowing me down—twice. Not like they'd give me directions even if I'd had a chance to ask them. Plus it's dark as fuck there. I could barely see my hand in front of my face."

Gwylla frowned, suddenly focusing on me. "Hunters? At night? And they were after the stag? Were they Unseelie fae?"

I shrugged. "You all look the same to me. Why?"

She ran over and started sorting through the miscellaneous bling on the ground, finally lifting up a silvery crown with sapphire and onyx stones. "Oh no."

Oops. I'd told her I'd never made it to the palace, but a crown and tapestries would probably not have been lying around in the woods. Time to lie. Well, to lie more.

"*That* was not my fault." I pointed at the crown. "None of that stuff was my fault. The stag teleported us out of the forest and into a castle, and snagged all that shit on his antlers. We did end up in a dressing room, and I was looking for the correct jewelry box and drawer, but someone screamed and the fucking deer teleported us before I could...leave the ring."

Gwylla let out a breath, her wide eyes meeting mine. "I'm glad you didn't. Return the ring, that is. Because I sent you to the wrong kingdom. Somehow I managed to put you in the Unseelie court instead of the Seelie court."

Damn it. That meant I'd left the note in the wrong kingdom. It was the Seelie queen who would want to negotiate for the return of the ring, not whoever the fuck ruled that other kingdom.

"Wrong kingdom!" I threw up my hands in frustration. "Middle of the fucking woods in the wrong kingdom, with the wrong castle, the wrong dressing room, and the wrong jewelry box."

This whole thing was a giant clusterfuck. And for once, *I* wasn't to blame.

She blushed. "I'm so sorry. There's a good chance next time you'll end up a distance from the castle as well, but I'll try to ensure I open the gateway into the correct kingdom."

"And maybe draw me a map?" I suggested.

"I could go with you and provide guidance." She bit her lip and frowned. "If I use a glamour and a few charms, I might be able to remain undetected."

I weighed the benefits of having a native guide with the chance I might end up returning with her corpse. I got the impression the fae would kill her if she was found in Aerie. And if they didn't, I might kill her myself. One hour and I was ready to murder the woman. A few days or a week would truly put me in a stabbing mood.

"Nope. A map will work just fine," I said.

Even with glamour and charms, Gwylla's presence would put a big target on our backs, and I didn't need that.

"Or I could go," Nyalla suggested.

"You?" I sputtered.

It was clear by Nyalla's offended expression that my interjection was the wrong thing to say. I wasn't sure how else I was supposed to react, though. Nyalla was human, and thus very breakable. And very killable. She did have the angel-gifted ability to see into people's hearts, and knowing motivation did come in handy sometimes, but it didn't outweigh the risk of her getting killed.

"At least *I* can read a map," she snapped. "Remember that time you drove us up to New York City, and we ended up in downtown Philadelphia? Or the time you tried to drive us all to Hershey Park for Austin's birthday party and we ended up in downtown Philadelphia."

I did seem to end up in downtown Philadelphia a lot, even when using GPS.

"Even when you teleport, you still wind up in the wrong place sometimes," Nyalla went on.

"How was I supposed to know Kansas City was in *Missouri*?" I demanded. "Or that there's a Portland *Maine* in addition to a Portland Oregon?"

Okay, maybe I shouldn't be throwing shade on Gwylla for her location issues. Nyalla was better at navigation, but that still didn't outweigh the fact that she was a fragile human.

"Fae are particularly skilled at enchantment," Gwylla said. "The elves used fear and isolation to keep their human slaves obedient, but we find it much easier to enchant them into appropriate behavior. I could provide you with a charm to resist this, but as a human, you'd still be susceptible to falling under the spell of the stronger fae."

Nyalla looked a little ill at that, but gritted her teeth and nodded. "I'll be okay."

"Yes, you'll be okay because you're staying here," I told her. "I won't risk you getting killed, or enslaved."

"I fought demons and angels, a power-hungry elf, and a dragon," she pointed out. "Remember that angel Harper and I took down and restrained? I'm not as helpless as you think, Sam. You need someone to help read the map and keep you focused so you don't come back with an albino deer, a torn tapestry, and the ring you were supposed to return. Plus I'm human. I won't be out of place there, and they'll ignore me thinking I'm a servant girl. They'll under-estimate me, and you've taught me that's a huge advantage."

I *had* taught her that. And she wasn't wrong about the map and the focus thing. Still...

"So it's settled," Nyalla announced far before I consid-ered the matter settled. "Gwylla will embed a gateway spell into an object for Sam to carry, so we can return whenever we're done with the task, and wherever we happen to be in Aerie. She'll craft a charm that will make me less suscep-tible to enchantment, and put together a map of the king-doms. And in one week, Sam and I will go to Aerie and return the ring."

It was not settled. But I had a few days to convince Nyalla to stay home. And if I couldn't convince her, then I'd find a way to ditch her and go to Aerie alone.

9

By the next morning, I realized I'd acquired a creepy new stalker—one with a huge rack of antlers and glowing eyes. Before teleporting home I'd made a pitstop in Seattle to walk along the waterfront and visit my old nemesis, the gate guardian. I spotted the deer across a busy street, people walking around it as if they saw a giant white stag on the sidewalk every day. Then it was on the roof of a building by the gate to Hel, and in a back alley near the wharf. Each time the thing stood and stared at me. It was unnerving, but when I teleported home and caught sight of it out in the horse pasture, then later staring at me through the kitchen window, I'd had enough.

"911, what is your emergency?"

"I'm being followed," I told the woman. "He's staring at me everywhere I go. I just caught him looking at me through my kitchen window."

"Is he still there?" the operator asked, the clack of her fingers typing in the background. "I'm sending the police right out."

I looked over at the kitchen window, my gaze meeting

the glowing one of the deer. "Yep. Still staring at me through the window."

I verified my address, and answered the door ten minutes later to two uniformed officers—one of which I recognized.

"Usually we get called out here because someone's complaining about *you*."

That was true. Mostly because I could handle just about anything that trespassed on my property with ill intent far better than human law enforcement. But I wasn't sure what sort of abilities this creepy deer might be packing. Better to see it take out a few cops and gauge whether I'd be able to kill it myself or if I needed to call Gregory and plead for his help.

Honestly, I didn't really want to kill the deer. I'd fed it Skittles, after all, and kinda saved it from those fairy hunters. But the stalking thing was getting on my nerves. And demons did tend to resort to murder when annoyed.

"So, where's the stalker?" the other officer asked me, after shooting a reproving look at the asshole who'd been at my house too many times to count.

"There." I opened the door wide and pointed across the great room to the bank of French doors leading to my back patio and pool area. Standing inches from the middle door was my nemesis.

"It's a deer," Asshole-cop announced. "A really big albino stag."

Idiot. "I know. It came through the gateway from Aerie and has been following me ever since. If it just hung out in the pasture with the horses, I'd be okay with it. It's the staring at me through the windows and doors thing that's getting to me. That and showing up wherever I go. Grocery store? There it is in the produce section, munching on

Romaine. Bar? It's by the pool table underneath the taxi-dermy head of his cousin. It was looking through my bedroom window this morning, and my bedroom is on the second floor."

"Shoot it," Non-Asshole cop said helpfully. "You've got a huge spot over your fireplace, and that thing has to be a twenty-pointer at least. And it's an albino. Would look really great over the mantle."

He had a point. But it was kinda hard to kill something I'd been feeding candy to just yesterday. Plus I felt a little guilty that it was here and not in Aerie. I'd urged the thing through the gateway, and while it was safe from the fae hunters, it was in a strange place, where I was the only person it knew.

A lonely deer. Fuck, how had I become so sentimental? I was going to blame Gregory. It was all his fault. Falling in love had turned me into a mushy softie of a demon/angel.

"I don't want to kill it," I told the officers. "Can you just arrest it and charge it with stalking? Or trespass? Isn't it illegal to look through people's windows? It's a Peeping Tom. Or Peeping Deer."

"You can't charge wildlife with trespass, or peeping," Non-Asshole cop informed me.

"We can call animal control," Asshole cop suggested. "They get rid of nuisance raccoons and bats and stuff. Although I'm not sure they'd think a deer in a rural area of the county to be a nuisance animal."

I thought about that, but the idea of the stag sad and even more lonely in some cage bothered me. And if they set it loose somewhere else in the county, it would be back here before I could brew a cup of coffee.

"How about you all just chase it off?" I asked. "And

maybe issue a stern warning? That might be all it needs to stay away from me and go bother someone else."

Asshole cop snorted. "It's not our job to run around after a deer, yelling at it to stay away. Just call animal control."

I dug in my pocket and pulled out a couple of fifties. "This change your mind?"

"Yes, it does." Non-Asshole cop snatched one of the bills from my hand.

Asshole cop reluctantly took the other one. "Are we allowed to club it? Or tase it?"

I thought about that for a second. "Yeah. Sure. As long as you don't kill it."

Of course, I didn't know exactly what might constitute lethal force toward this animal, but I was willing to bet anything from Aerie would be heartier than the average deer.

The two cops went around to the back of my house, while I watched from inside. At first the stag ignored them, only glancing over when they started yelling and waving their arms at it. The thing didn't even budge when Non-Asshole cop ran at it. Clearly deciding more than threats were needed, Asshole cop pulled out his Taser and shot the deer.

I winced, then realized the deer was absolutely unaffected by the electrical current. Actually, he *was* affected. His reaction was annoyance. He turned toward the officers, snorted, then lowered his head.

"Run!" I shouted, happy I was safely inside behind safety glass.

It was well worth a hundred bucks to watch the deer chase two police officers around my yard. The stag managed to get close enough to Asshole cop to hook him with his huge antlers and toss him into the horse pasture where Diablo decided this was a fun game and took over running after the cop. The other one jumped in the pool to try to escape, but this stag apparently didn't mind going for a swim. He jumped in after the officer, deer-paddled after him, and bit him on the ass as he tried to climb out. Finally both cops managed to get back around the front of my house and into their police car, where they tore off down the drive, the stag in pursuit.

Either the cruiser had a higher top speed than the teleporting fae deer, or the animal got bored because half an hour later it was back staring at me through my windows and doors with its freaky glowing eyes.

I had no interest in running around my back forty being chased with a deer, and I figured the thing deserved some peeping time after the entertainment he'd provided, so I let him be. My angel and Lux were coming home in time for dinner after having spent the last day doing some father-son bonding. I'd give the stag a bit of a reprieve, and if he was still creeping around my house by the time they got here, I'd make Gregory get rid of it.

Not kill it, because I still felt weird about murdering something I'd fed candy to. But maybe Gregory could send it back to Aerie, or somewhere else it wouldn't be able to teleport back from. And if not, I'd drive it down to Columbia in the morning and shove it through the gateway to Hel so it could harass the demons.

"What's going on?" Joe asked as he came down the stairs from his bedroom. "I saw the police here. Did someone try to break in?"

His voice cracked a bit on the last sentence, making it clear that he worried it was the fae trying to break in.

"I've got a stalker." I pointed to the French doors and the stag.

Joe sucked in a breath. "That's...I've never seen a deer like that before. Are its eyes *glowing*? Do albino deers' eyes glow?"

"It's from Aerie," I told him. "I had some business there among the fae, and it came through the portal with me when I left."

No need to tell him I was riding it, or that a bunch of fairies had been hunting it.

"It's a fae deer?" He eyed it and backed up one of the steps.

"It's from Aerie, so it's some sort of fae deer. But don't worry," I assured him. "It's not a deer-assassin or a deer-spy. A bunch of Unseelie fae were hunting it, so it's kind of a refugee like you."

Which meant I was probably going to end up housing the thing. Damn it.

"How do you know it's an Unseelie fae stag?" Joe backed up an additional step.

"Gwylla said the stuff caught in its antlers was Unseelie, but I don't know if deer is native to only that kingdom, or if they can be found all over Aerie." I frowned, wondering if deer had political alignments, or if they differed in the Seelie and Unseelie areas of Aerie.

"Who is Gwylla?" Joe didn't seem reassured. In fact, he looked poised to bolt up the stairs any second.

"A fae woman." I held out a hand as his eyes widened. "Not here. She's not here. She was exiled from the Seelie kingdom a long time ago and currently lives up in Alaska. I promise you she isn't involved at all in the kidnapping of humans. At least, not anymore."

His shoulders slumped in relief. "And you're not going to let that fae deer in the house, are you? It's not sleeping inside?"

"Absolutely not," I lied. There was no telling what would happen when Nyalla got home. Or Lux. The little angel really loved animals and might decide Jager needed to stay in his room.

Thankfully my answer seemed to satisfy Joe. It didn't calm him enough to let him descend the stairs and walk across to the kitchen under the stag's intense gaze without trembling, but at least he managed to get a soda and a bag of chips before bolting back upstairs.

As for me, I got some chips and a soda of my own, then sat down to watch television.

"Hope you like *American Loggers*," I told the deer as I turned to the lumberjack show. "There's a snowstorm and I'm looking forward to seeing some trucks sliding off embankments and flipping down hills."

I heard the deer snort, took that for agreement, and settled in to watch my show.

10

The *American Logger* episode didn't disappoint. Even Jager seemed to approve. In anticipation of Gregory and Lux's arrival, I went upstairs to shower. Since my bathroom didn't have any windows, the deer was forced to stand out in the pasture and stare up through the one near my bed. I was beginning to think bringing him into the house would be better than him staring at me through the windows all night. Maybe I could lock Jager in a bedroom or in the basement so I could have sex without a fae-deer voyeur watching us.

Gregory and Lux entered by the front door instead of teleporting into the middle of my kitchen as they used to do. Lux had been obsessed with *I Love Lucy* lately, so he not only insisted on entering and exiting via the door, but in shouting "Lucy, I'm home!" in a Cuban accent every time he arrived.

I was a mediocre cook at best, so our family dinner tonight was raw oysters, steamed Bay crabs, and a quart of German potato salad all courtesy of Lighthouse Seafood and Deli.

I took some up to Joe, who had locked himself in his bedroom, no doubt to remain safe from potentially murderous fae-deer. Lux and I ate while Gregory drank coffee and munched from a bag of potato chips. I did manage to convince him to sample the potato salad, but he refused the crabs and oysters. Actually he looked somewhat revolted as Lux and I slurped raw shellfish and ripped apart the crabs with our hands.

"Oye-stars! Yum!" Lux shouted as he reached to snag another one from the platter.

"Eat your fill, buddy," I told him. The kid might be an Angel of Order, but I was raising him right.

"So what did you all get into yesterday?" I asked as I snapped the legs off a crab and sucked the meat out.

"We explored the asteroid belt of this solar system, and analyzed the atomic composition of the various rings of Saturn," Gregory told me.

"Black hole," Lux said as he chased his oyster with a mouthful of fresh horseradish.

I swear my heart stopped. "Black hole?"

Gregory shot me an embarrassed smile. "We took a quick side-trip to another galaxy, and while I was discussing the differences in the energy output of various stars, Lux slipped away. I don't blame him. Black holes are fascinating."

I felt lightheaded at the thought of my little angel being sucked into the event horizon, stretched and crushed. Angels were immortal, but they *could* die, and I was pretty sure that black holes, super nova, and other shit could kill even an archangel as powerful as Gregory.

"He didn't get too close," Gregory quickly informed me. "When I caught up to him, we became beings of light so we could experience the effect. Then I gated us away. There was no risk to either of us."

I glared at him. He'd given me serious shit that time Lux had nearly gone through the chipper shredder, and here he'd almost let our kid get sucked into a black hole? Totally the pot calling the kettle black kind of scenario here.

"Never visit a black hole without Daddy," I informed Lux.

He nodded, eating another spoonful of horseradish. "Not wifout Daddy. Got it."

"And what did *you* do yesterday?" Gregory asked, obviously eager to change the topic of conversation.

"Uh." Now it was my turn to squirm. "Went to Aerie. Brought back some bling, a torn tapestry, and a stag that's stalking me."

The archangel scowled. "Why were you in Aerie? Did you take a truckload of Durfts and drop bears with you? You need to tell me exactly what happened when you were there."

I glanced over at Lux, thinking it was best if he didn't hear this. No sense in putting even more chaos ideas into the little angel's head. "Honey, why don't you go into the kitchen and get a popsicle out of the freezer? You can eat it by the pool."

"Yay!" The little angel was gone in a flash.

I waited until he was safely outside with the door closed before I turned to Gregory. "Remember those rings Lux stole? And how you think his going to Aerie might be what broke the contract between the angels and the fae? Well, this fairy friend of Raphael and Ahia's said that returning the ring would stop any invasion and all-out war from the fae. And that if I returned the ring, I might be able to negotiate a peace."

The archangel rolled his eyes. "As you would tell me, 'this fae woman is smoking crack if she believes that.'"

"I know. I didn't intend on returning the ring," I told him. "I was going to leave a note for the queen, telling her I had her artifact and that if she wanted it back, we needed to bargain. But Gwylla, that fae woman friend of Raphael's and Ahia's, opened a portal into the wrong kingdom, and I ended up leaving the note with the Unseelie instead of the Seelie."

He snorted. "Figures. I don't like you going to Aerie. It's one thing for you to quickly run vicious animals through the gateways while I wait on this side, it's another for you to go through a portal some random fae woman created. You could have been killed or taken prisoner, and I wouldn't even have known where you were."

"Nyalla was with Gwylla at the portal," I said. "If I hadn't come back, she would have let you know what happened. And although Gwylla is pretty shitty when it comes to her portal locations, she'd probably be able to give you at least a vague idea of where she sent me."

"How could she give me a vague idea of where she sent you? She intended to open a gateway to the Seelie kingdom and instead put you in the Unseelie one. I would be frantically searching the wrong kingdom for you if you hadn't returned."

He had a point.

"I don't doubt your power, Cockroach," he continued. "What I doubt is your ability to broker any sort of peace. You're an agent of chaos. Everything you touch falls into pandemonium."

"Pandemonium which eventually turns out for the best," I reminded him. "Tell you what, if I manage to get the note to the right kingdom, and the queen wants to negotiate, I'll bring you on board. Deal?"

His eyebrows shot up. "You're going to Aerie *again*? Through one of their gateways this time, I assume?"

"No, through another one Gwylla is going to create. She told me I'd be in less danger using hers than the ones the fairies make," I hurriedly added.

"Less danger." The archangel glared at me. "She sends you to the wrong kingdom, but you're going to trust her to somehow send you to the right one this time?"

"No. But this time 'll have a map," I told him. "So if I get lost, I'll be able to figure out where I am and how to get to the Seelie court."

His eyebrows shot up. "You? A map?"

For fuck's sake. "Nyalla offered to go with me, to read the map and help me stay focused, but I'm not going to let her. You'll just have to trust that I'll figure it out myself," I snapped, annoyed that he too was insulting my directional capabilities.

"How long will this note-leaving take?" Gregory asked. "I need to know when I should start to worry and prepare to invade a hostile realm to rescue you."

I rolled my eyes. "You keep your ass this side of the gates. An archangel in Aerie is *really* going to piss them off. I might be able to fly under their radar, but you definitely won't."

His lips twitched. "Okay. Fine. But if you're not back in two weeks, I'm coming to Aerie with my sword."

"I don't think your sword is going to show up. Mine didn't when I tried to summon it. I couldn't teleport either," I told him. "Although I'm sure you don't need a sword to murder two kingdoms of fairies and rescue me from a dungeon."

He smiled, his eyes glowing a bit. It reminded me that

there really wasn't much of a difference between us when it came down to it.

"I'm teasing you, you know," he told me. "You'll survive, and somehow it will all work out in the end. It always does. The journey is always incredibly painful, but journeys of transformation always are."

I wasn't sure he meant that as a compliment or not, but I chose to accept it as one. Getting up from my chair, I went over to sit on his lap, wrapping my arms around his neck and digging my Old Bay and crab encrusted fingers into his hair. "What do you say we send Lux to bed early tonight? Or make him go muck the stables for a few hours? I think you and I need a little private time."

"Doggie!" Lux shouted from the back of the house, illustrating my point.

"Don't let him inside," I shouted back to the baby angel. Boomer had rolled in something dead and stinky this afternoon, as hellhounds often did. I really didn't want him in the house until I'd had a chance to hose him off with the pressure washer.

"Too late," Lux said cheerfully.

"Damn it." I twisted around on Gregory's lap, expecting to see, and smell, my fragrant dog. Instead there was that fucking stag, staring at me from ten feet away with its glowing eyes. Lux stood beside it, reaching up to pat the thing's shoulder.

"Nice doggie," he informed me.

"Get out of—" The last word was cut off with a squeak because Gregory had risen from the chair with lightning speed, dumping me on the floor. Before I could take a breath, he'd summoned his sword—his fiery sentient sword that was raining sparks down on my custom-made, solid-maple table.

"Do *not* burn down my furniture!" I got up and stood between him and the table, my own sword appearing unbidden in my hand. "Or my fucking house. And don't kill the deer. It's a stalking pain in my ass, but I fed it Skittles and somehow that's made it mine."

Gregory's sword vanished and he stared at me. "Is it the Skittles? Or the act of feeding something that marks a being as claimed? Because I know of no Angel of Chaos or demon where that has ever been the case."

"It's a me thing," I told him, not certain how that had occurred either. It's not like I had any idea why I claimed certain things and beings as mine, or how it happened. It just happened.

"That's not a normal deer," Gregory informed me, his gaze shifting back to the stag.

"Well I figured that, what with the glowing eyes and the giant rack of antlers and the albino color," I replied. "It teleports too. Isn't that cool? It came through the portal from Aerie and is stalking me. Probably because I fed it the Skittles. And maybe because it's lonely."

"Was it being hunted?" Gregory asked.

"Yeah, in the middle of the night by some absolute assholes on horseback."

He sighed and sat down. "Deer hunted by the fae in their wild hunt are convicts that have been transformed into deer."

I looked over at Lux with concern, but he was still petting the thing's back, and Jager was nuzzling his pockets. As I watched, the deer pulled out a small packet of Skittles and ate the whole thing, wrapper and all.

"Like a theft kind of convict?" I asked the archangel. "Because this deer seems a bit gentle to be a murderer or a rapist, and I can imagine the fae would be insanely strict with their punishments for what here would be misdemeanors."

Gregory shrugged. "From what I've been told, this particular punishment is used for the crime of treason, but the fae consider many things to be treasonous."

"So...theft deserves capital punishment." Wow. I was even more determined to take the rap for Lux's theft. Being turned into a deer and hunted by a whole lot of fae wasn't that bad of a sentence for me, but I wouldn't want Lux to have to endure that.

Actually I liked my odds of surviving that punishment a whole lot, since I was pretty good at evading capture, and killing off my pursuers.

"But from what you told me, this would have been a night court hunt." Gregory frowned at the deer who was nuzzling Lux's other pockets. "This being is a transformed Seelie fae. Not an Unseelie one."

I stared at him, open mouthed. "You can *tell*? Not only do you know it's a transformed fae, but you know which kingdom it's from?"

He frowned at me, his tone turning reproachful. "There are some physical differences in fae of the different kingdoms, Cockroach, but the true tell is their energy signature. Seelie and Unseelie fae have different specialties and abilities, and their energy is distinct."

I waved that away. "So what's the big deal with a Seelie fae being hunted by the Unseelie? I mean, a convict is a convict, isn't it?"

He shook his head. "The kingdoms are almost constantly at war. They would not swap prisoners for this crime, because part of the hunt contract involves being hunted by their own kind. The convict agrees to the transformation and the hunt instead of facing an ignoble death or an eternity in their horrible prisons. They are free, as long as they can remain one step ahead of the hunt. The only reason I can imagine for a Seelie fae to be transformed and the prey of an Unseelie hunt is if they were caught in the Unseelie kingdom as a spy. Even so, I don't believe they'd be offered this honorable death instead of just being imprisoned and tortured for all of eternity."

Gregory seemed to know a lot more about the fae than I'd expected. And he was able to communicate that knowledge in a succinct manner, as opposed to long-winded Gwylla.

"Is there some way we can transform him back?" I asked, glancing again at the stag. Maybe I could cut a deal where we broke the enchantment in return for Jager being my guide in Aerie. That way I'd be able to leave Nyalla safely behind plus not have to cope with my questionable orienteering abilities.

"We would need to consult with your fairy acquaintance before attempting such a thing," the archangel told me. "Perhaps she can break the spell. If not, then once we have a good grasp of the structure and nature of the spell, we could attempt to unravel it ourselves."

Great. I wasn't looking forward to seeing Gwylla again this soon, and I was worried that this might delay the work she needed to do on crafting the other spells we'd need for our trip. But if the deer could be transformed back into a fae, my chances of delivering my note to the correct fae royalty would increase.

"I'll have Nyalla arrange for her to visit." I picked up my phone and sent off a quick text. "But what should I do with this deer in the meantime?"

"My room!" Lux announced as he fed the deer from a

huge bag of Skittles that had somehow appeared in his hands.

I didn't really want to trust this stag in my child's bedroom, especially since I didn't know exactly what sort of crime had caused him to be transformed and hunted. On the other hand, I didn't want to lock it in the barn with the horses, just in case my best chance at getting around the fae kingdom colicked overnight or impaled himself on some farming implement.

"No. My room." I sighed, thinking that my plans for an evening full of sexy-times had just gone out the window.

11

The deer snored. And every time I dozed off, it got onto the bed and snuggled up against me, stabbing me with its antlers and knocking me off the edge of the mattress with its hooves. The thing also had no consideration for personal space. It watched me brush my teeth and shower, and even tried to watch while I was taking my morning shit.

We were up before Lux, so I made pancakes with chocolate chips and brewed a large pot of coffee. Joe popped into the kitchen as I was cooking, took one look at the stag wedged in the corner between the fridge and the sink, and left. His loss. Pancakes rocked, but if he would rather hide in his room and eat stale chips from last night, so be it.

When I flipped the last pancake out of the fry pan, I put the stag's breakfast on a plate and its coffee in a bowl.

FYI, fae convicts-turned-deer evidently like two spoons of sugar and a healthy splash of cream in their coffee. It wasn't a teeth-clenchingly sweet as Gregory liked, but it was damned close.

Lux came down just as the deer and I were on our

second cup of coffee. The little angel chatted with the stag as he ate his breakfast, and by the time I was clearing the dishes off the table, Gwylla and Nyalla had arrived.

Nyalla couldn't teleport, but she had Gabriel wrapped around her pretty little finger, and he seemed more than happy to transport her anywhere she wanted. Since the stodgy archangel wasn't present, I was assuming he'd dropped Nyalla off in Alaska where Gwylla had her sanctuary and that the fae woman had magicked the two of them back here, probably with one of those portals. Although this time, her navigation appeared to be working.

The fairy took one look at the stag and frowned. The deer eyed her, snorted, and backed up.

"No. No." Lux held out his hands to the deer, petting it reassuringly. "Friendly fairy. Friendly."

The stag looked down at him, then back up at Gwylla. I could swear its eyes narrowed menacingly, making me question my assumption that its crime had been non-violent.

"I've been told the deer is a Seelie fae who was given the option of being transformed and hunted as opposed to a dishonorable death or imprisonment," I said to Gwylla. "Since I was in the Unseelie kingdom and it was their people hunting it, I'm assuming this was some sort of spy that was caught and convicted of treason?"

Gwylla tilted her head. "That is often the case, but this... this fae is young. Very young. Children are not often given such a sentence for their crimes. I'm sorry I did not realize this was a transformed fae initially. I was thrown off by your unorthodox arrival through the portal, and the deer vanished directly afterward, so I didn't get a good read on it. These white deer are very rare, but they do exist naturally in the wild, so I just assumed it was a native animal and not the product of a spell."

I wasn't going to blame Gwylla. Yes, she'd screwed up the location of her gateway, but I wasn't exactly in a position to throw stones on that. And this stag had only been there a split second before teleporting away.

"This *is* a transformed Seelie," she went on. "Young. No more than the equivalent of fifteen or sixteen human years. And from what I can see of the spell, she has been transformed for a very long time."

Nyalla gasped. "She's only fifteen or sixteen?"

I knew Nyalla was thinking of her own experience with the elves, but something other than Jager's fairy-age surprised me.

"She?" I stared at Gwylla, then turned to stare at what I had thought was a stag with his big-ass rack. "*She?*"

A girl. The stag was a girl. Which I guess meant she technically was a doe? But what kind of doe had huge antlers like that? The does around my property didn't have antlers at all, so how was I to know she was female? Let alone that she was actually not a stag, but a doe?

"She." Gwylla gave me a sideways smile. "Fae deer all have large sets of antlers and no visible genitalia. The fairy is definitely female, and the animal she has been transformed into is a female is well.

"Fifteen or sixteen." I did the math, using my fingers. "And you said the spell was cast a long time ago. So this child was how old when she was convicted of a treasonous crime? Eight or nine, I'm assuming?"

The fae woman wrinkled her nose and stared at the deer. "I'm guessing she was the equivalent of five or maybe six human years when the spell was cast."

"*Five* years?" I exploded. "How is a five-year-old fae child guilty of treason? How is she able to consent to this sort of punishment? And how was she able to evade capture by the hunt for the equivalent of ten or eleven human years?"

"Treason is not the only reason for transformation," Gwylla explained. "And no, we would not convict a five-year-old child of treason and subject her to the hunt. We would strip her of rank and place her into a lifetime of indentured servitude."

"A *five*-year-old child?" My voice raised to nearly a shriek.

"Not because of her actions, but because of her parents' actions." Gwylla winced at my expression. "Parents are responsible for the crimes of their children, and a parent's crime is often passed down to their offspring for punishment, especially if they are elderly or die before a sentence can be issued. I don't necessarily agree with this. I'm just telling you how the legal system works in Aerie," she quickly added.

"Okay, then under what other circumstances would a young child wind up transformed into a stag?" I asked.

"For protection," she responded. "If the parents committed treason, or some other crime, and they were about to be caught, they might have paid a high-level fae to transform their children. That way their offspring could evade capture and not be punished for their parents' crimes. If the parents somehow managed to escape, they would release their children from the spell when it was safe, or they could send their transformed children to a trusted friend or relative to be released from the spell when they arrived. I think that might have been the situation with this child."

"So I'm assuming the parents didn't survive, and the friends or family never found her, or possibly died themselves?" I asked.

Gwylla shrugged. "That definitely could have happened. I'm surprised she's survived this long on her own as a deer."

"Why a *white* stag, though," I asked. "If that's the form they condemn criminals to, if that's the animal that's hunted, then why would her family choose to make her a white stag, or hart, or whatever? Why not a sparrow, or a squirrel or something?"

"I'm assuming her family lacked the magic to do any other form. Honestly, they probably bought the spell, and this might have been the only one available." She shrugged again. "I'm not even sure *she* will know, given how young she probably was at her transformation."

"Can you reverse it?" I wondered if it might be better to leave the poor girl as she was, especially since she'd seemed to have spent more of her life as a deer than as a fairy.

Gwylla shook her head. "This is not a kind of magic I am skilled in."

"Gregory said he might be able to do it if you could let him know the specifics of the spell. The Archangel Michael, I mean," I said at her puzzled expression.

"I would not presume to know the abilities of an archangel, but from what I have learned, *demons* are particularly skilled in transformational magic." She eyed me. "I am fairly certain you could return her to her fae form yourself."

I laughed. "She might end up a troll or a cow or something if I do it. I don't know enough about fairies to risk it. Elves maybe, but fae? No."

"We're not so different." She took a step toward me and extended her hand. "See for yourself."

My eyebrows shot up. "Uh, you do realize that I won't be just feeling up your hand? I need to go *inside* you, to examine not just your genetic makeup, but how your spirit connects to your corporeal form. It's invasive and intimate."

She nodded. "Normally I would allow no one this kind of liberty, especially a powerful demon. But it's the only way you will know how to return this child to her true form."

I hesitated, but she kept her hand extended so I took it, diving my personal energy down past her skin, allowing my spirit-self to explore her. That's when I confirmed that her human form was indeed a façade. There were similarities between Gwylla and the elves I'd snatched deep glimpses of in my life, but there were also differences. Her spirit had more in common with those shadowy creatures that had attacked Gregory and me at the gateway. It was oily, slippery, and complex. The genetics of her corporeal form were fairly straightforward, but her spirit wasn't as deeply embedded as with humans, or as distant as with angels. It was fluid, shifting and changing as if her body were merely an outfit, easily removed. And between the body and the spirit was something more insubstantial with flexible bone and fangs for teeth. It took me a second to realize that this was the fae woman's true form. The beautiful icy-haired beauty with pointed ears and delicate features was a carefully constructed mask, hiding the monster within.

I pulled back, realizing that Gwylla had truly allowed me a level of knowledge and intimacy that she probably had not allowed anyone ever before.

"Thank you," I told her.

She nodded, giving me a wobbly smile. "I hope that helped. And I hope that you will keep my secrets."

I smiled back, a little nauseated at the oily darkness of her spirit self. "Every living being varies in ways that go beyond their physical self. The strengths and weaknesses I discovered will only be used against my enemies. You are an ally, Gwylla, not an enemy."

"Thank the Goddess," she breathed. "Do you know enough to return this poor girl to her true form?"

Probably not, but I knew all I was going to know, and at this point I was the best chance she had at not being a deer for the rest of her life. If I screwed up...well, Gregory could always fix my mistakes.

Hopefully.

"Yep." I cracked my knuckles and walked toward the deer. "Lux, you might want to go over near Gwylla for this."

"Okay. Nice doggie." He patted the deer's shoulder once more, then skipped over to stand next to the fae woman.

The stag, or hart or whatever, nuzzled me, putting her velvety nose in my palm and looking into my eyes with her weird glowing gaze. As I'd done with Gwylla, I sent my personal energy into the beast, diving below the furry hide and searching for the fairy inside the animal.

It took a while to find her, hiding deep inside the strange anatomy of the antlered doe.

It's okay. I'm going to help you. I felt the deer flinch, but the fairy girl inside reached out toward me. *Stay there. I'm going to surround you and protect you, so you'll be safe when I change your corporeal form.*

She tensed, then relaxed, allowing me to encircle her fae-self with my own spirit. Holding her safe, I grasped and dissolved the corporeal form of the deer, recreating a similar structure to what Gwylla used to house herself. There was a moment of indecision when I was done, a moment of doubt. If I released her and I'd screwed up, she'd die. But I couldn't shelter her forever. I had to trust in my own skill.

But...she was too young to die.

I felt the girl reach out to me, tentatively touching my spirit self.

*I trust you. You saved me once, and I know that you will save
me thrice more.*

Well, fuck that. Thrice more? Seriously? Did this count
as number one? Was this some fae prophecy? Because I
didn't like the idea that I'd need to rescue this deer, or girl,
in the future.

But she was right. I needed to let her go, and to trust. So
that's what I did, pulling back from her fae-self, through the
corporeal form I'd created. I felt her extend, claim the physical being with that insubstantial, lethal form just under the
surface. By the time I'd retreated into my own body, she'd
claimed this other one as her own. For a second I saw her as
she truly was, the shifting smoke of her body, the oversized
glowing neon of her eyes, the sharp bones, the pointed
fangs. Then I blinked and before me stood a beautiful
teenager whose golden hair was streaked with white. Her
eyes were a bright mossy green, her skin a dark burnished
tan.

And she was stark naked. Which didn't really bother me
since I spent as much time naked as possible. It didn't seem
to bother her or Gwylla either.

"Pretty doggie-girl!" Lux squealed, clapping his hands.
"Good job, Mommy."

Good job indeed.

"Hi." I released her hand and smiled. "I'm Sam."

She swallowed a few times, then said something with a
rusty voice—something I didn't understand.

Gwylla stepped forward to interpret. "She says her name
is Iselle." She said something else and Gwylla frowned. "She
said that you can still call her Jager if you want."

I laughed at that.

There were a million questions I wanted to ask this girl,
but she clearly needed rest and then some more food. The

transformation had probably been fairly traumatic, and she'd spent most of her life as a deer, fleeing bands of hunters. This was going to take time to adjust.

She might not be recovered enough to act as my guide in Aerie. Actually, I wasn't even sure she *could* guide me around the kingdoms. First, language would be a barrier in communications between us. Secondly, she might not know anything beyond the areas of the forest where she'd hidden as a deer. Even though she'd teleported us into various rooms of a castle, that might have been an accident, a panicked random location she'd picked in an attempt to get us to safety.

Even if she wasn't of any use to me in negotiating the return of the ring, she might have information that would help us get the upper hand against the fae. And if not...well, I seemed to have a habit of collecting strays and making them part of my household. Plus Nyalla would be thrilled to have another young woman in our house—one who might have had similarly traumatic experiences at the hands of others.

Iselle said something else and there was a weird chiming noise that had me looking around the room.

"She says she owes you a debt," Gwylla translated.

"Okay." I shrugged, not sure what a teenage fae girl could do for me beyond act as my guide in Aerie when I needed to return.

"I'm not sure if you fully understand the significance of her statement." Gwylla looked back and forth between me and the fae girl. "For us, the commitments we make as part of our bargains are physically binding. We can prevaricate, but we cannot lie. Even as young as she is, this girl did not pledge herself to you lightly. She owes you more than a favor, she owes you her life."

I squirmed, more than a little uncomfortable with that. Here I'd been thinking the fae were like a cross between demons and elves, but we had no problem lying, and while breaking a vow had consequences, our promises weren't magically binding.

"Can I release her from this?" I asked.

Iselle's eyes widened and she shook her head, saying something to Gwylla, who interpreted.

"You can, but it distresses her that you would consider such a thing. This is a matter of honor to her. She has no living family in Aerie to turn to, and you are the only one she trusts here beyond the little angel. Binding herself to you through a debt of honor provides her with much needed safety."

Well shit. I hadn't thought of that.

"Stay," Lux insisted. The little angel came forward and took my hand, tugging it so I looked down at him. "Pretty doggie-girl stay."

Well, that settled the issue.

I turned toward the teen and smiled. "Then I welcome you to my household, Iselle-Jager. We're your family now."

Tears glistened in the girl's eyes and she nodded, her lips wobbling.

"I can take her home with me," Gwylla offered. "The sanctuary I've created might be more familiar and comforting to her. After she is recovered, I can return her here to fulfill her vow."

"Let it be her decision," I told Gwylla. "I'm happy for her to stay here, and Nyalla knows how difficult it is to adjust after living your life in a different realm. She'll be happy to teach and help her, even if she doesn't speak Iselle's language."

Gwylla turned to the teen, gesturing around the room.

Iselle replied at length, then Gwylla spoke again before turning to me.

"She wants to stay with you. She trusts you, and I can tell she doesn't quite trust me—which I completely understand given her circumstances. You fed her. You defended her from the hunters. You removed the amulet that blocked her magic."

I frowned. "You mean the necklace she was wearing? That was an amulet?" I hadn't known, but then again, Aerie and fae magic felt very foreign to me.

Iselle nodded, then said something more in her language, clasping her hands over her chest and bowing.

"She has been quickly learning your language over the last day, and hopes to be able to speak directly with you soon. Even though she was very young when transformed and has been restricted from her magic for a long time, she will do all she can to assist you and be of service."

She was fae. She at least knew that one forest area of the Unseelie kingdom. She could teleport—which would be really fucking useful.

But she was a girl the human equivalent of fifteen, and I wasn't sure I felt any better about risking her life than I did about risking Nyalla's.

12

Joe was even more alarmed about sharing the house with a Seelie girl than he was with a fae deer. I began to feel guilty that he was spending so much time up his bedroom, so I loaned Iselle some clothing and sent her off with Nyalla and Lux to shop. After they left, I went upstairs and let him know the house would be fae-free for the next three hours.

He made himself lunch, did the dishes, then went outside saying he wanted to walk around the pasture and the wooded area near the boundary of my property. I watched for a while as he petted the horses, slipping them some peppermints he'd taken from a bowl Nyalla had in the kitchen exactly for that purpose. I had no idea how long he'd be remaining here. Probably until he felt confident that the fae weren't going to snatch him up again, or send assassins after him. From his reaction to Iselle both in her deer and Seelie form, the guy was obviously traumatized. He might never leave.

The thought annoyed me. I'd built a separate house for my Lows and visiting household from Hel to stay in just so I could have some privacy here. Maybe Joe could shack up with them? Or maybe I could put in an apartment over the barn? Because if he was still here after my wedding, I was going to have to figure out some other arrangement for him. Nyalla would have a fit if I kicked him out, but I now had her and Lux and Joe and Iselle all shacked up in my house.

The best idea might be for *me* to find a new house and let everyone else stay here.

Just in case, I researched homes for sale, favoring a few promising ones in Switzerland, Argentina, and Portugal. Joe came back from his walk an hour later, made himself a plate of sandwiches, and took it along with a cooler full of ice and sodas upstairs to his room.

Nyalla, Lux, and Iselle returned laden down with shopping bags, the human girl and the little angel happily chatting away to the younger fae. They all went upstairs and by the time they descended for dinner, the Seelie girl was looking like she'd walked right out of a local high school. Her sunshine-colored hair hung in beachy waves, covering the points of her ears. Her moss-green eyes were subtly highlighted with eyeshadow in shades of pink, the lashes darkened with mascara. Her dark-gold skin was perfect by nature, but it now bore a sparkling sheen. Her jeans were snug on her slim frame, and her printed silk shirt flowed artfully around her upper body in boho fashion. The gold chain around her wrist had green stones dangling from it that matched her eyes.

"Ta-da!" Nyalla stood aside, her hands framing the other girl.

Iselle smiled shyly. "Pretty?"

"Pretty!" Lux shouted his approval.

"Beautiful," I told the fae girl, not caring at the dent

Nyalla had probably put in my credit card. "You look just like a human teen."

Her smile broadened at that and she nodded, clearly having exhausted her command of the English language with that one word.

"Dinner." I clapped my hands to break the awkwardly sappy atmosphere. "Let's go into the kitchen and see what our new friend might like to eat." It had been a long day for Iselle and I knew that her transformation and the newness of her situation had taken a lot out of her.

Newsflash—Iselle might not be strictly a vegetarian, but her taste in food certainly leaned that way. I wasn't sure if it was a cultural thing, or because she'd spent most of her life dining on acorns and grass, but either way it left her with few options in my fridge, which was mostly stocked with meat and meat byproducts.

Thankfully I still had that stalk of fresh Brussel sprouts and a bag of kale that Gabe had sent home with Nyalla a couple of days ago. I wasn't about to feed the poor girl that nasty stuff raw, so I roasted both vegetables in the oven, tossing them in olive oil and a mixture of spices. It was pretty basic stuff, but Iselle wolfed it down like I'd served her a prime cut rib eye.

Lux demanded that he be in charge of the dessert. Iselle's eyelids were drooping when she'd finished her vegetable dinner, but she perked right up when Lux slid a bowl of chocolate ice cream in front of her. It was topped with fresh strawberries and whipped marshmallow. Once she was done, Iselle was darned close to falling asleep at the table, so we escorted her upstairs where Lux insisted on giving up his bed to the girl. I showed her where the bathroom was, hoping that after all the years as a deer she actually knew how to use a toilet. Just in case, I made sure the front door wouldn't accidentally lock behind her if she went outside to do her business.

A few hours later Lux curled up in my bed with me for the night. I loved having him close, and felt a profound sense of peace and calm when Gregory slipped into bed with us before dawn. As much as I liked our adult, sexy-time antics together, this family sleeping thing was pretty damned nice.

Better than nice. It filled a space in my spirit-being that I'd never before realized had existed.

I WOKE at dawn to an empty bed, and the sound of voices downstairs. Throwing on some clothes, I went down to see Iselle and Lux sitting at my dining room table, each of them bundled up in a blanket while Nyalla plied them with hot cocoa and rum-butter muffins. Gregory was on one side of the fae girl, and Lux to the left.

"Coffee," I muttered to them, heading into the kitchen. I liked cocoa, but this early I needed the jolt of caffeine that only a triple espresso could bring.

As my morning elixir was brewing I heard the murmur of voices from the dining room, and was surprised to hear Iselle speak in halting English. Was it a fae thing to learn languages quickly? Or was she just particularly gifted this way?

By the time I came back in with a mug of coffee, Nyalla had supplanted Gregory from his seat and was holding the girl's hand.

"Can you tell us how you were turned into a deer?" Nyalla asked.

"Spell. For safety." The fae frowned for a few seconds

choosing her words carefully. "We had to flee our village one night, my mother and I. I think there was a war and the soldiers were killing people and burning towns, so we left. We hid, staying in one cottage then another. My mother was afraid—very afraid. One day she told me this was the only way I could be safe, and that she would find me and reverse the spell once she could."

Nyalla squeezed the girl's hand. "I'm guessing you never saw her again."

Iselle shook her head. "I waited in the general area, worried that if I journeyed too far, she would not be able to find me. I even went by the cottage after a dozen moon cycles to see if she was there, but the place was burned to the ground and there were decomposing bodies. I forced myself to look, but I could not tell if any of the dead were her."

Nyalla made a sympathetic noise. "All those years and you had no one. And being transformed into a deer as well? How terrifying that must have been for you."

The fae girl nodded, her moss-green eyes sparkling with tears. "There are beasts in the woods that feed upon deer and other animals. I could not trust any fairies since I do not know who were our enemies. One night, I fell to a hunter's dart and thought this would be my end. Instead I awoke unhurt, wearing the amulet that kept me from using my magic. Every new moon since then I have been chased by the hunt. There are other deer that look like me who wear the same amulet. Many of them did not survive more than a few moon-cycles. I do not know how I managed to escape the hunters for so long, but I feared I would soon be dead myself."

Lux leaned over and put his head on the girl's arm. "Safe now. Mama will keep the deer-girl safe."

She smiled over at me. "I know. I trust her with my life."

Yikes. That was a scary thought. But I had other things I wanted to ask the girl, and I didn't want to dwell on the responsibility for yet another life resting on my shoulders.

"Do fairies normally have the ability to teleport? Or is this something that's a rare magic among your kind?" I asked her.

She frowned. "I don't know. I cannot remember my mother being able to do so. But I remember always having the skill to move my physical body over great distances with only a thought. It scared my mother, and she pleaded with me not to use that magic."

I made a sympathetic noise, thinking how disturbing it would be if Lux took to vanishing halfway across the world. Luckily I had the ability to follow him with only a thought myself.

"And the other deer?" Gregory asked, continuing the questions. "You said they wore the amulet as well? And that the amulet kept the wearer from using any magic?"

Iselle nodded. "The only other albino deer I came across also wore the amulet. Perhaps it was only an identification or tracking device for the huntsmen, but I could teleport before it was put on me. And when it was removed, I could once more."

Lux patted the girl's arm. "Pretty fairy-deer is strong and powerful."

She laughed. "I do not feel powerful. I feel helpless and scared."

Nyalla gripped her hand. "I understand. I was scared too. I was so scared that I felt like my heart might burst out of my chest. But it turns out I'm stronger than I thought. And I have friends—friends that will always be there for me. You have those friends as well."

Iselle sucked in a breath, then nodded as she slowly let it out. "I will try not to be scared."

I thought of Joe upstairs, hiding from this scared fae girl and realized that everyone had baggage—myself included. Friends and loved ones. They were the ones that helped you find the strength to carry the baggage. Hopefully both my new houseguests would find that strength.

"You're a Seelie fae. How did you end up in the Unseelie kingdom where Sam found you?" Gregory asked Iselle. "I'm assuming that you *and* your mother were living there when you were transformed?"

She thought about that for a few seconds.

"I do not remember living anywhere but in what you are calling the Unseelie Kingdom," she confessed. "I know that I am Seelie, but I don't know if my family has always lived in the place where I was found, or if there were circumstances that caused us to move either before my birth or shortly thereafter."

"Where did you live before you went into hiding?" Gregory asked. "I mean, was it a castle? A house in a large city? You mentioned a village, but had you lived somewhere before that?"

Iselle frowned. She looked down at her mug of cocoa. "I vaguely remember seeing long golden halls with a magical forest indoors when I was very little, but maybe we visited this place, or I saw it in a dream or a book. Before my mother and I fled to the forest, we lived in a village above an herbal shop where my mother worked."

"That sounds lovely," Nyalla said with a smile.

The fae girl relaxed for the first time since we'd begun these questions. "We had a garden behind the shop where my mother grew most of her herbs. We'd go into the forests on days when the store was closed and forage for special roots, fungi, and plants. She'd dance with me, sing me songs, teach me her magic." Iselle smiled. "I felt special, adored, protected." The smile faded. "But then the enemies came and we had to hide. And I had to become a deer."

"I'm so sorry," Nyalla said. "I'm sorry you lost your childhood so young."

I was the one who teared up at that, thinking that at least Iselle had a childhood to remember. Nyalla had none of that. She'd been a slave since her first memory, and while the elves adored babies, once she'd been able to toddle around, she'd needed to earn her keep. And Nyalla's experience had been particularly horrible since she had no innate ability for magic. A changeling was expected to be valuable through their ability to learn and perform magic for their elven owners. Nyalla instead was a disappointment, condemned to menial tasks and scorn, until she was eventually sold to a demon.

Thankfully that demon was me. I'd bought her as a present for Wyatt, bringing his long-lost changeling sister home to him. And in the process, she'd become like a daughter to me—a daughter and a best friend.

"You said your mother taught you her magic. Do you have any other magical abilities besides teleportation?" Gregory asked.

The girl tilted her head and pursed her lips. "I remember instruction in weather manipulation, turning night to day for brief periods of time, influencing animals, and creating plant life."

"And speed-learning languages," I added.

She tilted her head and looked at me. "That is a skill everyone has, no? As for the other things, I think I have the ability to learn and do much more, but I had no instruction or the opportunity to practice anything when I was a deer."

"Your education was stunted," Gregory agreed. "But the fairy-folk have long lives, and here you have the opportunity to continue learning. Gwylla has offered to assist you, and I am more than happy to arrange for an apprenticeship with a high-level elf, or a human sorcerer."

Iselle scowled. "Elves are not to be trusted. They are horrible creatures, and there is good reason they are banished from Aerie."

My eyebrows went up because the elves told a different story. According to them, they'd left of their own free will, and chose not to return because they hated the fairies that ruled Aerie.

"Some humans are very skilled at magic, but their methods are different and they will most likely not have experience in the same areas as your talents," Nyalla told her. "Perhaps living with Gwylla for a while would give you the best chance to catch up on all the things you've not been able to learn while you were a deer."

The girl bit her lip. "This Gwylla bears the mark of exile. I'm not sure I can trust her either."

"You were a Seelie fae living in the Unseelie Kingdom and on the run," I pointed out. "Probably not a good idea to judge Gwylla too harshly. Plus if it wasn't for her, you'd still be a deer. I couldn't have changed you back without her help."

Iselle squirmed. "I'm sorry, but I feel safest with you. And the little boy-angel. And the human woman."

Of course she felt safe with Lux and Nyalla. They were kind and compassionate beings who loved deeply. Me? I was a chaotic violent erratic being, but I would give my life for those I'd pledged to protect. And for some reason, the deer I'd fed Skittles to, the fae girl who'd stood before me naked and afraid, was one of those I now felt bound to guard and defend.

"You are welcome to stay here as long as you wish," I told her. "I consider you part of my household. I'm just letting you know that I probably can't help you develop any of your fae abilities."

"Maybe you can do Zoom lessons with Gwylla," Nyalla spoke up. "Video conferencing. That way you can learn from her without ever leaving the house. Although I don't think Gwylla has computers. Or internet. She can create a portal to visit here, but I think it's emotionally painful for her to leave her sanctuary."

"Maybe in the future I will be able to visit her, but for now, I want to remain here, with Sam." Iselle smiled at Nyalla, then turned that smile to me.

"More clothes," Lux spoke up. "Shoes. Shopping."

For fuck's sake. How many more clothes did the girl need?

"Oh, absolutely." Nyalla clapped her hands. "But we don't have to deal with the car and the mall this time. Internet shopping is awesome. When you're done with your hot chocolate, come up to my room and I'll show you my favorite online retailers. We can get you some dresses for clubbing, a few bathing suits, workout clothes, shoes, soaps, moisturizers, and all sorts of other things."

I downed the rest of my coffee, not wanting to think about the credit card bill. "I need to run out with this asshole archangel here to do some work. You three have fun internet shopping. Nyalla, show Iselle around the property, order lunch delivered, and sit out by the pool to relax or stream some movies. Lux, no bothering the neighbors, and no riding the mower around the field unsupervised. And try to convince Joe to come downstairs. I've seen him peeking over the banisters, but the guy needs to get over this shit and start learning to live with Iselle or he's going to have to spend his life in a tiny room."

"Okay," Lux said with a grin.

Nyalla shot Gregory a quick glance then looked over at me. "And this afternoon? Are we going to...do the thing?"

I couldn't very well leave Iselle here alone, or with Lux and the freaked-out Joe as her only companions, but I worried she might not be onboard with "the thing."

"Maybe," I said. "It's going to depend..."

Gregory seemed clueless and uninterested in this vague talk, but Iselle turned to face me.

"I am willing to assist you with any task. You broke the collar that bound my magic. You saved me, you transformed me, and so I am in your debt. I owe you my life, and I belong to you."

There was a weird chiming noise that again seemed to come from nowhere and everywhere at once. I looked around, wondering if it was a malfunctioning appliance or if one of my smoke detector batteries was running low.

"Hey, no problem," I said. "Like I told you, you're a member of my household now, so there's a responsibility on my side as well. Besides, thanks to you, I scored a few things in Aerie. I came away with a new crown, a torn tapestry, and some other bling, so it's all good."

"I mean it," she said, her voice a bit stronger. "I am in your debt."

Another damned chime. I needed to find that broken smoke detector before it woke me up at three in the morning with this shit.

"Okay. You and Nyalla go buy everything on the internet. I'll deal with 'the thing' later," I told her as I climbed up on the dining room table and summoned my sword so I could poke at the smoke detector mounted on the ceiling.

An hour later Gregory had helped me change the batteries in every smoke detector we could find, and we were off to close the interdimensional gateways that the fae had once again opened into my world.

13

"Do you think these connect to the Seelie Kingdom or the Unseelie one?" I asked as the archangel and I stood in front of the gateway we'd located outside of Belfast Ireland. The cage next to me rattled and the sound of snarling came from it. I'd sent pairs of Durfts through the portals in Spain and Scotland this time, and was ready to dump four demon-badger hybrids through this particular gateway.

"Although I can tell the difference between the two races of fae, I don't know enough about their kingdoms to pinpoint where the gateways lead to," he responded.

I frowned. "Gwylla has said the whole time that these incursions are the Seelie queen's doing, that the contract between the Seelie fae and the angels was broken when Lux went to Aerie and took that ring from her jewelry box. But were there separate contracts between you and each kingdom? If Lux inadvertently broke the bargain with one Kingdom, does that mean the other kingdom is still bound by the agreement or not?"

"We negotiated with both kingdom's representatives and

they were considered separate agreements. Although at the time they were not at war and were united in fighting against us." Gregory sighed. "I believe having a common enemy brought them temporarily together."

"But do you think Lux's trespass was enough to bring them together again?" I mused. "Are we only fighting the Seelie queen, as Gwylla implied, or has the Unseelie king joined in this as well?"

Gregory frowned in thought. "I honestly don't know. The attacks so far have born the energy signature of the Seelie kingdom, but the shadow fae we encountered are found in both courts," he said. "That doesn't mean the Unseelie consider their contract with us to be broken."

"So everything so far has been from the Seelie court?" I asked.

"All the energy signatures my angels and I have noted have been Seelie," he replied. "But a few of the gateways we've closed have held a mix of Seelie and Unseelie energy."

"Are the kingdoms working together?" I wondered

"I hope not," he said, echoing my thoughts. "The fae kingdoms are powerful on their own, but together they are a serious adversary."

"I just need to know if I'm dealing with one kingdom or two," I said.

I'd disrupted the Unseelie hunt, stolen their prey, whacked one of their hunter's horses on the nose with the butt end of a spear. Then I'd ridden a stag through their castle, stealing a crown, a tapestry, and some other random shit. Then I'd left what amounted to a ransom note on top of a jewelry box. We may have started out dealing with the Seelie fae, but my well-intentioned attempt at ending this might have ended up pissing off the other kingdom as well.

Hopefully all this shit I was shoving through their

portals was only annoying the Seelie kingdom, because a divided fae worked to my advantage.

"I don't know what I'm doing," I confessed. "My idea was to annoy the fae with my guerilla attacks then offer them a deal in return for the ring. Now I've got a rescued kidnapped human and a teenage Seelie fae, who has lived most of her life as a deer, in my house. I don't know who I'm fighting. It's all turning into one giant shitshow."

Gregory wrapped his arms around me, his spirit-self brushing mine. "Darling, you should act as impulse drives you. That is your gift, your power, your destiny. I trust that whatever guides you is what should be. And I will always honor that and support you. Yes, I express my reservations and my viewpoint, but whatever action you decide to take, I will always be by your side. You can count on that."

I hugged him back. "Sometimes I seem to make things worse."

He squeezed me tight. "Then that's because things need to become worse before they transform. Remember the glass horse you made from the beer bottles, the bottles you smashed into shards at the campground? Destruction is the only way to transformation. Creation can only occur through an act of destruction. Butterflies only are born because a caterpillar dissolves into a gelatinous form."

None of that seemed particularly reassuring, but I felt relieved to know he'd always support me, no matter how badly I screwed shit up.

"I'm going to continue to throw crap through the portals," I warned him. "And I'm going back to Aerie in an attempt to get this fuckhead of a queen to negotiate with us. It might backfire, but it might work."

He laughed, kissing the top of my head before letting me go. "I'm always here for you, Cockroach. And if I need to, I'll go through a portal and murder everything I see to rescue you."

I smiled. "Same. I mean, just in case you end up at the other end of some portal and I need to rescue you."

I needed to do something to make these fae beg to have the contract back in place. Something happened ten thousand years ago to make them hustle to the table and agree to a bargain that wasn't in their favor. And I was determined to make it happen again, no matter what it took.

"Are you ready?" At Gregory's nod, I outlined the gateway. "It's right here. But wait a sec. I want to pop through to the other side with these demon-badgers to drop them off and take a look around. I'll be right back."

The angel scowled. "There may be those shadow fae on the other side, or guards, or other monsters. No taking a look. Just dump the demon-badgers, and hurry back through the gate."

"These gateways are most likely in different locations all over the Seelie kingdom." I rolled my eyes. "There's not going to be shadow fae waiting at every one of them. And the last ones were only there and came through because Joe escaped and ran through the portal."

"There might be something there worse than shadow fae," he told me.

"Maybe. Maybe not. I doubt they're guarding these portals. They don't expect any of you angels to go through them. These gateways are a bold fuck-you, a way to snatch humans at will. I'm only going to pop through, check things out, and show them the error of their ways."

He sighed. "Cockroach, *please* be careful. Just take a quick look around while staying close to the gateway. And get back here in no more than ten minutes."

"Will do," I told him, knowing that I probably wasn't going to follow any of those "suggestions."

Not waiting for him to reply, I dragged the crate of demon-badgers through the gate and instantly found myself inside some sort of conservatory. Lavender-colored crushed-stone walkways wound through the giant building between artful displays of plants and trees. The fragrance was subtle and elegant. Small wooden benches were strategically placed to allow fae the best view of the plant life.

It was gorgeous. And I felt only slightly guilty at what I was about to do.

Pulling a small set of clippers from a pocket of my cargo pants, I got to work, snipping flowers and lopping huge chunks from the plants. No one came into the building, but I went as quickly as I could until every bush was hacked and chopped, and trees were defaced with lewd carvings from the knife I'd also smuggled in. One green hedge I cut into a penis shape, and another was a fist with the middle finger raised. That done, I quickly ran to the benches, carving "Fairies are troll-fuckers," and "The Queen gives her humans blow-jobs. And swallows" all in Elvish.

Then I let the demon-badgers loose. Unlike the Durfts, they didn't attack me, but ran around the conservatory, knocking over sculptures and crushing flower beds.

I stood back for a few seconds to admire my handiwork, then decided there needed to be one final touch. Picking up a good-sized paver from the side of the walkway, I threw it through the glass of the conservatory.

Alarms shrieked. Which was my clue to get the fuck out of here. Running, I dove through the gateway, shouting at Gregory to close it. He complied, and I collapsed on the ground, laughing.

"You were gone twenty minutes," he scolded me. "I was on the verge of coming to get you."

I composed myself and stood. "No need. I can't believe I got all that done in twenty minutes, though." Telling him what I'd done, I laughed again. "The fae are going to be so fucking pissed."

He shook his head. "Assuming you've gotten all that out of your system, let's go to the next gateway."

Not surprisingly, I hadn't gotten it all out of my system. Instead I snuck through each gateway, leaving a trail of chaos behind. Mosquitos. Stink bugs. Japanese beetles. A Volkswagen full of rattlesnakes.

The last portal opened up into a forest whose trees were not quite as aggressive as the one where I'd met Iselle. Still, I was reluctant to go carving into them. Instead I popped out to make a quick side trip to Hel and back, then reentered the gateway to release the four Durfts along with an invasive species of sentient briar into the woods. Another gateway landed me in a giant kitchen with rows of artistically arrange foodstuff lined up on a marble counter. I could hear voices nearby, so I quickly smashed the food, and spat in a few of the bowls before dashing back out the gateway.

"My work here is done," I told Gregory as he closed the final interdimensional door.

"So your strategy involves angering them until they what? Give up?" he asked with a smile.

"Yep. Every time they create a gateway, I destroy shit and then we close it. Eventually they'll think twice before opening another one."

"Or they'll decide every gateway needs to be guarded," he pointed out.

I shrugged. "I'll dash in, throw a Durft in their faces, then run back out. Trust me, they'll eventually get frustrated with my impish guerrilla warfare and give up. They're no match for me," I bragged.

"I don't think it's a solid long-term strategy, but I'm happy to see some offensive action as opposed to defensive ones." Gregory made a frustrated noise. "I know you're in favor of a demon army storming Aerie and winning this through a military victory, but after millions of years, I've finally come to realize that a military victory isn't usually a victory at all. Destroying their civilization will only create generations of enemies determined to avenge what they see as an unfair attack. It would only set us up for endless war with the humans in the middle of it all. Any other course of action is preferable."

I stared at him in shock, because Gregory had always been the first to thrown down the gauntlet and whip out the sword as far as I knew. This was a huge change. And I honestly thought he was right. Warmongers loved fighting and killing for the experience of it all, but even they eventually realized there was no positive outcome to war.

There were plenty of times when violence was the only answer, especially when immediate action was needed to save a group of people or even the planet. But those situations didn't come along often.

"It won't reduce the number of humans being kidnapped, though," he added.

I smirked. "I've got a plan for that. Nyalla agreed to put out a press release and humans are going to be educated on fairy prevention. No one is going gently into a fucking Seelie portal ever again. They'll fight with every bit of bullets, pepper spray, and Tasers they can get their hands on."

"Pepper spray?" he raised his eyebrows.

"I've been told that the fae have sensitive noses," I informed him. "Gwylla nearly went into anaphylactic shock when I put Tabasco on her veggie hash last week. And while Tasers won't kill a fae, it might startle them enough for a human to get away. Same with guns. And emptying a magazine into a fairy is going to at least give someone a chance to get a good running head start on these fuckers."

Gregory wrapped an arm around my shoulder. "Have I ever told you how much I love you? How brilliant you are? How ruthlessly sneaky and diabolical you are?"

I felt myself blush. Demons were not normally fond of praise. Our forms of affection were usually couched in insults and slander. But I'd changed just as Gregory had, and hearing these compliments warmed my heart.

14

I waved a pointer at the white board where I'd drawn a bunch of arrows and a series of crude stick figures.

"Do we all understand the plan?" I asked.

Snip's hand shot up. "Mistress? If one of us corners The Dolly before *you* manage to, what should we do? I have heard she is a hell of a fighter. She could easily overpower us."

Hmmm. I hadn't thought about that. My plan was to grab Dolly Parton, teleport her to my house, and eventually lock her in the guest bedroom once I'd evicted Joe. Joe wouldn't be happy, but if he wasn't ready to go home yet, he'd need to set up a cot in the basement, or in the barn. My wedding was in less than ninety days, so if he was still hanging out at my house by then, he could always move back into the guest room.

"I really don't understand why you don't just send Dolly Parton a letter," Nyalla complained. "Or approach her agent with a booking deal. I thought that's what we were going to do. I'm not really on board with this whole kidnapping thing."

I let out my breath in a whoosh, trying to keep my temper in check. "I'm Satan. From what I've seen on social media, Dolly Parton is a devout follower of this Jesus guy. I doubt she'd agree to any sort of gig that involved Satan. And even though she might be partial to the Archangel Michael, I really don't think she'd want to officiate his marriage ceremony to Satan. We're just going to have to kidnap her and either convince her to do this, or somehow threaten her into compliance."

Nyalla made a disapproving sound, folded her arms across her chest, and turned her head.

"Back to Snip's question, if you encounter The Dolly and I'm not nearby, stuff something into her mouth so she can't scream and duct tape her arms and legs." I made a mental note to supply him with duct tape and a sock capable of silencing The Dolly.

"Sam!" Nyalla glared at me. "You can't gag and bind Dolly Parton. Or any other person."

Crap. "Fine. No duct tape or gags. We'll just nicely convince her to come with us." I was totally bringing duct tape and a gag, I just wasn't going to let Nyalla know about it.

"Your wedding isn't for months," Snip pointed out. "Isn't that a long time to keep a human captive? I'm not particularly strategic, but I think that might allow her lots of time to plan and execute an escape attempt."

I glared at the Low. He'd been reading a lot ever since he'd fallen in love with the gate guardian in Columbia. She liked to buy him books, and discuss the literary classics with him, thus his vocabulary had increased. It annoyed the shit out of me.

"Between my household members and Boomer, I'm hoping any escape attempt will be thwarted. Plus Dolly *needs* to be captured this week. It's the perfect opportunity. She's staying at a friend's house and there is very little security. She'll be alone between the hours of six and eight tonight according to my source."

My source was Samael, who was even more excited than I was at the prospect of Dolly Parton officiating my wedding. He'd done some intelligence gathering for me in return for permission to put together the reception playlist. Our musical tastes aligned, so I happily ceded that task to him.

"Are we ready?" I asked. "Because I'm teleporting us at exactly six fifteen." That should give us some cushion in case her friend is a little late leaving the house.

Snip nodded. Nyalla shook her head. "I'm not going along with this one, Sam. It's too risky."

"Seriously? You're willing to go with me to Aerie where they enchant and enslave humans, where you know nothing about the landscape or what we might encounter, but kidnapping Dolly Parton is too risky?" I huffed.

She nodded. "Yes. I live here. And I want to stay living here. Getting arrested for kidnapping will make that difficult."

I didn't point out that her main squeeze, Gabriel, could easily make any legal trouble go away. He adored Nyalla and as much as he was a stickler for the rules, he wouldn't hesitate to wipe the memories of law enforcement and teleport her right out of jail. She'd probably get a scolding for it all, but she'd be quickly forgiven.

I'd get chewed out for years for being a bad influence on Nyalla, but it wasn't like that was anything new. I didn't care what Gabriel thought of me, and we were due for another brawl anyway.

I secretly loved our brawls. Even if sometimes I lost the fight.

"Besides, someone needs to stay here with Lux, Joe, and Iselle," Nyalla pointed out.

True. Lux tended to get into trouble when left alone, and I didn't want to come back with a hog-tied Dolly Parton to find the police were at my house investigating reports of illegal fireworks, or complaints that a young flying angel was dropping bags of horse poop on the neighbor's house. Iselle I was less worried about. She could teleport and had managed to survive as a deer. She'd be fine, although there was a chance she'd burn my house down trying to microwave leftovers. Joe...well he was a human and knew how to operate the microwave. He'd be fine on his own.

But Nyalla clearly needed an excuse not to go on a kidnapping trip, and I probably shouldn't leave my young angel alone with a fae teenager and a human guy I'd met less than a week ago.

"If you're staying behind, can you finalize the brides-maid dress orders tonight?" I asked Nyalla, hoping to check one more thing off the wedding to-do list.

It had taken us months to come to an agreement on suit-able dresses. I'd initially wanted hoop-skirted, *Gone With The Wind* gowns in a white satin artistically splattered with red. I'd liked the zombie-bridesmaid vibe, and surprisingly Nyalla had agreed with the design saying the fabric and dress style was a perfect metaphor for how the wealth of pre-Civil War South had been built on the blood of slavery.

Candy had nixed the idea, saying that while she approved of the message, she looked horrible in a hoop skirt.

Samael had wanted a skin-tight, leopard skin backless dress that was slit up the side to the waist. Leethu had heartily approved, but Nyalla and Uriel had strongly voiced their disapproval.

As had Candy, of course.

Candy's pick looked like a fucking business suit. Uriel's choice was a tux just like the guys were wearing. Nyalla's was reminiscent of an elven dress, full of floating gauzy panels with one boob exposed.

Leethu and Samael gave that one the thumbs-up as well. Gabriel had caught a glimpse of it on Nyalla's laptop and quickly vetoed that suggestion.

We were running out of time, so I finally threw in the towel. I insisted on the red-splattered white satin, but gave up on any sort of design consistency. Everyone could pick whatever style they wanted as long as they used the fabric I'd picked out. Then I assigned my maid of honor, Nyalla, to get everyone's design picks and measurements and place the order. I'd paid through the nose to get five dresses custom made within six weeks so we could have them here in time for final fittings and my wedding. And as eager as I was to see what everyone had picked out, I'd decided that some things were worth waiting for. The surprise of seeing my bridesmaids on my wedding day would be epic.

Nyalla was in charge of the dresses, Samael in charge of my bachelorette party, Candy handling flowers, Leethu getting the cake, and Uriel arranging for the limos and hotels. That left me to get my wedding dress, secure the venue, and arrange for Dolly to officiate the ceremony, and maybe sing a song or two at the reception. All of that was done except for Dolly. And by tonight, that should be taken care of as well.

I wondered if Dolly Parton was a vegetarian? Did she like beer or whiskey? I'd need to find out so I could make her captivity here as pleasant as possible.

～

AT SIX FIFTEEN I armed Snip with a sock and a roll of duct tape, then teleported him roughly a quarter mile from the house where Dolly Parton was staying.

"She's older than she looks, so be gentle," I warned Snip. "I don't want her having to use a wheelchair at my wedding, or be so bruised up she can't pronounce us archangel husband and demon wife."

Snip nodded. "Got it. No rough stuff. Just a sock in the mouth and duct tape."

"The security system won't be on, but I'm sure the doors and windows are locked. I'll get us in the house, and our mission is to find her as quickly and quietly as possible," I reminded the Low. "If she knows we're in the house, she'll barricade herself in a bathroom and call the police."

Snip shrugged. "That still gives us fifteen minutes or so to break down the bathroom door and grab her. Human police can't teleport and it will take them that long to drive to the house."

"No, but some private security forces can be there in a minute or two. Dolly Parton has money. She might have one of those companies on speed dial, and they might be there before we can break down the door. They'll probably have magical weaponry too."

Snip shivered. "I don't like those nets. Or the bullets. I don't like the regular bullets either. Do you think Dolly Parton carries a gun on her person? Getting shot really hurts, and if she's got good aim, she might kill me."

That was a good point. I thought for a second. "From what I've seen, she favors fitted outfits. You'll be able to clearly see if she has a gun on her person. If she does, then just run and I'll take care of it."

I'd been shot plenty of times before. It wasn't fun, but I'd learned to quickly recreate damaged flesh, and to both survive and animate a dead body if my attacker managed a head shot. Better me than Snip who had very limited skills when it came to his corporeal form.

Waving for Snip to follow me, I made my way through backyards and bushes, trying to remain out of sight. Humans were nosy and were as territorial as any demon when it came to their residences. If one of them caught sight of us sneaking around, the police might arrive before we even managed to break into the house.

Thankfully everyone had mature landscaping, and we'd managed to remain undetected as we darted from shrub to shrub. It was six thirty-two by the time we crawled through the lavender garden, skirted the pool, and found ourselves at the back patio doors. They were locked, but with a small trickle of energy sent through the handle, I manage to pop the door open.

The faint sound of Glen Campbell's "Southern Nights" came through the speakers high up in the walls. The house had an open floor plan, with lots of windows and pillows everywhere. It looked comfy, and welcoming. The pictures of family on coffee tables and shelves as well as the magazines scattered across the sofa, made the place feel less like a developer's model home and more like a family's dwelling.

I pointed Snip toward the kitchen while I took the stairs, thankful that none of the flooring had creaked to announce our presence. Halfway up the stairs, I froze. There was a dog sitting at the landing. A Chihuahua.

His bulging little eyes met mine.

"Hi, cute boy," I whispered, knowing the futility of my attempt at friendship. These tiny little dogs were like fucking piranha. They hated everyone. They had damned sharp teeth. They were a whirlwind of snapping hell, and nothing deterred them once they decided to make a meal of you. Forget having a Rottweiler or Doberman for a guard dog; the best home security system was a Chihuahua.

The dog stood and growled. I held very still, figuring if it worked for rabbits, maybe it would work for me. If I didn't move a muscle, maybe the dog wouldn't see me, or get bored and leave.

At that moment a high-pitched scream came from the kitchen, followed by a slightly lower-pitched scream. The Chihuahua bolted down the stairs, sinking his sharp little teeth into my ankle.

I shrieked, kicking my leg in an attempt to fling the thing off. He sank his teeth in deeper, and I lost my balance, falling backward down the stairs. The dog stayed attached to my leg the whole way down. When I hit the floor, I kicked out my leg again, attempting to dislodge the Chihuahua. He let go just as my foot connected with a table, knocking it as well as a vase full of flowers over. The vase and flowers hit me in the face, water dowsing me and running into my nose and mouth. That was when the dog decided to bite my arm.

I was sputtering nasty flower-water when I heard Snip scream again as well as the very recognizable voice of Dolly Parton.

"You git outa here, you no-good varmint. Drop that corn-bread and skeedaddle!"

The two rounded the corner, Snip had a piece of corn-bread in one hand and was cowering and squeaking as a woman with big blonde hair wearing a floral silk robe and high heels whacked him with broom.

Getting to my feet I grabbed the Chihuahua with my free hand and tried to tug it loose. The dog dug in harder with his teeth and ended up tearing a chunk of flesh out of my arm as I yanked him free. I screamed and dropped the dog who immediately latched on to my not-yet-bitten leg.

Snip grabbed the brush end of the broom and tried to wrestle it out of the woman's hands. She let go, then reached behind her and grabbed a huge cast-iron skillet.

"Git. Both of y'all, git!" She swung the skillet and Snip dropped the broom, still holding on to the piece of cornbread. Then he ran, abandoning me.

I might be able to manage this Chihuahua, but I knew my limitations, and facing both a nasty little dog plus Dolly Parton wielding a cast-iron skillet was more than I could manage. Shaking off the dog, I took off after Snip, the dog and Dolly Parton on my heels. Thankfully neither one continued to chase me past the hedges marking the property perimeter. It took me a while to find Snip cowering under a well-manicured boxwood and eating the remains of the cornbread piece he'd stolen. The sound of sirens was growing louder, and a television van had already roared past us, pulling into the house's driveway, so I was thankful to have located the Low before either of us were arrested.

I teleported us home. Neither one of us fixed our injuries right away. Snip had good reason because he struggled to repair himself or even assume a different corporeal form. Plus, he told me that he was kind of proud of the minor bruises. How many Lows could claim that Dolly Parton beat the crap out of him with a broom?

I understood. Not that I had a valid excuse for staying bloody and injured myself. I could fix these wounds in a blink, and I didn't have any special pride in being chewed up by a Chihuahua. I guess it was a form of solidarity. If Snip was going to endure his bruises from this epic fuckup, then I probably should bleed on my sofa for another hour or two.

"Don't tell Nyalla," I warned Snip as I switched on the television. She, Lux, and Iselle had gone out for dinner and the note on the dining room table said not to expect then home until nine or ten tonight. She'd quickly realize everything didn't go as planned since there was no one locked in my guest bedroom, but I didn't want her to know we'd been embarrassingly run off, or how close we'd come to arrest.

"In tonight's news, a shocking home invasion at the house where Dolly Parton was visiting a friend. The intruders were driven off by the country singing legend, who was unhurt in the encounter."

Dolly Parton and an interviewer filled the screen. She was still wearing the floral silk robe and high heels, not a blonde lock out of place.

"This must have been such a terrifying experience for you," the interviewer said.

Dolly laughed. "Not exactly. I was startled, but after I shooed the two out, I started to feel kinda bad for them. I mean, what kinda robbers go into someone's kitchen and take a piece of cornbread? They probably were just hungry."

"Hungry?" The reporter looked like he wasn't buying it. That ritzy neighborhood wasn't exactly walking distance from where the homeless hung out. And I was a little offended that I'd been mistaken for a hungry vagrant. Snip? Sure. The Low totally looked like he should be digging through garbage cans for scraps of food, but even though my jeans and T-shirt were worn and not designer, I didn't think I looked *that* bad.

Except by the time Dolly had seen me I'd been on the floor, covered in stinky floral water and my own blood from that little shithead of a dog. So her impression was probably more on point than I wanted to admit.

"I've pledged to donate to the local homeless shelter and the soup kitchen as well as the food pantry," Dolly announced. "Those two poor folk reminded me that so many people go hungry. The next time someone sneaks into my kitchen, I hope I'm able to take a moment to think, then offer them a glass of sweet tea and a big plate of barbeque to go with the cornbread instead of chasing them out with a broom."

"I *love* her," Snip breathed, his eyes wide. "Tea and barbeque? I wasn't sure I was up to another kidnapping attempt, but if she's going to feed me barbeque, then she can whack me all she wants with that broom. Maybe even that skillet."

I loved barbeque as much as the Low, but we weren't needy humans, and I doubted Dolly would make the mistake of assuming we were harmless vagrants next time. No, she'd get a better look at Snip's crappy human form that screamed "demon" and reach for the skillet once more.

And there had to be a next time, because now I was absolutely obsessed with having Dolly Parton officiate my wedding. Clearly another home invasion was out of the question. Security would be tightened, and the singer would be more alert. No, I needed to grab her some other way.

Perhaps a carjacking? Or I could lure her out to an event? She clearly was very charity minded. Maybe if I came up with a fake Make-A-Wish kid, we could use that to lure her in. Snip could pose as a dying child, and I could dress in a nurse's uniform. Before any of her staff knew it, I'd teleport her away and have her locked in my bedroom.

It was an excellent idea—but one that would have to wait until I got back from Aerie.

15

"Dear Ms. Parton. I have Lowdemonitis, a genetic condition that greatly affects my lifespan. I drool, suffer from scaly skin, and jaundice." Snip looked up at me. "I think the jaundice is a good touch, because I *am* yellowish."

I nodded, rotating my finger in a get-on-with-it motion. Snip's early drafts of letters had him suffering from rare disorders like Hermansky-Pudlak Syndrome and Marcus Gunn Jaw-winking Syndrome. I'd accused him of making that shit up, but evidently he'd found some old medical book at the library and picked out a few things he thought sounded interesting.

I had scanned the letters, and while both disorders *were* interesting, the Jaw-winking one wasn't life-threatening, and Snip lacked the albinism to pull off the other one. I ended up telling him to just make something up, using his characteristics as symptoms.

"Currently I am on my deathbed at Snipville Memorial Hospital," the Low continued.

"Wait." I frowned. "She's going to have one of her people

Google Snipville Memorial Hospital, and then the gig will be up. Plus I don't think having you in a hospital is a good idea. We'll need to somehow manage to find an open room, and get you on the patient list. How about if you're convalescing at home instead? And don't say death bed. That sounds a little extreme."

Snip huffed out a breath. "That's the point of this stuff. My story is supposed to make her feel sorry for me, and have her worry that if she doesn't hurry up and grant my dying wish to see her, I'll be gone. And then it will be too late for her to do her good deed of making a dying patient of Lowdemonitis happy before he croaks."

I nodded. "Okay. Then keep the death bed thing. Let's find a nearby house that's abandoned or in the process of foreclosure or something, and use that as the address. Make sure you give her your actual phone number so when her staff calls to confirm, you can tell her how horribly sick you are. But not too sick. I don't want her trying to come see you before I get back from Aerie."

I was the only one who could teleport Dolly Parton from the abandoned house to the bedroom I'd prepared for her. Actually, I was the only one with teleportation skills willing to take part in this scheme. I wanted it to be a surprise for Gregory, so I wasn't going to tell him. Gabe would refuse. Raphael was busy doing best-man stuff for the wedding. And Samael was nowhere to be found right now. As usual. Every time I needed a truly amoral, highly skilled, Fallen angel to assist me, he was off grid. Once he'd put in his design choice and measurements for his bridesmaid dress, he'd vanished. The jerk better show up for my bachelorette party or I was going to be pissed.

I glanced at the kitchen clock. "Okay. I gotta run. You mail her the letter, email a copy, and "@" her on social media with your plea. Everything. Hopefully my trip won't take more than a day or two and we'll be able to put the plan in motion for Dolly Abduction, Stage Two."

~

"I STILL THINK I should go with you," Nyalla said. "Iselle only remembers Aerie as a deer, and most of that is the forested areas. You can't read a map, while I can. Plus I can keep you out of trouble."

Or get me into more trouble. Iselle at least was a fairy. She'd be less likely to be caught and assumed to be a runaway slave. Plus Nyalla was still dealing with the trauma and abuse of her life in Hel at the hands of the elves. She was feisty, and while I admired that, her coming with me was likely to end in a scenario where she was facing "punishment" and I was having to defend her.

"I *really* need you to take care of wedding stuff while I'm gone," I told her. "Samael is MIA, so you might need to step in on the bachelorette party stuff. The final food menu is due this week, and the caterer also needs to know the booze, beer, and wine selection for the reception."

Nyalla sucked in a breath. I could see the conflict in her expression. She loved organizing my wedding, but she clearly didn't want to stay behind while I went to Aerie.

"Here is the map." Gwylla handed a scroll to me. "Having been warned that you were directionally challenged, I spelled it to show where you are in relation to the landmarks, and to show an arrow for the direction you are heading."

"GPS!" I exclaimed. I still had the occasional issue with GPS, but I was more likely to not get lost with these modifications.

"And here is the portable gateway." Gwylla handed me an oval, gray, river-smoothed stone. "All you need to do is say 'home,' and it will transport you and whoever you are touching to your house. You remember where to place the ring?"

I wasn't going to replace the ring, but a note instead. Although, she didn't need to know that.

I nodded. "Sixth jewelry wardrobe on the left, third drawer down."

She winced. "Third jewelry box, sixth drawer down."

I glanced over at Iselle and she smiled mischievously. "I will remember, Sam."

"Just return the ring, then come home." Nyalla glanced at the expedition-sized backpack both Iselle and I wore. "Even if Gwylla's navigation is off, it shouldn't take you more than a day or two to complete your task."

I patted the side of my pack. "Can't trust that fairy-food, right? Or drink? Or any offer of hospitality. Everything comes with strings. So we're bringing our own stuff."

My backpack growled and I patted my stomach. "See? I'm already hungry. So let's get on with this thing."

Nyalla scowled. "Sam."

I opened my eyes wide, trying my hardest for an innocent expression. "What?"

"Almost eighteen years I spent in Hel. You think I don't know a Durft growl when I hear it?" she asked.

"Dinner," I informed her. "It's an acquired taste, I'll admit it, but there's nothing more satisfying than eating one of those vicious motherfuckers. Plus, if we're attacked, they'll make an amazing weapon. Better than mace. Certainly better than my worthless sword that doesn't seem to appear when I'm in Aerie."

Nyalla's lips twitched. "I love you, Sam."

My heart warmed at her words. "I love you too, Nyalla."

Iselle seemed enchanted by our exchange, but Gwylla rolled her eyes. "If you all are done, I need to open this gateway and get back to my sanctuary."

"Ready." I adjusted my backpack.

Iselle patted her backpack that squirmed at her touch. "Ready."

Gwylla stepped forward to the mound of earth, spreading her arms wide and chanting. A glow extended from her hands, and out of the swirling lavender fog, a doorway opened into the hill.

16

For a brief second I saw the remains of rotted-wood coffins inside the portal, bones spilling from their centers. Then it all vanished into a haze of lavender.

"The gateway is open," Gwylla said, her voice hoarse. "Hurry. I feel my kin approaching, and both you and the doorway need to be gone by the time they arrive."

I grabbed Iselle's hand so I wouldn't lose her in the portal, and the pair of us ran through, into the lavender mist.

We fell out the other side. Fell. For some reason, the portal twisted us around, and what had been the ground on our side was ninety-degrees from the ground in Aerie. Our momentum propelled us about six feet forward, then we crashed down onto our faces. Thankfully we were once more in the woods and our landing was cushioned by dirt and soft moss.

The trees took an alarmed step backward, then leaned forward. I spat moss, then scrambled to my feet, pulling an ancient grill spatula I'd bought from a flea market years ago from the loop of my backpack and brandishing it at the foliage.

I know, but none of my knives were long enough to stay in the loop, and the grill fork to the set had disappeared sometime last May. A spatula might not sound that intimidating, but judging from the way it had quickly rusted, it was neither stainless steel, nor chrome-finished.

It was iron. I could send my personal energy into an object and instantly know its atomic and molecular makeup. There was a bit of nickel in this spatula, but most of it was cheap, rust-instantly iron. Hopefully it would make an effective weapon against the fae. Iselle had broken out in hives when she'd touched it the other day, so I was betting the other fae would suffer the same reaction. And if they weren't sensitive to the iron, well I'd just use it as a bludgeoning weapon.

Killed someone with a grill spatula. I totally wanted to add that to my rap sheet.

I'd also shoved an iron railroad spike in my backpack along with a small iron skillet and the Durft. Hopefully the animal wouldn't eat them.

"Get back," I shouted at the trees, waving my spatula at them. Iselle got to her feet beside me, adjusting her backpack before jerking her head to look into the woods.

"We need to leave. Now."

I unrolled the map. "Let me just figure out where the heck we are."

"No." She grabbed my arm and yanked. "Hurry. They're coming."

I had no idea who "they" were. It wasn't night, and I seemed to remember someone telling me the Wild Hunt always rode in the dark for some stupid reason. My own horses had much better night vision than I did, but I still wouldn't trust them to gallop through the woods in the middle of the night without stepping in a groundhog hole or tripping over a fallen branch and tossing me into a briar patch. But Gwylla had said her kin, or whatever, were nearby, so I was guessing "they" were some sort of fae we didn't want finding us.

Iselle and I ran through the woods, while trees snatched at our clothes and hair, and tried to trip us. She was far nimbler than I, and I got the feeling she could run a whole lot faster than we were currently going. I could as well, but not without a high risk of face-planting into one of these moving trees.

There were a whole lot of crashing noises all around us. I wasn't sure if it was the forest making all that racket, or me, or whatever was chasing us. If we were being pursued by fae, then the commotion was probably a combination of me and the trees. Iselle moved with the silence of a whisper in the wind, and I assumed other fairies would be just as light-footed.

An arrow whistled past me, barely missing Iselle. The next one hit me, lodging in my shoulder. Numbness spread down my arm, but I halted the progression of poison before it could go farther. Iselle dodged another arrow that came at us from behind, making me wonder how sharp her hearing actually was, and how she could hear the missiles coming with all the noise my feet were making.

We raced around a corner, leaping over a tree that fell in our path. A second arrow hit my arm, which was flopping around and looking like a pincushion at this point.

It was becoming clear to me that we weren't going to outrun our pursuers—well, *I* wasn't going to outrun them.

Iselle probably had a chance if I wasn't slowing her down. And *I'd* have a chance if these fucking trees weren't out to get me, or if I could take to the air. Flight would have been a good option, but one well-placed arrow would have me falling from the sky. And with my arm and shoulder numb, I wasn't sure both wings would be fully functional at this time.

"Go," I urged Iselle as I tried without success to fix my numbed arm and shoulder. "Get to safety, and we'll meet up later."

She glanced back, her brow furrowed. "No. I won't leave you."

"I mean it. Go." How was she still running while looking back at me? Did she have eyes in the back of her head? Some sonic location ability?

Iselle bit her lip. I scowled at her. "Go." I repeated using as stern of a voice as I could. It wasn't easy since I was gasping for air. Evidently whatever poison was coating these arrows had affected my lungs. It was a good thing Nyalla hadn't come with me, because these arrows would have surely killed her.

The fairy frowned, then kicked it into overdrive. Her legs were a blur as she raced away from me, darting around trees. She'd vanished in seconds, right when a third arrow nailed me in the ass.

Unable to halt the poison in time, I crashed to the forest floor, skidding on top of rocks and fallen twigs, and coming to a halt when my back slammed into a tree. I reached back with my working arm and pulled the arrow out, removing a good chunk of my flesh and jeans with it. Rolling over I tried to do the same with the two other arrows, but only managed to yank the one from my arm before I was hauled to my feet.

One fae had me held tightly with my arms twisted

behind my back. Three more stood in front of me, with weapons in hand. They were all on foot, with no horses or any other sort of mount nearby, and they all wore a light-weight leathery armor that was probably enchanted.

The guy holding me—or girl, I couldn't really tell them apart—jerked my arms tighter and said something in a voice that was probably meant to be harsh and intimidating. It wasn't because their language was this beautiful lyrical thing, but the arm-jerking hurt. It hurt in both my arms, letting me know that whatever poison had been on those arrows was starting to wear off.

I tried to wiggle my right foot, because that limb was far more essential to my escape than my right arm. It moved, but not with the kind of coordination I'd need to run. Wings? It was an option, but I'd need to risk getting shot again—and taking an arrow to my wings would be far more painful and debilitating than taking two to the shoulder and one to the ass.

The fairy jerked my arms and repeated himself, louder this time, because everyone knows that if someone doesn't understand your language, yelling at them facilitates comprehension.

Maybe they figured I was just holding my tongue and taking the fifth. Just in case they happened to speak some-thing besides their fae language, I spoke to them in Elvish.

"I want my phone call. And a lawyer."

"Lawyer" didn't translate to Elvish very well, so I used what the expat elves living among the humans called the job—"defender of lawbreakers."

Not that it mattered. The fae just looked at each other, then they all started yelling at me.

Whatever. The more we stood here, the better my

chances were at getting enough feeling in my leg to make a break for it. I wiggled my foot again, happy that a pins-and-needles sensation was stabbing through my toes and heel. They kept jerking me around and yelling at me. I kept repeating my phrase in Elvish and wiggling my foot. Just when I was thinking I might risk an escape, another three fae appeared in the small clearing.

They were dressed like the ones who'd captured me, had been absolutely silent in their approach, and one of them had Iselle.

The girl was bruised, with sticks in her hair and scratches on one cheek. Her hands were also twisted behind her back, and she had an arrow sticking out of her upper arm.

"Police brutality," I shouted at them in Elvish. "Just wait until my lawyer gets here. We're going to sue you for everything you've got."

"Police brutality" was the translation of what the elves would call "abuse of authority," but it was close enough.

"Are you okay?" I asked Iselle in English, concerned that the arrow in her arm might cause more lasting damage than it had done to me.

"Numb. Can't do magic. Feel like I might vomit," she informed me in the same language.

Our use of English enraged the fae just as much, if not more, than my use of Elvish. They were all shouting now, hauling us back and forth before throwing both of us to the ground. One of them kicked me. Thankfully the blow landed in my still-numb ass so I didn't feel it.

Iselle saw the blow and shouted out something in the fairy language. That silenced all the yelling. The one who'd been holding me stepped forward and hauled her upright

by her good arm, saying something to her in a more modu-
lated tone.

"He wants to know who you are, and how you know a
language not heard in Aerie since the elves left," Iselle translated for me.

I blinked in surprise. "He knows Elvish?"

A faint smile twitched the corner of her mouth. "No one
knows Elvish aside from maybe the ancient among the
priestesses. But it has similarities to our language. I think he
guessed."

The fairy yelled at Iselle, then glared at me for second
before yelling at her again. I got the idea she was just
supposed to translate and not be having a side-bar conversation with me.

"Tell him I'm a monster that has killed many elves.
That in my realm I am much feared and respected," I
told her.

That earned me some serious side-eye, but she spoke to
the fae. Judging from his incredulous expression, I was
guessing she'd translated what I'd said accurately.

The fairy replied to Iselle, then looked at me
expectantly.

"They think you're a human, but one of those arrows
would have sent a human into cardiac arrest. Since you
confirmed you were speaking Elvish, they believe you may
be part human and part elf," she said.

I burst out laughing. If only she'd known how absurd
that was. The elves were total racist fucks, very concerned
with genetic purity. Amber was the only part-elf I knew,
born to an elven woman desperate to have a living child,
and a demon sire. After giving birth the elven woman had
realized the flaw in her plan. The infant could never pass as
a full elf until she gained better control of her powers, and

any slip would mean death to both the baby and to her mother.

Things had worked out for Amber, but not so much for her mother. But there was no way elves were running around breeding with humans. Or probably even having sex with them.

"Shall I tell them you're an angel?" Iselle asked. "Or a demon?"

I grimaced. "Hell no. Let's not cause any more problems between the fae and the angels. And I'm not sure he'd know what demons were. Just insist that I'm a powerful shape-shifting creature that knows many languages and has come here to..."

Crap. Obviously I hadn't planned this trip out very well because I had no idea what to use as an excuse for my presence here in Aerie. I didn't want to admit I had the queen's ring, and I didn't want to say anything about the issue between the Seelie fae and the angels.

"...see the sights," I finally completed my sentence. "I'm a tourist."

Iselle nearly rolled her eyes at that, then translated. I wasn't exactly surprised when my reply earned me a kick from a nearby fairy.

The seven of them then began a lively discussion amongst themselves. I wiggled my foot again, realizing I still wasn't quite recovered enough to make an escape attempt.

"They're talking about our backpacks," Iselle whispered to me. "And they're debating whether they should kill us and steal our stuff, or take us prisoner and steal our stuff."

The fae holding me jerked my arms aside and pulled the backpack off me, tossing it to another of his buddies. The one holding Iselle did the same. Then they all edged closer, watching as the two opened the backpacks.

The Durft in each pack burst forth, snapping and snarling. The fae screamed, throwing the backpacks and scrambling for weapons. In the chaos, I yanked free from my captor and dove for the neglected packs, grabbing the spatula with one hand and the frying pan with the other.

Iselle tried to pull free from the fae that held her, but he'd continued to hold her tight, pivoting to put the girl between him and the Durfts that were shredding the other fae. I dove at the fairies, hoping for the best as I swung the frying pan at the fairy's face and slapped him in the arm with the spatula.

He evaded the pan, but yelped as welts rose on his arm. Ducking my next swing, he pivoted again to use Iselle as a shield. The girl shrieked as I accidentally smacked the tip of her ear with the spatula.

"Sorry! Sorry!" I shouted.

I managed to hit the fairy guard on the arm again, this time with the pan, then dove between Iselle's legs in an attempt to get him to let go of her. Instead he kicked me, dancing backward and yanking the girl with him. She stumbled as he pulled her over me, and the fairy stumbled as well, thrown off balance by the shift in her weight.

I took that as my cue and jumped for the guy, driving my head right into his crotch. That made him let go of Iselle. She scrambled away and I proceeded to beat the shit out of the guy with the frying pan and the spatula.

The other fae were having no luck against the Durfts. Two of the hellish creatures against six fae wasn't exactly fair odds, but I didn't feel sorry for these assholes. They'd planned on killing us and taking our stuff, after all.

And the carnage made me happy that the Durfts I'd been shoving through the fairy portals were delivering the chaos I'd hoped. I really wanted to stay for the fight, but the better move would be to grab Iselle and get the hell out of here.

A fae managed to deliver a killing blow to one of the Durfts, who must have been immune to their poison from the number of arrows sticking out of him. The Durft sank his teeth deep into the fairy as he died, ripping out a chunk of flesh.

One Durft against six still-conscious fae—five if the one with the arm wound was out of commission.

I grabbed Iselle, pulling her to the edge of the clearing. "Can you run for it? Or better yet, teleport us out of here?" I asked her.

She flexed her arm and winced. "Not yet."

"Then we're going to fly," I told her. "Get ready. I'll reveal my wings, grab you, and take flight. With any luck, the Durft will occupy them enough that they won't be able to get off a shot at us until we're out of range."

Iselle's eyes widened in fear.

"Do you have any issues with altitude?" I asked. "Or g-force? Or motion-sickness? Although it might be a plus if you could dive-bomb them with puke."

Her eyes widened even more. "N-no?"

I revealed my wings, snatched her in my arms and flew for the sky. It wasn't as easy as it sounded. My wingspan was large and the clearing was narrow, and launching myself straight upward wasn't a skill in my wheelhouse. I flapped my wings, smacking tree branches on the way up. It slowed me, and the fae definitely noticed not only that their captives were escaping, but that I now had huge, black-feathered wings.

The fae yelled. Three of them left the other three to deal with the remaining Durft and scrambled for their weapons.

I flapped my giant-ass wings harder and the fae staggered from the wind my feathered appendages were creating, but in spite of the dramatic nature of our escape, it felt like it took me fucking forever to get us above the tree line. Iselle was heavier than she looked, and the trees weren't cooperating. They swung limbs in our direction, trying to impede our escape and bat us out of the air. Despite the size of my wings, I managed to avoid most of them. And the trees efforts served as a kind of shield against the arrows the fae were now shooting at us.

Iselle clung to my shoulders, wrapping her legs around my waist and burying her face into my neck. It made it easier to hold her, but her fear was causing her to dig heels and nails into my skin. Fae are damned strong, and I could feel the trickle of blood on my shoulders.

"Almost out of their range," I told her, kicking out at a tree branch and using it to springboard higher. An arrow whizzed past me, then another one tore through my wings.

It hurt like fuck. It had gone clear through, so I was surprised when I felt the numbness spread through that wing.

"Hold on!" I shouted as my one wing tried to compensate for the loss of the other. I kept altitude, but began to spin around, unable to control our direction. Iselle screamed and clung to me tighter. I wanted to keep my arms around her, but I needed to use hands and feet to grab tree limbs in an attempt to straighten us out and get us out of range of the arrows.

My whirlwind motion had kept the fae from being able to hit me with any more of their missiles, but slowing myself gave them a better target, and two more arrows tore through my other wing.

No wings, no fly.

Iselle screamed again as we plummeted to the forest

floor. I gave up trying to slow our descent, and wrapped my arms and legs around her, turning so I'd hit the ground first. Glancing over my shoulder, I saw a few panicked fairy faces, and smirked, hoping I landed on them and squished them all dead.

Then I slammed into the ground and everything went black.

17

I regained consciousness in some sort of camp area, hog-tied with magical ropes and surrounded two guards who both had arrows pointed at me. Years ago I would have died-died from an impact like that, but this time, even knocked-out, I had managed to cling to a deceased corporeal form until I was able to recreate it into something that was alive and functioning.

From the absolutely terrified looks on my guards' faces, that had freaked the fae out just as much as me sprouting wings and trying to fly away with Iselle.

The moment I'd opened my eyes, one of my guards had let out a high-pitched shriek and shot me with an arrow. That had killed me a second time, and when I'd regained life and consciousness once more, it was dark out.

Iselle was a dark lump propped against a tree ten feet away. I saw her stir, and hoped that she hadn't been horribly injured in our crash-landing.

"You okay?" I called out in English. My guards shouted and drew their arrows, quieting and jumping a few steps back when I snarled at them.

"I'm fine," she replied, sounding far from fine.

"What injuries do you have?" I asked, worried that they might be something neither I, nor the fae girl could repair.

"A few broken bones. They feel better, though, so I think I must have some healing magic in addition to my other skills. It's not surprising since my mother had minor healing magic in addition to her plant magic."

One of the fae guarding me barked out an order, turning to point his arrow at the girl.

I snarled again. "Touch her and I will devour you."

Iselle translated for me and both fairies' attention returned to me. They took another step back, their hands on the bows shaking slightly. I was sure Iselle hadn't translated that quite how I'd meant, and that the fae now thought I was going to chow-down on their still-alive bodies.

Whatever. Honestly, eating them was probably scarier to them than the devouring I'd threatened.

My bravado and survival skills might have cowed the fae, but I wasn't about to push my luck, so I stayed silent, watching Iselle and hoping she was able to heal by morning. I wanted to make another escape attempt, but that wasn't going to work if she couldn't walk or use her arms.

As the night went on, my guards changed several times, the other fae taking turns between watching me, scouting around the camp, and sleeping. I stayed awake, concerned about the fae girl and our safety in this strange forest with hostile captors who'd probably love to see us dead.

The morning arrived and brought a heated argument among the fae. Iselle seemed to be holding back a smile, although she didn't translate for me. Her amusement gave me hope that the fae weren't fighting over the best way to kill us, and that she might be healed enough for another escape attempt. After a while I realized that the fae were undecided on how to transport us. Judging by their gestures, a few wanted to make us walk with bound hands and hobbled feet. Others were advocating for dragging our hog-tied bodies through the forest. A few wanted to just slit our throats and be done with it. I got the impression that the slit-our-throats camp was only being overruled because they were concerned I had magic that made me unkillable and that if they murdered my companion, I'd hunt them down and end their lives in a long, painful, gruesome way.

They weren't wrong.

Our captors were looking worse than Iselle and I, which, no doubt, also made them wary of me. They seemed to have trouble quickly healing from the Durft damage. While the guy I'd bashed unconscious with a spatula and a frying pan had fully recovered, the others were all still covered with bites and scratches. The one who'd had a chunk taken out of his arm looked particularly worse for the wear. I made a mental note to step up my Durft-through-the-portals game.

Their injuries also made me think about biowarfare. I'd had some ideas in that direction, but should investigate using viruses and bacteria from Hel in the future.

Iselle's gaze began to turn worried, and I realized I needed to do something to prove our worth to them—something that would keep them from killing us long enough that we could escape.

"Tell them that the fierce animals are called Durfts, and that they are trained to attack their owner's enemies," I said to Iselle.

She interrupted the argument and relayed what I said. The guy who I assumed was their leader due to the fact that he had less injuries than the others tilted his head and narrowed his eyes in thought.

Iselle said something else to them before translating for

me. "I told them you are a very powerful being where you live, and that your kingdom will be willing to pay ransom for us that includes supplying them with their own pack of Durfts along with lessons in training them."

Very clever! She might have spent most of her life as a deer, but she clearly had retained enough memories from her early childhood to know how to bargain with her people.

As the fae began to talk amongst themselves, my stomach growled loudly. They'd breakfasted without offering anything to either me or Iselle. I was really regretting the loss of the food I'd packed in our backpacks. There had been an Italian sub, a bag of trail mix, and some chocolates. Oh, and a packet of Ho Hos. I really wanted those Ho Hos. Everything had been in a bear-proof canister that the Durfts hadn't even attempted to chew through, so I hoped that it would all still be untouched back in that clearing. Once we escaped, I was absolutely going back for that food.

"They want to know more about the weapons we were carrying," Iselle said, interrupting my thoughts of Ho Hos. "Especially the Durfts."

I shrugged. "I'm a tourist in a strange and violent land. Obviously I should be prepared to defend myself. And since I have killed many elves in my life, I assumed the weapons that are most effective against them would also work to protect me from any attacking fae. Durfts are often used by the nobility in my land to guard and protect. It made sense to travel with two of them. And the weapons I used were of a metal that the elves are allergic to."

Iselle translated, and this time I saw the fae exchanging speculative, and worried, glances.

"They are Unseelie," she whispered to me as they again talked amongst themselves. "I do not know which Kingdom we are in, but I do not think they will treat a young Seelie fairy as anything but an enemy. I believe they have only delayed killing us is because they don't know what you are and what danger you might pose."

"And the fact that I've died twice and come back to life has probably scared the shit out of them," I mused.

Iselle jerked back, her eyes wide from that. "You are *truly* unkillable? Is this some magic you possess, or a spell cast on you?"

I shrugged. "It's more like a learned skill."

But where I might be very difficult to permanently unalive, Iselle wasn't. So this talk of killing us needed to stop.

"Let them know that you are my paid guide and under my protection, and that if you die, I will torture and kill them, their families, their friends, and their loved ones. I will also cast a curse where their names will never be spoken, their lives never remembered."

Iselle translated, and now she was also eyeing me with a nervous fear along with the other fae. Great. I'd terrified my newest household member. It wasn't a great way to start our partnership.

The less-injured head of the fae party held up a hand, halting conversation among the others. Then he spoke to Iselle.

"He said they will take us to the capital of the kingdom so the king can decide whether to ransom us or not. We will walk with our feet hobbled and our hands tied, leashed to one of the fae." She frowned. "I don't know exactly where we are, but from what they've said when conversing amongst themselves, I believe we are in the borderlands between the Seelie and Unseelie kingdom. That would make for a very long journey to the capital. Several weeks or more unless they use magic."

The borderlands. Gwylla had once again fucked up her navigation. We were closer to the Seelie kingdom then I was last time, but probably weeks if not months away from the queen's palace.

A several week journey in either direction wasn't ideal. First, there was that deadline Gregory had given me. As hot as it would be to have him storm into Aerie and murder huge numbers of fae to rescue me, that didn't support my long-term strategy. Plus two weeks walking without food was going to be a serious annoyance for me, and possibly a deadly one for Iselle.

But that was something I'd deal with later tonight. I got the feeling I needed to accept this situation for now, and save any further negotiation for later, lest the fae decided killing us was a better option.

THE DAY'S march was slow-going. Our captors kept urging us to move faster than the hobbles allowed, yanking on our leashes, and forcing us to half run in short steps. As the sun reached its zenith in the sky the fae began to look nervously around, cringing every time I stepped on a twig or crunched through leaves. They kept us moving past sunset, which only increased the noise I made in comparison to their silent footfalls.

Finally we halted in a clearing and the fae tied each of our leashes to some sort of stake they sank into the ground. Unlike last night, no one magically started a fire, and four of the seven fae stood guard in the forest while the remaining three unpacked food and thin blankets that seemed to be spelled to blend in with the forest floor. It was a cool trick, and I wondered if the camouflage technique would work its magic in other environments.

I was more interested in the food, though. My stomach growled loudly at the sight of it. While I would be just uncomfortable going days or weeks without food, I knew that Iselle needed to eat something. And drink. They hadn't offered us any water since we'd been captured, and Iselle's thirst would be worse than mine. She might have healed her injuries, but a lack of food and water would definitely hinder our escape attempt, and eventually kill her.

The fae were beginning to heal from the Durft attack. I was bummed that the wounds weren't permanent, but the slowness of their healing from them was still a plus I hoped to use now and in the future.

My stomach continued to growl as they ate. The three fae who'd unpacked traded duties with the guards at one point, allowing the others to eat. The only one who remained in the camp during both shifts was the guy I was pegging as their leader.

Eventually he approached, sitting closer to me, a large knife out of its sheaf and in one hand. Glancing over at Iselle, he returned his gaze to me and spoke.

"He wants to know how you came to know elves and about your people's war with them," Iselle told me.

"It would be a lot easier for me to participate in story time if they untied me and at least fed us. I'm fucking starving," I snapped.

Iselle translated and the fairy laughed, shaking his head.

"He said since you're unkillable, you're not going to die from starvation and thirst, and that keeping me too weak to escape will ensure you stay here and behave. They believe you won't leave without me."

This guy was smarter than I'd thought. "True, but if you die I will make good on my threat, so they need to at least provide you with a sustenance level of food and drink."

She translated, and the fae thought about that for a moment before replying.

"He proposes a bargain. Food and drink for me in exchange for information from you."

I narrowed my eyes. How much food and drink? And how much information? "If they give you half the rations they eat themselves and as much water as you want, then I will answer three questions every night," I proposed, totally lowballing the guy.

We went back and forth, and finally agreed on half rations for Iselle during the journey and water in the morning and evening. In exchange, I would tell the story of my experience with the elves, tell them what I was, and answer three additional questions each night.

"They think you're some kind of angel, even though your energy is not that of an angel," Iselle told me as the fairy went to get her food and water.

"Have they actually met angels?" I asked her. I didn't know how long the fae lived, and wasn't sure how many of them had been involved in the war.

"From what they've said in my hearing, no they haven't met angels. But I know there are stories." Her lips twitched as she looked over at me. "I remember hearing a few of them when I was a child, before I was turned into a deer. The angels are like...I believe the human term is boogeyman?"

"And demons?" I asked, trying to decide which one I should claim being.

"I don't remember any stories about demons from my childhood," she told me.

Then demons it was. It would be nice to ride on the coat-tails of horror stories told about the angels, but I didn't want to cause any additional issues with the contract between the fae and the angels.

The fairy returned with a small chunk of dark bread that had what looked to be berries and nuts in it, and a large cup of water. It wasn't a lot, but Iselle tore into the meal and drank every last drop of the water. I waited until she was done to tell my tale since I needed a translator, and the fairy thankfully didn't insist she wait to eat. When she was done, the fairy spoke first.

"He asks again what you are," Iselle told me.

"I am a demon, specifically an imp," I began. "Long ago, before the angels and fae warred over the humans, the angels fought among themselves. Their war fractured the heavenly host, and half of the angels were banished to a place called Hel. I am a descendant of those angels."

Iselle translated and the fairy tried and failed to repress a shudder at that.

"The elves had left Aerie for a new home, but this home wasn't habitable for long, and when half of the angels were banished to Hel, the elves decided to go with them," I continued. "Over the millennia, the elves and demons became uneasy neighbors with strongly defended territorial boundaries. We had trade and commerce and alliances, but lived separate lives with very different civilizations and cultures."

"You're losing his interest," Iselle whispered when she was done translating that segment. "Get to the killing of elves."

Or he may decide to do something like piss on her food before giving it to her, was how my mind finished that sentence.

"In my childhood I grew up on the borderlands between

an elven kingdom and the demon lands. I was friends with a young elf, but I bit the top of one of his ears off, and after that things kind of went downhill."

The fairy gasped as Iselle translated. I wasn't surprised since even she'd recoiled with that confession. "You bit his ear off?" she asked.

I shrugged. "It seemed like a fun thing to do. Affectionate, even. How was I to know it wouldn't grow back?"

The fairy clearly didn't feel my reasoning was valid. I quickly continued with my story just in case they decided ear-biting was an offense worthy of death.

I told of the numerous times I'd outsmarted the elves, retrieving my stolen horse, and wiggling my way out of the bargains I'd made with them. I told them of how I escaped an elven prison. How my household and I were double-crossed by the elven king we'd agreed to fight with, and my epic one-on-one fight against their king that ended in his death. The fairy listened, then asked his three questions for the night.

"He wants to know about the creation and sourcing of this 'chicken wand' you used to help you defeat the elven king," Iselle said.

Of course he did. I'd dangled the idea of using Durfts as a weapon to keep us alive, so it was no wonder that he'd also be interested in a weapon that was powerful enough to send an elven king running in fear. Not that he knew the king was just phobic about poultry, and that for most, a chicken wand was just an entertaining bit of expensive magic that also could provide a distraction and/or dinner.

Although if you paid extra for a wand that produced only roosters, you would end up having a dozen or so angry, aggressive, fighting cocks with only the flick of your wrist.

"Human sorcerers and magic-users make the chicken

wands, and they are available for purchase." I eyed the fae, not sure if their currency would be acceptable in the human world. "Or equitable trade," I added.

Iselle translated and the fae glared at me, replying in a tone of voice that was obviously displeased.

"He doesn't believe you," Iselle said. "Humans have no magic. They are not capable of such things. You have lied and thus he considers the contract between the two of you to be broken."

"Wait," I shouted as the fairy rose to his feet. "Tell him humans were given all the gifts of Aaru all at once by the angels, and their evolution has been very fast. Tell him that the humans they are capturing are not the magically skilled ones. Tell him that when the elves tried to invade, the humans successfully defended their lands against them."

The fairy waited while Iselle translated, then replied and left.

"He's skeptical," Iselle told me. "The fae see humans as weak and easily enthralled. They do not believe they have evolved to the point where they will be a threat to the fae. They see humans only as servants, entertainment, and brood animals for those fae who struggle with infertility. And he does not believe you about the elves—either that humans have defeated an elven attack, or that you have fought them and won. He believes you have lied."

I hadn't. Well, I *had* embellished my story a bit, but I hadn't outright lied. And it was frustrating that one of the few times I'd told the truth, I wasn't believed. Now Iselle would be without food again. Hopefully what she ate tonight would sustain her enough for an escape attempt. I was fully healed, and from what I could see, she was as well. And I'd been probing the magic on the ropes tying our wrist as well as the ones used as our hobbles. The spells were good, but not as good as the elven nets or even what some of the sorcerers were producing. With continued work and a little luck, I hoped to be able to break the magic in the next day or two, set us free, then have Iselle quickly teleport us the hell out of here.

The next morning the fae packed up, tightened our magical restraints, and we began our forced march through the forest once more.

This time the trees parted. As willing as they were to let the Unseelie scouts through, I felt animosity radiate off them. Their smaller branches shivered, their leaves rustling softly as if they grumbled about the intrusion in their forest. All day we tromped without any hint of reaching the end of the vast woods. Shadows stretched long and we continued to walk even though the sky grew dark. I knew that the fae had great night vision, but occasionally even they stumbled. As I myself tripped, I realized what was happening. The trees with their passive aggressive shit were doing all they could to stick it to all of us.

Finally the march stopped, and the group made camp. Iselle and I were able to sit down, still bound and unfed. The fae were hushed, whispering among themselves as they put down bed rolls and pulled food from their packs.

"They're worried," Iselle leaned over to tell me. "We're still in the contested border zone between the kingdoms, but something has them spooked."

"You think it's the trees?" I asked. "The forest isn't thrilled with any of us being here."

She shook her head. "Fae forests can be deadly, but this particular forest tolerates travelers. If someone did more than collect fallen wood, they would attack. If we tried to live here, they would kill us. But beyond threatening, tripping, or catching our clothes and hair with branches, there is nothing to fear from these trees."

"Then an army? A Seelie army?" I looked around, half expecting to see a bunch of pointy eared motherfuckers swarming us from the forest.

"They would have heard if a large group were moving through the forest." Iselle looked around as well. "And we would not be camping."

So then they were probably concerned about other scouting groups—Seelie ones. Either this area was a spot where incursions from both kingdoms were frequent, or there had been actual sightings of Seelie in the area.

We watched as they gnawed on bread, dried fruit, and drank water, then took turns sleeping. After the first shift change Iselle slumped against my shoulder, her breath deepening into soft snores.

I didn't sleep, and I'd become rather in tune to the trees around us, which is why I realized we were about to be attacked even before the Unseelie fae did.

18

Our captives shouted a split second before bright light exploded in the clearing, blinding us all. Iselle and I hit the ground, unable to take shelter since we were still bound and magically tied to a stake. As arrows and magic filled the air, I worked on the gaps I'd discovered in the magic, trying to widen them enough to get free. Iselle shrieked as the ground near her started to burn with a blue flame, and I decided the time for caution was over.

Breaking magic with brute force doesn't usually end well, and this was no exception. I shouted for Iselle to stay down and tried to channel the explosion away from her. As a result, the three fae thirty feet in front of me were blown to bits, and four trees were splintered and blackened as if they'd been struck by lightning. I wasn't all that worried about the fae dying, but the trees... I wasn't sure what their buddies would do in retaliation for my killing four of their forest mates, but I was probably about to find out.

Scrambling to my feet, I ran to Iselle and checked on her.

She was undamaged from the blast but still bound, although the magic tying her hands was weakened.

"I'm going to break this," I warned her. "I'll try to redirect the blast away from you, but you might have some serious burns or lose a hand."

She sucked in a breath at that, then ducked with fairy-speed to evade an arrow. "Go ahead. If we don't get out of here, I'll lose more than a hand."

Our captors were quickly being overcome by their more numerous opponents and I wasn't sure I was going to like what would happen to us when the fighting ended, so I threw myself over Iselle, dove my spirit-self into her to protect her as best as I could, then broke the magical bonds. When the dust cleared from the explosion, I looked up to assess the damage.

Iselle was okay outside of a few burns on her hands and ankles. This second blast had seriously injured two fae who were blistered and moaning on the ground. I'd also taken out two more trees.

"Can you teleport?" I asked her.

She reached out to touch my arm, then began to cry. "I can't. I can't do it."

I hugged her. "It's okay. You stay here and stay safe. I'm going to grab some supplies then we're going to get the fuck out of here."

I hated to leave her side, but if we were going on a long hike through a hostile, sentient forest, we were going to need supplies. As I dodged magic and arrows, I dove for the packs and started grabbing anything that looked reasonably useful. Hopefully Iselle's inability to teleport came from fear, the pain of her injuries, and dehydration, and her magic would come back online in the next few hours. If not, then I might have to risk flying us out of the forest once we'd put some distance between us and the fae. We'd be a target in the sky, but judging from the way the trees were rattling their limbs and pulling up their roots, getting shot down was the least of my worries.

Stuffing everything I could find into two packs I turned to run back to Iselle when an earthquake knocked me on my ass. It also knocked the fae on their asses, bouncing them from the forest into the clearing like those ping pong balls in the lottery drawings. After a few seconds the earthquake stopped, but the ground continued to shift and slide. I struggled to my feet, kicking a fairy in the head and grabbing his sword as the trees advanced. A branch hit me in the stomach, knocking me into another fairy who I inadvertently stabbed with the sword.

Now in addition to the arrows and magic, tree limbs were clocking fae, sending them flying. I dodged another branch and ran for Iselle, but one of the attacking fae got to her first. She screamed, thrashing as he tried to drag her to her feet. I threw the sword I'd stolen, hoping my aim was good, but before it reached them they were gone.

Gone. Vanished.

My sword thwacked into one of the trees. One more thing that would make this forest hate me and want me dead.

Time seemed to freeze in place for what felt like an eternity. They were gone. Teleported. The attacking fae could teleport, where the ones who'd captured us clearly didn't have that magic handy. But why? Why Iselle?

I assumed the attacking fae were Seelie and because they were at war with the Unseelie, they'd ambushed the scouting party, but why take Iselle? Why abandon the fight that had cost them a good number of their squad to teleport a young Seelie away? Did he realize she was a captive and felt the urge to protect a teenage fairy from their enemy by removing her from danger? It was the only reason that made sense, but in spite of the supposed good-intentions, Iselle was mine, and I was responsible for her safety.

I had no idea where she was. I couldn't speak the language here. I didn't know where the fuck I was because that map Gwylla had made for me was in my backpack along with my Ho Hos. I was hungry, pissed off, and ready to kick some fairy ass.

Starting with the guy who was rushing me right now with a glowing sword in hand.

Fuck this dude. I screamed, running toward him Berserker-style. His eyes widened and he stopped, swinging his sword. He was fast, but I had frustrated anger on my side, and that made me a force to be reckoned with. I blocked the swing with one of the backpacks I was holding. Food, clothing, and cutlery spilled from it as I twisted, wrapping the torn fabric around the glowing sword and jerking the weapon from the fairy's hand.

Then I reached out, grabbed him by the shoulder, dove my personal energy deep inside and pulled.

In less than a second I'd extracted his soul, spooling it into me and neatly slotting it where so very many souls had once lived. I'd not Owned since I'd let my collection of souls go, when I thought I was dying in Hel. I hadn't replaced them mostly because I knew how much Gregory hated it. But I was beyond caring about that right now. All I wanted to do was murder as many of these fuckers as I could, then go find Iselle.

After I'd retrieved the map, the portal stone, and my Ho Hos, that is.

After I rescued Iselle, then I'd leave a modified, more threatening note and go home, because fuck these assholes.

They didn't deserve a diplomatic solution. They deserved to be nuked into space.

I dropped the dead fairy, picked up his sword with the backpack still wrapped around it, and ran to the next fairy. One of the trees got to him before I could, stabbing him through his chest with a pointed branch. I tried to grab his spirit-self, but I was too late and it slipped through my hands as the fairy died.

I had equally bad luck with the other fae I tried to engage. Either one of the opposing fairies got to him first, or the trees did. Soon the clearing and the trees were wet and sticky with blood, bodies littering the ground.

Spinning around, I eyed one of the Unseelie fae who'd captured us—one of the only fae left standing. He blasted the last Seelie scout with a white stream of magic and took off as I ran for him. I was going to let him go, knowing that these fae could run faster than I could, but one of the trees smacked him back into the clearing. He plowed into me, and by the time we hit the ground his soul was mine.

The forest fell silent, the trees looming over the dead— and me. I crouched down in the thick red blood that coated everything and eyed them.

Were they eyeing me back?

"I don't want to hurt any of you, or even stay in this forest," I told them. "Let me gather some stuff, and I'll get out of here."

I picked up another two packs, slinging them over my shoulder. Stuffing the short sword through the tattered belt loops of my jeans, I began to strip the fae whose clothing had suffered the least damage. I could easily assume the bodies of the fairies I'd Owned, but clothing was something I still struggled to create. Sneaking into the Seelie court would be easier in the form of a Seelie fae, but only if I could stroll in wearing their traditional clothing instead of filthy, torn jeans and a blood-soaked AC/DC T-shirt. The trees rumbled, and I got the impression that they were discussing whether they should kill me or not. Worried they were not going to rule in my favor, I tore clothes off the fae as quickly as I could, wrapping and tying them around the straps of the packs

As I worked, the ground opened up and the dead bodies slid down into the holes, dirt and moss covering them. There wasn't a trampled blade of grass or anything beyond the remaining packs and supplies to suggest something other than plant life had been here for centuries. I ran for the two somewhat intact packs, putting one on my back, and the other on my front, adjusting straps to ensure my wings wouldn't rip the nylon apart. I adjusted the other packs with the clothing tied around them and picked up the sword that was no longer glowing.

The remaining supplies disappeared into the ground just as the bodies had, letting me know that the forest was running out of patience.

Pulling up the memories of the Unseelie fae I'd Owned, I revealed my wings, and took to the skies.

THE SEELIE FAE I'd killed and Owned hadn't been more than a grunt, a disposable member of a scouting party, but the Unseelie one was that guy I'd assumed to be their leader. I was right, although in the overall hierarchy of the Unseelie kingdom, he was insignificant. His name was Aethell, and he'd grown up in the capitol where he continued to live as a bachelor in a tiny row house when he wasn't out on patrol. He was career military, assigned to the borderlands and a scouting party because he wasn't politically connected in any way that would garner him a better assignment. Smart, but forever doomed to a shitty job because his family lacked money and influence. It was a tale as old as time.

The good thing about Aethell was he had an excellent sense of direction and had come to know the borderlands like the back of his hand. I flew high enough that the trees couldn't reach me, but low enough that I wasn't visible from miles away. Keeping my eye on the ground, I watched for any other scouting parties as I retraced our path to where the fae had abandoned our backpacks.

Word of the battle clearly hadn't spread through the forest to these particular trees, because they didn't attack me as I spiraled down to the clearing. The air was heavy and I could feel their scrutiny and wary dislike as I landed, but beyond some menacing rustling of leaves, they did nothing threatening.

On the ground I hid my wings and untangled the four packs I'd looped around me, untying and sorting the clothing before stuffing it into the most spacious packs. Checking our own packs, I was thrilled to find that not only had my Italian sub gone unmolested, but my trail mix and other food was still there. And best of all, the Ho Hos were uncrushed in the bottom of the bear-proof canister.

I'll admit that I sat and took some time enjoying the Ho Hos. There was a good chance they might not survive the coming days, and I didn't want them eaten by some fae creature or eventually decomposing on the forest floor. After I was done, I tossed the wrappers aside, filled the large backpack with the fae food, cutlery, sleeping pad, and the map Gwylla had made me, just in case I ended up somewhere my Owned souls were unfamiliar with.

The battle and my flight had taken up a good bit of the

morning and afternoon. The sun was dimly filtered through the trees, letting me know we were approaching evening. I went through the remains of the packs, pulling out the stone Iselle and I were to use to open portal home as well as my note about the ring, newly written in the fae language thanks to Iselle.

Pulling some paper from Iselle's backpack, I rewrote the note in a far more threatening tone—in the fae language thanks to the two dickheads I'd just Owned. Stuffing it into the pocket of my jeans, I held up the stone.

This I could not lose. It was our ticket out of here. Neither of the fae I Owned knew where the gateways to the human realm were located. Without the stone, Iselle and I could spend months or even years wandering around looking for a way out. I'd kept it in my backpack and it had been left behind when we'd been captured. I couldn't let that happen again. I needed a safe place for it, and the pocket of my jeans wasn't any safer than my backpack.

So I shoved it up in my vajayjay. My box of love. My hoo-haw.

Judging from our recent capture, the fae didn't seem inclined toward invasive strip searches, so I was betting it would go unnoticed there. Plus, thanks to the Kegels I'd been doing and my exploration of those Benwaballs that Leethu had left at my house, my snatch was tight as a trap door. That stone wasn't getting out until I let loose those muscles and released it.

I put the large backpack on, adjusting it to my front so it wouldn't hinder my wings. Then I took to the air, switching my focus from Aethell to the Seelie fae I'd Owned named Rowill. He was significantly lower in status than Aethell, but the guy's family were palace guards. He'd only been stuck with this distant assignment after a rather disastrous incident involving fae-fire at a royal banquet. That he hadn't been put to death was due to his family's long service to the court and his father's pleading.

Rowill might be inept as shit, but through him I knew how to get to the Seelie palace, and I knew the basic layout of the place.

Even more, I knew why Iselle had been taken, and it hadn't been for the heroic reason I'd supposed. The Seelie squadron had been sent to retrieve her. It had been a mandate from high within the court, a priority when there should have been other priorities during a war with the Unseelie.

Why her? She'd spent her life as a deer and no one had come for her besides the Wild Hunt of the Unseelie. Yet now the Seelie knew she was in Aerie, knew where she was, and for some reason made capturing her a priority.

Whatever that reason was, it wasn't good. I needed to get to Iselle. And then I needed to get her the fuck out of Aerie as quickly as I could.

19

As I left the borderlands and entered the Seelie territory, I had to give up flying for walking, and likewise abandon my more familiar form for that of Rowill, since it would be disastrous to be seen wandering around looking like a human. Rummaging through the pack, I pulled out the mismatched clothing from the Seelie attackers and changed out of my jeans and T-shirt.

Just in case I ended up caught and searched, I hid my threatening note in my shoe. I gave serious consideration to sticking it up my honeypot along with the portal stone, but figured the conditions in there weren't idea for inked paper. Giving up on sleep, I jogged day and night toward the capital city where Rowill's memories told me they were to take Iselle. Because of this, I arrived at the city gates, sweaty, exhausted, and generally pissed-off at everything. I'd gotten used to the convenience of teleportation, and cursed the inability of the fae to develop useful technology like a fucking car or at least a public bus service.

At this point, I'd take a damned bicycle. And if I had come across a farm or any place with a horse or something reasonably close to a horse, I would absolutely have stolen it to shorten my journey.

Waiting in line to cross through the gates into the city, I realized that my attire must be some sort of military uniform based on what everyone else was wearing. There were fairies bringing carts and baskets of goods into the city, and some walking with families and children in hand. Fancy rich people in magically floating and self-propelled carriages went quickly through another line. Watching the vehicles, I realized that they did have their own version of cars, and that I was just unfortunate enough not have encountered any to steal on my trek here.

I stayed mixed in with the commoners, hoping to slide through unnoticed. It worked. The guards took one look at my tattered, stained uniform and waved me inside without a second look.

The city was a maze of curving streets, quaint houses, and stores. I cut through an open-air marketplace on my way to the giant Cinderella-looking castle that towered on a hill, looming above the city. As I drew closer, I realized that there was no way I could slip into the palace or its grounds dressed as I was, so I wandered the streets until I found a man alone in a quiet lane, clocked him upside the head, stripped him naked and stole his clothes. The uniform I stashed in the back corner of an alley, just in case I needed it later. Smoothing back my hair and rinsing off my face in a backyard decorative fountain, I headed for the palace.

There was a line at the main gates composed of those magical carriages and fae in fancy-dress. Circling around to the back, I went in through the servants' entrance instead. My priority was to find Iselle, and having wasted way too much time jogging through the wilderness, I wasn't about to waste any more here. The palace staff probably wouldn't know where she'd been taken, but I was willing to bet there was some military muckety-muck at whatever social event they were having, and he or she might know where Iselle was being held.

I grabbed a bottle of wine from the kitchen, then went down the narrow back hallways the servants used to go from room to room. Accosting the first fairy I saw, I asked her how to get to the ballroom.

She frowned, looking down at my clothing.

"I'm supposed to bring a bottle of wine to Lord Mfllmwm." I slurred the name, hoping she wouldn't ask me to speak more clearly. My Owned fairy, Rowill knew the royalty and some of the powerful people in the Seelie Court, but I was sure name-dropping any of them and claiming to be their servant would blow my disguise.

She ignored the name, dropping her gaze to the bottle in my hand before gasping. "That's cooking wine. Do you have the wits of a human? Take that to your Lord and he'll have you beheaded before you can pull the cork."

Yanking the bottle from my hand and grabbing my arm, she dragged me out of the passageway. She plonked the wine on a table as we passed by, then led me down a maze of corridors to a room with a guard.

"Give him a bottle of Golden Peschet-Mossen." She stomped her foot when the guard looked back and forth between the two of us. "Hurry it up now. You know how these Esch Lords get. We're to make sure they're happy and drunk, so if you don't want to spend the rest of your life in the dungeon, get the wine."

We waited while the guard unlocked the door and went into a room that was floor to ceiling with wine racks, each of them filled with bottles.

"Why are the Esch Lords supposed to be happy and

drunk?" I asked, figuring I might as well dig around for information while I was waiting for a more believable prop to carry to the ballroom.

She shrugged. "It's not my place to ask questions and I'd suggest you do the same. These parties are usually to raise money for the war, though."

"Think we'll beat the Unseelie?" I asked, pushing my luck.

The fairy barked out a laugh. "Eventually. The queen won't rest until she rules all of Aerie, and at the rate we're going, I'll be old and toothless before we beat them. Just be lucky you're serving some minor landowner and not sent out to fight."

The guard came out of the room and handed me a bottle. Before he'd finished locking the door, the servant was once more dragging me through the hallways and down the narrow corridors between the rooms. I stumbled trying to keep up, and nearly got whiplash when she opened a door in the wall and shoved me out.

"Ballroom is there." She pointed to the left where there was indeed an arched entrance to a giant room full of elaborately-dressed, dancing fae.

I turned back around to thank her, and saw nothing but a seamless wall behind me with the occasional painting breaking up the expanse of creamy gold paint. I reached out to feel the wall and could not tell where the door had been. Knocking around didn't reveal any opening or even a space under the plaster. I walked down to the nearest closet which had an actual door with hinges and a sparkly glass handle, opened the door, and eyed the thickness of the walls, noting that there was no way a walkable passage should fit between what seemed to be a wall less than a foot thick.

Magic. And a pretty ingenious use of it in my opinion.

Walking back, I snuck in the side entrance to the ball-room and hugged the wall, taking a few minutes to see what was going on and to decide who among these fae might know where Iselle had been taken.

I'll admit that I was afraid. I'd spent too long on the journey here and I didn't want to face the possibility that she'd been interrogated and put to death while I'd still been running through the forests.

"What are you doing?" A fairy wearing a sky-blue and gold uniform hissed to me. "Get that bottle of wine out there before someone sees you standing here like a witless human."

Okay, the human bashing had to stop, but he had a point. I needed to get my ass in gear.

I began to walk the perimeter of the ballroom, trying to decide whether one of the jewel-encrusted fairies would have more knowledge than the guards at the edge of the dais. Finally I picked my mark, approaching a gaudily dressed fairy who'd just come off the dance floor and taken his leave of an equally gaudily dressed fairy.

"My Lord," I said with a bow. "Lord Mfllmwm would like to talk to you regarding...gems and artwork and his possible donations to support...stuff." I held up the bottle. "He would like you to accompany me to somewhere private where you both may share this and discuss his contributions to...stuff."

The guy eyed the bottle and nodded, strutting along behind me as I took him out the side ballroom doorway and down the hall to the closet. Opening the non-magic door, I shoved him inside.

He was dead and I'd Owned his soul before he even stumbled over the stack of buckets and mops.

Yeah, why the fae had old-school mops and buckets

when they could magic passageways inside their walls was a puzzle—a puzzle I had no time to solve.

I kept my average-joe-fairy appearance because I didn't want to have to strip this guy and struggle into his ornate clothing. Leaving him in the closet, I left with the bottle of wine, sorting through the fae's memories as I made my way back to the ballroom.

The fairy was a high-ranking government official's son. He had no idea why Iselle was taken, or what had been done with her, but he did know the layout of the queen's private chambers because he'd been screwing one of her ladies-in-waiting. I filed that away, then re-entered the ballroom to pick my next prey.

Six fae later the closet was getting rather full of dead bodies, and I was no closer to knowing Iselle's location or fate. Feeling a bit desperate, I lucked out and spotted a fairy I assumed was a general or something from the metal-covered sash across his bejeweled jacket.

The general wasn't all that interested in the bottle of wine, but when I told him that Lord Mfllmwm had information about a Unseelie spy in their midst, he practically ran me over in his haste to get to the closet. Owning him gave me the first decent knowledge I'd had all night.

Someone had delivered information to the queen's military advisors that the attacker sending vicious animals through their portals would be entering Aerie to launch a stealth attack. The attacker would be accompanied by a young Seelie girl who had aligned herself with the enemy. The birthdate of the Seelie girl seemed oddly important, and there were instructions from the queen to bring us both to the Court. If I could not be captured, then I was to be killed, but the girl *must* be delivered alive to the queen for interrogation.

I hoped she was still alive. Iselle, that is. Not the queen. In fact, I regretted I hadn't been able to stuff the queen's dead body in this closet with the other fae.

I'd been sending Durfts and other shit through their gateways lately, so it *was* possible there was a hit out on me, even this soon, but the military dude I Owned knew this very detailed information from an unnamed, unknown spy.

How did they know about me? About Iselle and when as well as where we were entering Aerie? The Unseelie scouts that caught us wouldn't have been communicating with the Seelie, and even if they had a spy among them, none of them should have known that Iselle or I were the ones dumping Durfts, drop bears, and demon-badgers into their kingdom. Unless someone on the human side of the world told them what I was doing, but the only ones who knew that were members of the Ruling Council and some of my household.

I had a traitor in my midst, and while I could be wrong, I had my suspicions on who this traitor was.

But more important than the identity of the spy, why did they want *Iselle*? Did they think that she was somehow key to our counteroffensive against them? Did they fear her involvement with me indicated a wide-spread Seelie rebellion? None of the idiots I Owned seemed to know. She was supposed to be captured alive and brought to the queen for interrogation, and because she really didn't know anything, they probably would have tossed her into the dungeon.

Which meant I needed to get to the dungeon. Unfortunately none of the Seelie bozos taking up space inside me knew exactly where that was. I could maybe grab a few more of the ballroom guests, but eventually someone was going to notice a bunch of fae were missing and someone else would remember seeing me lead them out into the hall-way. And then they'd find the dead bodies.

No, I needed to get into the dungeon immediately, and the easiest way to do that was to get arrested, or whatever the fae equivalent to that was.

Even though I knew where the queen's quarters were, I would have no time to deliver this note to the exact jewelry box in the correct drawer. So instead I took one of the medals off military-officer-guy, and pinned the note into his chest before leaving the closet.

I had to lean on the door to get it closed. It was hard, but I managed. Then I went back into the ballroom and ran into the middle of a giant fairy square-dance, knocking over whoever was in my way. Popping the cork out of the bottle of wine, I took a swig, then dropped my drawers and mooned the entire crowd.

The wine actually was pretty damned good, so I stood up to take another big swig before bending over to wiggle my butt once more. Some fae screamed. Others laughed. But I hadn't managed to drink more than a third of the bottle of wine before two guards grabbed me by the arms and haul me out of the ballroom.

I let my feet drag, my trousers around my ankles. I almost dropped my bottle of wine, then I realized that spilling it on the floor might mean servants had to mop, which would send them to the closet where I'd stored all the dead bodies. Eventually they'd find them and the note I'd left, but I had hopes that event would be delayed until Iselle and I manage to get safely back home.

20

___

The guards moved with inhuman speed, and I'll admit my brain was a little fuzzy from rapidly drinking a wine whose alcoholic affects were magically supplemented. I had this vague scheme to escape from my cell, find Iselle and break her out, then use the magical stone up my lady-bits to get us back home. Hopefully I'd be able to do use the rock from the dungeon, but I worried that there could be some blocking magic that wouldn't allow Gwylla's spell to work either. If so, I'd need to somehow get us out of the dungeon and to a place where I could activate the stone.

I bounced down the stairs, dragged by the two fae. With one hand, I managed to grab my pants to keep them from completely coming off. I still couldn't create clothing, and it would be hard to escape half naked.

"Is this just for the night?" Because I needed to know how long I had to rescue Iselle. "You guys will come let me out in the morning once I've sobered up, right?"

One of the guards snorted. "The only way you're getting out of here is in a bag. You disrupted the Queen's ball. It doesn't matter whose servant you are, you're down here for the rest of your life."

Well, at least I didn't have to rush this rescue, although I'd been counting on their coming to release me as a last-ditch escape chance.

"I hope that wine was good." The other guard glanced down at the bottle in my hand, mostly empty after I'd spilled a good bit being dragged through the castle hallways. "If disrupting the ball and showing your buttocks to the guests didn't get you life in the dungeon, stealing and drinking that wine would. That's only for the royals and their guests."

It *was* pretty damned good. Better than the elven wine. Better than the human wine. If I were Dar, I'd be arranging for some inter-realm commerce right now. If there was any way I could snatch a bottle before leaving, I'd really like to take him one.

We hit the bottom of the steps and I landed with a thump before being hauled forward down a wide stone passageway with especially dim lighting. Twisting my head side-to-side I tried to get a good look at the cells we were passing. I'd expected magically enhanced metal bars, but all I saw was solid stone. Correction—solid stone broken by rusty metal rectangles and ovals.

We paused after I'd counted fifty-three metal rectangles. One of the guards pulled an amulet-bracelet from under the cuff of his shirt and slapped it against the metal oval. The stone shifted, then slid sideways revealing a dark room.

The pair tossed me in, and the guard with the amulet slapped it against the metal oval once more.

I scrambled to my feet and rushed the door, only to have it slam in my face, leaving me squinting to see in the darkness. Feeling around, I couldn't tell where the door ended and the stone wall began, but I could feel both the metal oval on my side as well as the metal rectangle. I poked the rectangle with my fingers, surprised to discover it was a slot like what a postman would slide mail or a box through. It had a metal hinged cover that swung both to the outside of the cell and the inside. Pushing it out, I peeked through but there was nothing to see other than the stone hallway, and the stone of the walls and prison cell doorways.

My eyes adjusted to the darkness and I turned from the door to look around.

I'd been in a lot of dungeons in my life and this was *not* the worst. Still, it wasn't exactly a suite at the Hilton. The stone floors were uneven and damp. The walls seeped water and there was a weird glowing moss along the ceiling. A heap of torn and filthy rags formed a mound in the corner— discarded clothing from former residents, no doubt.

The bundle of rags stirred, and a face appeared from their folds.

I jumped and nearly screamed.

An old woman unfolded herself and stood. Her head barely reached my shoulder, and her back was hunched with age. Brown eyes set deep in a nest of wrinkled skin regarded me.

"We're doomed," she croaked in a rusty voice.

"Kinda looks that way." I poked again at the mail slot in the door. "I'm sure I'll think of something though."

"The forest waits. It lives and waits for the Chosen One," she said.

At least, I think that's what she said. Her speech was so garbled that I could barely understand her even with all the fae I'd Owned.

"You don't want to go back to that forest." I started

inspecting the walls again for weaknesses or cracks. "Those fucking trees will kill you. I barely got out of there alive."

"The forest. It waits."

Great. I was going to be stuck in here for who-knows-how-long with a smelly, insane, chatty-Cathy.

"How long have you been in prison?" I asked, hoping I could get some useful information out of this old bag.

She didn't reply. Instead she picked something up off the ground and put it in her mouth. I hadn't seen a bug since the guards had tossed me in here, so I assumed it was a dropped piece of whatever food she'd been last served.

No bugs and no light besides the glowing moss suggested to me that there wasn't an opening I could squeeze through, even in an alternate shape. But this oozing water had to come from somewhere, and I'd gotten good at surviving while in a whole bunch of weird forms over the last few years. Gregory was particularly fond of smokeless fire. He'd worked hard at getting me to practice that form, but my fire tended toward the smoky variety. Fire might not help much right now, but smoke could squeeze into all sorts of tiny places. I just needed to find those tiny places.

I examined the floor and the walls with close detail, but found no cracks. The stone was similar to granite. The water was a saltier variety of what came out of my tap back home. The moss glowed from phosphorescence and didn't seem to require any sort of light to grow. I dove my personal energy into a small piece and found it to be inedible in terms of providing nutrients, but not poisonous.

I tossed the piece of moss to the floor and the rag woman snatched it up, stuffing it into her mouth. Clearly if you were hungry enough, you'd eat anything.

It seemed the only way out was through the door—or rather through the mail slot in the door. I'd just need to change my form into something that could squeeze through the opening, wait for a guard to come down, kill him and Own him and take his amulet key thingy that would allow me to open Iselle's door once I found out which cell she was in.

Piece of cake.

The stamp of a boot on stone sounded through the thick walls and my roomie ran for the door, squatting to bring her face level with the mail slot. She remained there, quivering like a dog waiting for a treat while footsteps and metallic bang noises filled the air. Suddenly a tray shot through the mail slot, nearly hitting the woman in the face. She grabbed it and scurried off to her corner, immediately hunching over the tray and eating whatever it held.

Another tray came through the slot, clattering on the ground and sliding halfway into the room. My roomie froze, eyeing the second tray then looking over at me.

"Eat my dinner and I'll stuff your dead body through that mail slot," I warned her as I went over to pick up the tray.

It held a chunk of bread that was both stale and moldy, and a cup of greasy water whose lid had come off when the tray hit the floor. Half the greasy water was in the tray, soaking the nasty bread.

"I changed my mind. Help yourself," I told the woman.

She dove for the food. I watched her eat and drink, then she carefully shoved both trays through the mail slot in the door. I'd wanted to keep them as potential weapons, but in her rusty voice, she'd told me, "No tray, no food."

While my roomie was busy relieving herself in the same corner where she apparently slept I decided I should get out of this cell and position myself in a spot where I could grab the next guard who came down here.

A ferret would be tall and agile enough to get through the mail slot. And in the dark of the dungeon, I could easily find a spot to curl up and hide. And wait.

But when I tried to rearrange my molecular and genetic structure, nothing happened. I tried again, then a third time, but still remained squatting by the mail slot in that idiotic fairy's form that I'd been wearing most of the day.

I'd expected some sort of magic-dampening spell down here, or powerful fae prisoners would be making walls vanish and teleporting out of their cells. I hadn't expected the fae spell to block my ability to change my form, though.

Just in case this spell was selective, I tried to create electricity, tried to teleport, tried to summon my sword, and tried to crumble the stone walls, all to no effect.

So much for my great escape plan. And so much for being able to use the portal stone up my hooha to get us out of here. It seemed the only magic that worked in this dungeon was the guards' amulets that opened and closed the doors.

Which sucked, but it gave me an advantage as well. All I needed to do was get out of this cell, and the fae guards would be vulnerable. I could beat the shit out of them, and snap their necks without fearing any sort of magical defenses or attacks on their part. Of course, none of that would matter if I couldn't get the fuck out of this cell.

I examined the mail slot again with greater scrutiny. Fingers and part of my arm could be stuck through it with no ill effects. Wiggling a little, I got my elbow through, then patted around to see if I could reach anything I could use in an escape attempt. If I stretched my arm to the point of nearly dislocating my shoulder, I could manage to reach the metal oval that served open the cell door, but without one of the guards' amulets, that wouldn't do me any good.

I pulled my arm back inside and thought some more. If I could somehow get a guard in here, overcome him, then grab his amulet, I could open the door. Or if I could somehow disable the guard within reaching distance of the mail slot, I could maybe manage to get his amulet and open the door myself.

If only I could zap him, or stab him, or...something.

Wondering the limitations of this magical warding, I revealed my wings and was relieved to see their feathered lengths expand as far as they could in the cramped cell.

"Ooo, pretty," the old woman cackled. "Deep in the nightmare, an angel appears. A being of darkness and light to bring peace and save us all."

I hid my wings once more. "I'm all darkness, and I'm not interested in saving anyone besides myself and a one particular fairy right now. Everyone else in Aerie can fuck themselves."

"Eons ago the deal was struck," the woman announced, her voice becoming stronger. "Overthrow comes only from inside. Kingdoms may fight, people may die, but the crown falls only to its own."

"Uh huh," I said, only half-listening as I dug through my pockets for anything the fae who previously owned these pants might have been carrying.

"A curse falls upon those who break the bargain. Lies. Lies and war. Endless war until the wrongs of the past are made right."

Nothing. At least nothing beyond the belongings I put there myself before hiding my jeans and T-shirt in some back alleyway. Which consisted of: an almost-empty Skittles packet with a smashed red one in the bottom. Some lint. A hair tie.

And a ring.

What. The. Fuck.

I'd left it behind. Home. In my underwear drawer. I hadn't intended to actually return it, only to leave the threatening ransom note, so I hadn't bothered to bring it. But here the thing was. I stared at it, turning the ring in my hand. It hadn't been in my jeans pockets before when I'd changed into these pants, and I knew the nobody-Seelie I'd Owned and stolen these clothes from wouldn't have it, or even a replica of it.

And this most definitely wasn't a replica. I wasn't a jeweler, but I'd stolen enough shit in my life to know this was the exact ring I'd left back home.

"And then it was foretold. Two crowns were needed to bring peace. Two crowns."

I slipped the ring onto my finger, half expecting to become invisible because the fact that it clearly had followed me and suddenly appeared in the pocket of pants I was wearing sounded eerily like that long book about Hobbits and Elves.

"Two crowns," the old woman shouted, waving a grubby index finger from each hand in my face. "Two."

"Can you see me?" I asked, ignoring the fingers.

She blinked, as if surprised to see me there, and her eyes were suddenly sharp and clear. Her gaze lowered to the ring on my finger.

"That doesn't belong to you. Only the Seelie queen can wear the ring."

"Well, my finger hasn't fallen off yet, so I think I'm okay. What exactly is this thing supposed to do?" I asked.

"Fire and loyalty." She looked up at me once more, her eyes clouding again. "You cannot wear it!" she shrieked. "Only the queen can wear it. Only the queen."

"If this ring ensures the loyalty of her subjects, then why

the fuck isn't the queen wearing it twenty-four/seven?" I wondered. If I had a ring that would ensure the loyalty of my demon subjects, I'd never take that thing off.

"Pretenders cannot wear the ring," she screamed in my face.

I wiped spittle and bits of food off, backing away from the woman.

"Are you saying the queen is a pretender? Or that I'm a pretender? Are you implying the current Seelie queen isn't born of the royal line? Is she impersonating the queen with some kind of spell? Or did she overthrow your regular queen, and take the throne?"

I sorted through all my Owned Seelie memories and discovered that the current queen had gained her throne as part of a coup in which the previous royals had supposedly died in a murder-suicide pact to avoid imprisonment.

I was calling bullshit on that last bit, but my Owned souls seemed to believe the story.

Either way, I really didn't care who was running the kingdom, but my threatening ransom note wouldn't do much good if this current queen couldn't even wear the damned thing. No wonder it had been stuck in some jewelry box where Lux had found it.

Even more importantly, this ring didn't matter. Gwylla was wrong. The queen wasn't about to come through a gateway with an army for a piece of jewelry that was completely useless to her.

The old woman's only response to my questions was to look at her fingers and nibble on a hangnail. Clearly her usefulness in terms of information was over.

But magically appearing useless for blackmail ring or not, I still needed to get out of this cell, then find Iselle and get her to safety. I couldn't give up.

Another sweep of the cell didn't reveal anything I'd missed before. Reaching up to grab another piece of moss, I planted my foot into water that had puddled along one wall. When the ring on my finger touched the moss, light flashed around my hand, traveling through my body and into the water.

I yelped and flung the moss away. Then I stared at the ring.

Electricity. Something in the ring had reacted with the moss and sent a charge of electricity through me. It was enough of a shock that it would have killed a human.

Was it enough to kill a fae? I was in the body of a fairy right now, and it hadn't killed me, so I doubted it. But it gave me an idea. And that idea was the only one I had on how to escape this cell.

21

I spent the rest of the time until our next meal scooping the nasty water up in my hands and pouring it out the mail slot. I'd found another decent-sized puddle of water in a corner that might have been pee, and hoped that between the two, there would be enough liquid on the floor in front of our cell to conduct electricity.

There was one worrisome flaw in my plan. The guard shoved the trays through, so I couldn't exactly grab his arm to make the connection. The tray was metal, but I had no idea if that particular sort of metal here in Aerie would conduct electricity. If it did and I zapped the guard and it managed to either kill him or knock him out, then I'd need to hope I could reach my arm through the slot far enough to reach his wrist and get the amulet. Hopefully the amulet worked from the inside of the cell, otherwise I'd need to stretch my arm through the slot far enough to unlock the door from the outside.

Okay, more than *one* worrisome flaw.

Trying to increase my chances of success, I pulled down as much moss as I could reach and jammed it through the mail slot. Most of it fell to the other side, but I got a decent amount to stick in the slot. Balling more moss up in my hands, I waited.

The old lady raced to the slot as soon as we heard the footsteps. I hip checked her out of the way, wanting to ensure I was in position to grab the tray and electrocute the guard. She shrieked, slapping me and pushing me as she tried to get in front of the slot. I pushed her back and snarled.

"Sit the fuck down. You'll get your food. I'll even set you free if I can pull this off," I whispered to her.

What I'd said must not have registered in her prison-addled brain because she started screaming and pulling her hair. It drowned out the sound of the footsteps and mail slots, and I wouldn't have known my chance was coming except the guard paused to complain about the water and moss piled up outside our door.

Not wanting to wait for the tray, I shoved my hands through the slot, grabbed hold of something, and squeezed the moss against my fingers.

The burst of light was so strong it streamed into the cell through the mail slot and temporarily blinded me. It caused my roomie to shut up, but everyone else in the dungeon was now screaming—including the guard.

He thrashed, but I held on. I heard the trays clatter to the floor, smelled the horrible odor of something burning, and felt the lick of flames blister one of my wrists. Within seconds, his body was a dead weight, held up by my aching arms. I shifted around, trying to peer through the slot to see what part of the guard I was holding on to and how I might be able to possibly grab the amulet. What I saw was a bit alarming.

The dungeon was on fire.

Evidently I'd used too much moss, and the greasy water had something ignited because flames were snaking up the sides of walls and along the floor. Stone shouldn't be burning, but I guess this particular kind of stone was flammable, because I could see the flames crawling across the dungeon floor.

The old woman in the cell with me went back to screaming her damned head off about the fucking food, but I ignored her and tried to focus on getting the amulet.

Realizing my one hand was holding the guard by the arm, I shifted my other hand to feel around for the amulet on his wrist. It wasn't easy to get off the fairy's arm, but I finally managed to pull it free.

I was afraid to let the guy go, so I held on with one hand, brought the amulet through the mail slot with the other, and reached up to smack the amulet against the metal oval on my side of the cell.

The wall began to slide open, so I dropped the guard and yanked my arm through the slot to dash out of the cell in case the door began to close. My roomie ran after me, dropping to her knees amid the stanky water and flames to shove the spilled food into her mouth. I had other plans. Grabbing the guard once more, I spooled his soul into me, Owning him and taking his form. Then I pulled his clothes off, stamping out the smoldering pants before stripping and putting it all on.

HIs memories filled my mind, and I looked around, realizing that my situation had gone from bad to worse. The dungeon was on fire and I needed find Iselle before she asphyxiated or burned to death. *And* before something alerted the fae in the palace that their dungeon was on fire.

Once I found Iselle, I hoped the portal stone Gwylla had created worked down here because the fairies had already found the stack of dead bodies in the closet and were panicking over the idea of a murderer in their midst. They'd increased security, but at least they hadn't connected the country-lord's servant who'd gotten drunk on royal wine and mooned the peerage with the dead bodies.

Although it was probably only a matter of time before that connection was made. Good thing I'd ditched that form for this guard's or I would have found myself at the end of an executioner's magical rope.

But I didn't have any time to ponder any of that. I needed to find Iselle.

While my roomie chowed down on the discarded food meant for the other prisoners, I began opening every cell door, letting the prisoners out and shouting for Iselle. Just in case she was hurt or unconscious, I hurriedly searched each cell, flipping over any prisoners who hadn't rushed out to make sure I didn't inadvertently leave her behind.

The dungeon was still on fire. Smoke began to cloud the air and burn my lungs. That was no way for any prisoner to die, so I tried to encourage even the injured ones to make for the staircase. The imprisoned fae were emaciated and filthy, but every one of them managed to make it through their cell doors. The hall was crowded with them, coughing and staggering in a mass past the burning walls.

I'd doubled back and was opening the cell doors on the other side of the dungeon when a fairy jogged back to me. The guy wore tattered pants that were pretty much shorts at this time, and no shirt. His hair was long and matted, dark gold mostly covered with dirt. He was thin with bruises on his bare legs and sores on his blood-streaked chest. In spite of this, he appeared strong and alert.

"The door into the palace is locked," he told me. "How did you plan for us to get out?"

I blinked at him.

"You're releasing us as part of the uprising, to take our place in the rebel army?" he said, as if smoke had clouded my mind and made me forget my mission.

Ah. He assumed I was a member of a rebellion that had infiltrated the castle guards and was organizing a planned jail break. Turning, I continued to open cell doors as I answered him.

"I was going to open the door once I let everyone out." I was totally making it up as I went along, but he didn't need to know that. "If everyone can hang on, I'll let them out."

His eyebrows knitted together. "But the dungeon is burning fast, and everyone is starting to panic. I don't think many of us are in any physical condition to fight with your army in the palace. But we'll do our best."

Damn. There was no army, no coup attempt, no rebellion occurring in the palace. There was just me, in a burning dungeon, looking for the young fairy I'd accepted into my household so the two of us could get the hell out of here.

And leave all these prisoners free of their cells to burn in a dungeon.

"Is there any other way out?" I might be able to open the door out of the dungeon for them before Iselle and I use the portal stone, but they'd all be slaughtered by the fae on the other side since there were no rebels to assist them.

He looked around the smoke-filled dungeon. "We could take the chute they use to dispose of the dead. It goes under the city, then through a portal into the sea. Those of us who are stronger can help the injured ones to shore."

"Do that." I opened up another door and looked inside once the fairy prisoner limped out. "Get everyone out of here as quickly as you can. We can handle things in the palace."

He clapped a surprisingly firm hand on my shoulder. "Thank you for not forgetting about us in the dungeon. Those who are strong enough will head for Wynn to join the rebellion. I hope that your forces can take the palace and unseat the Queen. If not, we'll be there to fight by your side."

"Awesome. Vive la révolution," I muttered, continuing to open doors in my search for Iselle.

I continued to work my way through the smoke-filled dungeon. The flames had moved to the ceiling, and some of the cells on the other side were beginning to collapse as the fire consumed the stones making up the walls. Vague people-like shapes were vanishing through a hatch in the floor as voices yelled "Go! Go!"

I could barely breathe or see through the smoke as I opened the last cell door. Iselle hadn't been in any of them, and I was beginning to panic. Had she been killed? Had she died down here, her body shoved down the shoot that led to the sea? I staggered toward where I thought the staircase that led to the palace was, feeling until my hand connected with the railing. I was glad for my ability to survive just about anything, because the acrid smoke was worse as I climbed. This fire sucked, but it also gave me the perfect distraction.

Slapping the amulet against the metal oval, I burst through the door, startling the two guards on the other side.

"Fire," I croaked. "Prisoners. Escape. Fire."

That spurred a flurry of activity. The room was suddenly filled with uniformed fae, some armed with wands and others with amulets. The wand fairies went first, no doubt their version of a SWAT team to clear the area of potentially deadly attacks from emaciated and weakened prisoners. Then the ones with the amulets went down the stairs. Steam started to come through the door. I found myself ushered away by a fairy dressed far too nicely to be expected to go into the filthy dungeons. He told me that the Queen's Security Advisor wanted to talk to me about the possibility that the jailbreak was connected to "other events."

I.E. The dead bodies in the closet, and the note I'd left about the ring.

Shoving my hand behind my back, I wondered if there was some way I could manage to get the ring off my finger and hide it where it wouldn't be found. Maybe up my vajayjay with the portal stone? Unfortunately, we were practically running through hallways and invisible doors hidden in walls, and there was probably no chance I'd be able to claim the need for a quick bathroom break or a moment to change my clothes.

Before I could even voice the idea, the well-dressed fairy shoved open a huge wooden door with actual living leaves and flowers on it and waved me into a room. There was another fairy dude, this one older and clearly of some importance, standing behind a long live-edged table, his back turned to me as he looked out a giant, six-foot-square window. Glancing past him, I saw the view wasn't of the palace grounds or the city below, but a rugged mountain area with wind-bent, stunted trees and furry, goat like creatures hopping across the rocky ledges.

My escort left and I quickly sorted through the Owned souls' memories to determine the correct protocol for this meeting.

Remain standing. Eyes lowered and chin up. Act nervous, but as if I were trying not to be nervous.

The Queen's Security Advisor spun around, glaring at me. "What happened?"

"I...I was delivering the food trays, and there was an

explosion," I said, faking a stutter. "It knocked me out, and when I regained consciousness, the whole place was on fire, the cell doors were open, and the prisoners were gone."

Hopefully the actual guard's body was too burned for identification by now, or I'd need to ditch this form for another pronto. I eyed the Security Advisor, thinking that a fairy in his position might be one of the few who knew if Iselle had died in the dungeon or had been taken elsewhere. Although where would I hide the guy's body? I couldn't exactly drag it down the hallway to another closet and hope no one noticed, but there wasn't anywhere in this room suitable for body disposal.

"Huh?" I blurted out, realizing that the Security Advisor had asked me a question. Thankfully he didn't seem to actually expect a response, because he continued talking as he paced back and forth behind his desk.

"...must find whoever infiltrated our defenses. It's a disgrace. The Queen is furious that someone murdered nine prominent Seelie fae right under our noses, and had the audacity to leave a note threatening her! We searched the palace and grounds, and were convinced that the traitor had fled, but the release of the prisoners and destruction of our carefully constructed dungeon means he must still be here, hiding in our midst. How did the rebels defeat the magic of the dungeon? How was the attacker able to not only release the prisoners, but remove them from the dungeon without setting off any of the alarms?"

He paused and glared at me, this time clearly wanting a response.

"The traitor must have some powerful teleportation magic." How did this idiot not know about the body disposal chute? Whatever. If he thought I was able to defeat the spells on the dungeon and transport all the prisoners with a snap of my fingers, so be it. Anything that added to my rep as a terrifying badass would hopefully convince the queen to take my threat seriously and negotiate with me.

The Security Advisor fisted his hands, but not before I saw them tremble. He was scared too. Good.

I walked forward until only the desk was between us. "What if this isn't a rebel? What if it's a monster from the other side? An angel, come to take revenge for those who have been killed and for the humans who were taken in defiance of the contract."

He stepped to the side, eyeing the door before focusing his attention back on me. "Angels are weak and stupid. *They* broke the contract, not us. And they are too scared of us to attack us in Aerie."

"This one isn't too scared." I revealed my wings, tearing through the guard's singed clothing and jumping across the desk to tackle the Security Advisor.

I'd spooled his soul into me before he could scream. Then I assumed his form, changed into his fussy, gaudy clothing as best as I could without assistance, and shoved the fairy's naked body along with the guard's clothing under the desk.

Wedging the chair in to better hide the dead guy, I sifted through his memories as I looked in the desk drawers for anything that might be of use to me. These fae were much easier to kill that I'd expected. Maybe it was because I wasn't meeting them on a battlefield, but surprising them. Owning them and assuming their forms clearly was an effective attack strategy. Too bad I couldn't do it on a large scale.

There was some pretty cool stuff in the desk. Self-writing pens that could produce six different officials' signatures, beautifully colorful folders that compressed massive documents to one page thickness for easy storage, a blow-up sex doll.

Well, the fae equivalent of a blow-up sex doll. It was the size of a Barbie and shoved into the back of a bottom drawer that also contained a bottle of that special wine and an amulet that produced Viagra-like effects. When I pulled the doll out of the drawer, it flew from my hands and became a gorgeous, naked fairy woman with pale skin, black hair, and silvery eyes.

Oooo, naughty boy! Not only did the Special Advisor like getting nasty with a magical partner, he liked getting nasty with an *Unseelie* magical partner. And now that I'd Owned several of the fae, I could finally tell the two apart.

I kept searching as the naked Unseelie sex toy proposed all sorts of lewd activities in a sultry but somewhat robotic voice. "What's this?" I wondered as I pulled something out of the center drawer that looked like a television remote. I pushed a button and the mountain scene in the window behind me changed to the palace gardens, then to an ornate bedroom, then to another ornate bedroom.

Holy shit, this wasn't a magical window, it was a screen of camera views, just like the humans had, only created with fairy magic instead of technology. I cycled through the images, noting that this Security Advisor was one sick fucker from the amount of bedroom surveillance he had going on. Bedroom. Kitchen. Bedroom. Dungeon door. Bedroom. Ballroom. Mountain fortress. Seaside with a bunch of raggedy-dressed fairies staggering around. A grouping of towers in an isolated meadow. Another Bedroom.

Wait. I backed the view up to the towers and mentally grabbed hold of the Security Advisor's soul.

What is this? It's important. I felt you panic when I saw this. Tell me what it is.

He squirmed, resisting. But no one resists for long when you have their soul in your devilish little hands. It only took seconds before the fairy had opened the vault of his memories to me, this time without restriction.

Towers of the Foretold.

For some reason the queen had ordered that all young girls born on a certain day, in a certain season, of a certain year be brought to her for questioning and then imprisoned forever in these towers. This is where Iselle had been taken, where she was being kept.

Iselle and two dozen other young fae women.

22

O nce more I was glad that I'd ignored Gregory and Owned a bunch of fae, including this particular dude. Not only did I now know where Iselle was, I knew how to get there without having to tromp through miles of murderous forest.

All I needed to do was walk through this window. It needed to be showing the place where I wanted to go. Only the Queen's Security Advisor could use the window. And he needed to be holding that key that I'd seen with all the self-writing pens in the top desk drawer.

I ransacked the drawer, took out the key, and gripped the remote in the other hand. There was a chance this wouldn't work. So far the fae hadn't been able to realize I wasn't one of them when I had assumed an Owned fairy's form. I was good at hiding my energy signature, good at burying myself deep inside a physical form. And with all an Owned soul's memories, I could answer any tricky questions about their life. But the one thing I couldn't do was their magic. Walking through this window would work if it just required the key and this fairy's genetic makeup. It wouldn't work if magic was needed to use the window portal. What would happen if I failed the test was something even the Queen's Security Advisor didn't know. I could just bounce off the window or be dumped in a random place in Aerie. Or I could die.

Risk of dying hadn't stopped me from doing shit before, so I took the chance, closed my eyes, and jumped into the window. I didn't bounce off but I did trip on the sill and fall, opening my eyes just as I face-planted onto a lawn. Scrambling to my feet I saw that I'd landed in a courtyard with short, feathery-like grass in iridescent shades of green. Surrounding me were a series of three-hundred-foot-tall towers that reminded me of grain silos. Behind them were another row of towers, and behind them another. They were windowless with smooth cream-colored marble sides and domed golden roofs. I walked to the nearest one, circling it and not finding any entrance.

Dude. How the fuck do I get inside? And which one has Iselle?

The Queen's Security Advisor didn't know which girls were in which tower. He didn't know how to get inside either. Evidently the girls were magically sealed up inside once the queen had spoken with them. Food and drink were delivered magically, and I assumed there was some sort of waste management system in place. This asshole didn't know anything about that either. He was the big picture guy, not the detail guy, and beyond having the information to get me here, he was completely useless.

Except he *did* know about the dragon.

I jerked back to full awareness, looking frantically around for any sign of this dragon. The Security Advisor didn't know what it looked like, or how large it was, but judging from the dragons I'd met so far, I doubted it would be able to hide behind one of these towers unseen. Dragons were powerful, scary, smart, and were happy to incinerate anyone who tried to walk off with anything they considered to be their treasure.

But there was no dragon here to be seen, nor anything a dragon might consider to be "treasure." I mean, the towers were probably valuable real estate, but I'd expect them to be more blingy, with shiny, sparkly, collectable stuff embedded in the marble or heaped around the bases if they were going to appeal to a dragon. Perhaps this particular dragon had a spartan aesthetic? Or maybe he'd gotten bored of the tower vibe and taken off to find something more his style.

She.

I spun around at the voice inside my head.

And I can't leave. These fairies have bound me here. I can't even fly off to find a few paintings to pretty the place up a bit.

The air shimmered, and a huge silver dragon appeared in the middle of the clearing. She was lying down, her wings tight against her sides and her breath stirring the tips of the grasses in front of her.

I froze, realizing that I was in the form of a Seelie fae—a high-ranking Seelie fae that the dragon might decide should die either because of her captivity or just because she was bored.

Relax. You're not a fairy. You're one of those demons from Hel dressed up as a fairy. And while I'm bored enough to eat you, I'm hoping you'll be more valuable as entertaining company.

I walked closer to the dragon, changing my form back to Sam. "I'm assuming they brought you here to guard the girls in the towers?"

Yep. Not that they need me. No one comes here. They've been bringing in food for me. Horrible stuff. Tastes like cow that's been dead in the field for a few days.

"How did they capture you?" I asked, impressed that the

fae had no only managed to kidnap a dragon, but magically bind it.

The dragon snorted, setting a patch of grass on fire, then tamping the flames out with a paw. *A trap. I was sunning on a beach and they lured me through one of their portals with sea glass jewelry.* She sighed. *I love sea glass jewelry.*

So did Nyalla.

"I'm here to rescue one of the girls. Her name is Iselle."

The dragon shrugged. *I don't know their names. I don't even know what they look like. One day a tower appears with a fairy girl inside, and that's it. I can't let you take her, though. I'm bound here until they all die, then I'll be set free. If I let even one escape, the fairies will never let me go.*

"How will they know if one escapes?" I glanced around. "There are no doors or windows. How the hell is one even supposed to escape or be set free? And from what I can tell, these fae motherfuckers are pretty close to immortal. You could be stuck here a long time, eating rancid cow and staring at these boring plain towers, without a beach or sea glass in sight."

The dragon's green eyes gleamed, and she grinned, showing me all her white, pointed teeth. *Do you have an alternative to propose? Because I've been here what feels like an eternity and I'm ready to consider any options.*

"I've got a way to open up a portal. You might not be able to leave whatever area you're bound to here, but I'm willing to bet a portal would circumvent that magic."

She narrowed her eyes. *Not necessarily. Fae magic is very powerful. I'm not sure an angel-created portal will be an exception to the binding spell.*

"A Seelie fairy created it," I told her.

The dragon thought about that for a few seconds. *I'd like to see it and assess the magic myself before I agree to anything.*

"Uh, no." I wasn't digging the stone out of my nether regions until I was ready to use it.

How do you expect me to trust you without seeing the device? Demons lie, even ones that feel more like an angel than a demon. I could help you, and end up stuck here for all eternity.

"Or you could trust me, help me get the girl out and potentially escape." I shrugged. "I can't teleport in Aerie, and you're faster. If I try to run off you'll have me for lunch before I'm past the last line of towers. Plus I've got no reason to betray you. I want to stick it to the Seelie every chance I get, which includes setting their captive dragon guard free."

The dragon nodded. *Okay. Deal. I'll help you get the girl out, and you make sure I get through the portal out of here.*

She got up and strolled over to the closest tower, stood up on her hind legs and shook the building with her front legs. Chunks of marble broke free from where her claws dug into the stone, and the tower began to sway alarmingly back and forth.

"Stop!" I shouted, waving my hands at the dragon. "You can't just knock the thing over. You'll kill her. Or seriously injure her."

The dragon glared at me. *You didn't say she needed to be unhurt. These things don't have doors or windows. The only way to get the girl out is to knock it over and break the stone.*

"Can you just punch a hole in the side or something? A hole big enough for me to at least get inside?"

She rolled her eyes then extended a claw and jabbed it into the side of the tower she'd been shaking. Repeated jabs resulted in a cat-sized hole in a building that now strongly resembled a windowless leaning Tower of Pisa.

It would be a lot easier just to knock the tower over, the dragon grumbled as she began an alternating one-two punch that widened the hole considerably.

"Consider it a workout," I replied. "Upper body day. Bag work. That kind of thing."

Finally the hole was big enough. I climbed inside while the dragon began work on the next tower over. Rubble and marble dust was scattered across a winding staircase that took up the entire width of the tower. I started climbing, wondering why the fuck the fairies had put a staircase in a doorless tower. If I intended on trapping someone in a giant phallic marble column without any entrance or exit, then I'd just make the lower half of the thing solid. Why bother with this shit when no one would ever use these stairs? If the fae were too damned cheap to use solid marble, then at least leave it empty. It would make any rescue or escape attempt more difficult, although with a dragon standing guard, the fae probably figured she was their insurmountable barrier. Little did they know the dragon was bored and pissed off, and just waiting for an opportunity to get the fuck out of here.

When I reached the top of the tower, I realized that I had been mistaken. There was one door in the place—one from the staircase into what I assumed was the captive's room.

"Stupid fucking fairies," I muttered as I undid the simple locks and chains on the wooden door. Staircase. Wooden door. Bolt locks and chains like I'd find on the inside of a New York apartment.

I braced for some sort of magical blast when I flung the door open but there was nothing. The fae must have had faith in their marble tower and dragon to not bother with any additional security.

The room was actually nice. Magical widows showed a variety of pastoral scenes. A low bed with fluffy pillows and blankets stood in a corner. An intricately patterned woven rug covered the stone floor, and a couch along with a table and chair took up the rest of the space. I didn't see a kitchen, bathroom, or clothes washing facilities, so I assumed that was all done via some sort of fairy magic. The Seelie fae girl inside certainly didn't look dirty or starved, or like she'd been wearing the same clothes for a decade, but then again, since she was huddled under the table, it was hard to tell.

"Are you here to kill me?" Her voice wobbled a bit but she crawled out from under the table and stood facing me with her shoulders back and her chin raised. She had dark brown skin, and forest-green eyes. Her reddish-gold hair curled around her pointed ears and cascaded over one shoulder to her waist. She looked to be about fifteen years old, and she very obviously wasn't Iselle.

"Nope. I'm looking for a fairy girl named Iselle. Any idea which tower she's in?'

The girl shook her head. "There are other girls? Other towers? I barely remember the guards taking me from my father's arms and locking me in here. It's been so long…"

"Damn it. I'm going to have to go through all these towers looking for her," I blew out a frustrated breath, then gestured toward the doorway. "Grab whatever you want and come on out. You're free to go."

She looked around, snatched up a blanket, then ran for the door. She was out the hole in the side of the tower before I was halfway down. When I exited, I found her huddled on the ground, shaking as she stared at the dragon.

"What's that?" She whispered.

"Another captive here—one who helped you get out." The dragon had moved on to a third tower, so I walked over to the second one and jumped up to grab the jagged edge of the broken marble.

"These are all filled with girls like me?" The Seelie fairy girl was close behind me as I hoisted myself inside.

"Not filled. There's one girl in each tower." I started up the stairs. "I've got no idea why you all are being kept here, or why you were captured. I'm just looking for my friend."

"I don't know why either, but there are a lot of towers," the girl commented as she followed me.

Yeah. A lot of towers. And with my luck, Iselle would be in the very last one.

Seelie fairy girl number one helped calm down the panicking not-Iselle fairy girl in this tower, explaining that this human dressed as a high-ranking member of the royal court along with a giant winged monster were helping them all escape.

"Why would a human do this for us?" Girl number two asked as the two fairies followed me down the stairs. "Why would a slave set us free?"

I didn't bother to explain the situation because the dragon was a few towers ahead of me and I needed to catch up. For all I knew, the fae had some sort of alarm on the place that was now screaming out an alert that these girls were being released. The one good thing was that I was sure the alerts were going to the Queen's Security Advisor's office, and his body was under his desk. Plus I not only had the device to get through the magic window, but also the remote for the thing, so even if someone noticed the alarm going off, it would take them a while to create a portal or teleport here.

That was one more thing I'd learned Owning all these fae—teleportation as an innate magical ability was very rare. Iselle was more special than I'd thought.

The gaggle of Seelie fae girls following me had grown considerably by the time I reached the third ring of towers. Each time I found another girl in various degrees of panic or fear, and each time I left her in the hands of the others as I searched one more tower. As I'd expected, I didn't find Iselle until I'd climbed the stairs in the very last tower. I'll admit that I was a little scared the Security dude I'd Owned had been wrong and I would have spent all this time developing my quads with an insane StairMaster routine only to find my girl wasn't here. It had been that way with the dungeon, and I was pessimistic that I would again be met with failure. But when I unlocked that last door, I was greeted with a delighted squeal instead of screams of fear.

"You came!" Iselle launched herself into my arms and I hugged her tight, burying my face in her shining hair.

"Is that her?" The crowd behind me clapped their hands, hopping on the steps in excitement.

"It's her." I rocked Iselle a bit, then pulled away to smooth my hands through her hair and look her over. "Are you hurt? Did they injure you? Torture you?"

She shook her head. "No. After the attacking fairy grabbed me, he transported me to some sort of palace. I was interrogated by a number of people, then sent here to this room." She hugged me again. "I was worried you wouldn't be able to find me, that I wouldn't ever see you again."

"Is that the human language she's speaking?" One of the Seelie fairies behind me whispered to another.

"I'll always find you," I told Iselle, switching to the fae language. "But we need to hurry. I don't know how much time we have."

Iselle looked at the other girls. "Are they coming with us?"

Oh, hell no. "They probably want to stay here."

But it was too late. She'd replied in the fae language as well, and all the other girls were chattering excitedly about how they should all stick together, that they wouldn't even know how to find their families after all this time, and how they had nothing—no food or water or money to make any sort of journey on their own.

"I don't know why we were all taken and held here, but there's a good chance they'll just be captured and imprisoned once more if we leave them behind," Iselle said, this time in English.

Crap. I really didn't want to have to deal with two dozen teenage fairy girls, but Iselle was right.

"Okay," I said, tugging at her arm. "But we need to hurry."

Hurry evidently involved herding a bunch of excited girls down the tower stairs and out the narrow hole the dragon had made in the wall. Then they all waited with the dragon while I dropped my pants and dug the stone out of my honey pot. That act rendered everyone speechless and clearly shocked.

"I was worried about being searched," I told them as I wiped the stone on the edge of my fancy, gold-trimmed tunic. "Oh, like *you* wouldn't have done the same."

I addressed the latter comment toward the dragon, who had wrinkled her snout in disgust.

I wouldn't. No one searches a dragon.

Whatever. Walking to the center of the clearing, I held the stone in my hand, clicked my heels together and thought about home.

A narrow rift appeared in the air before me, sparkling with orange and gold.

"Go." I waved the girls through first, waiting until they'd all vanished before gesturing for the dragon to go. It was a tight squeeze since the rift was only evidently able to open so far, but the dragon managed. Then with a quick glance around me, I stepped into the rift, through a graveyard barrow, and out into a damp, foggy Irish morning.

The fairy girls were huddled together, shivering. The dragon was examining her scales for any damage the narrow portal might have caused. Gwylla looked like she'd jumped out of bed to get here, with her tousled hair and bare feet. She quickly closed the portal, then turned to glare at me.

"What have you done?" she demanded, waving a hand at the girls. "What in the name of all that's green and growing have you done?"

23

M y to-do list was expanding, and that hadn't been my intention when I'd started this shit with the fae. I still had wedding plans to finalize, including Snip's and my second attempt to secure Dolly Parton. I needed to meet with Dar and Amber regarding a fucking brilliant idea I'd had to further piss off the fae. I needed to somehow convince Joe that he wasn't being hunted and urge him to go live somewhere other than my house.

And now I had to find lodging for two dozen teenage fairies.

Nyalla dropped her phone to the table and ran a hand through her hair. "The Motel 6 has a ten-room block available, and the Red Roof has a six-room block. We could split the rest between the Super 8 and that Econo Lodge."

I frowned, thinking it wasn't a good idea to split the girls up, but I might not have a choice. My Low house was at maximum occupancy, plus lodging a bunch of teen fairy girls who'd been cooped up for most of their lives with my Lows might end in disaster. The hotel lodging might end in disaster as well, but at least it would all happen fifteen to twenty miles from my house.

"They should probably have a chaperone for each group." Nyalla glanced out the French doors to the pool patio where the girls were blasting music, drinking prosecco, and frolicking naked in the pool.

Maybe I should be looking at hotels sixty miles away, because even with a chaperone there were going to be arrests. Drunken, gorgeous teen girls who didn't speak English and had a propensity for nakedness? Girls who could punch any annoyingly lewd human into the next county? Definitely arrests.

"I've got an idea." Nyalla smiled at me. It was her naughty smile where her dimples came out and her eyes twinkled with mischief.

"Lay it on me," I encouraged.

"Talk Uriel and Leethu into taking them in." She sat back in her chair, her grin widening.

I shook my head in confusion, then I realized what she was saying. Uriel had gone missing from Aaru and the Ruling Council for a while, supposedly to deal with grief and guilt and other emotional shit. When she resurfaced, she and my succubus foster-sister were an item, and they'd purchased some Unibomber-sized ranch in the mountains where they lived with the A-Team of street-smart girls they'd rescued from a human trafficking ring. Uriel had resumed her duties on the Ruling Council with the other archangels, but she and her girl-band also ran around the world kicking abuser, pedophile, and trafficker ass, then sheltering their growing household of rescued women and children.

"The fae are girls, and they're teens in their age equivalent to humans," I mused. "They were captured by an evil queen and her minions, and kept isolated in towers until I set them free. It's perfect. All I need to do is spin some horror story about what the Seelie queen intended to do with the girls, and Uriel will swoop in for the rescue. That giant fucking ranch of hers has plenty of room for all of them. Neither she nor Leethu will care if they're naked and drunk either. Hell, Leethu is probably naked and drunk most of the time herself."

Nyalla nodded. "They'll keep the girls safe. Uriel will blow up half the state if the fae try to take any of them back to Aerie against their will."

My own girl seemed to have a fascination with blowing shit up lately. Not that I found any problem with that.

"Can you call Uriel?" I pushed back my chair and stood. "She'll believe you, where she'd think I was trying to prank her. Tell her it's urgent, that the girls aren't safe here because I'm such a fucking disaster, and that she needs to get them right away."

Nyalla gave me a thumbs-up, then picked up her phone. I went outside and took Iselle aside, pulling the fae ring from my finger and sliding it onto hers. "I'd like you to wear this and not take it off. And if anyone asks tell them that it's a family heirloom that had been stolen and was recently returned to your possession."

She tilted her head as she looked at the ring. "My family never could have afforded something like this. And it carries magic. If it's a family heirloom, it's certainly not mine."

"It belonged to the former Seelie queen," I confessed. "It's a long story, but it ended up in my possession, and at first I thought this whole mess was because of the ring. Turns out the current queen can't even use it. Only someone in the previous royal family could."

The ring had let out an electrical charge when in contact

with that phosphorescent stuff in the dungeon, but I wasn't sure if that was magic or just some weird chemical reaction. I definitely wasn't a member of the former royal family, so it must be the latter.

"It has powerful magic," Iselle said. "Persuasion magic. Enchantment magic. And fire magic. Surely there must be someone from the previous queen's family who should have this—a distant relative perhaps."

"They supposedly were all killed in a suicide/murder pact when the current queen and her forces breached the city gates." I was pretty sure the current queen or her minions had killed them, but I understood the need for the lie. Murdering not only the current ruler, but her children too wasn't a great way to endear the public to your claim on the throne.

Iselle frowned. "I remember that. I was very young, but I'd heard stories about the new queen and that there was a princess who had escaped before the palace was taken. She was supposed to be my age, and I was sad thinking how alone and afraid she must be."

Memories from my Owned souls floated into my awareness. A lost princess. A true heir who'd been spirited away, another nameless fairy girl dying in her stead. The stories spread like wildfire, and the Seelie populace had become enthralled with the idea of a girl who would one day walk from the forest to claim her throne.

As far as information went, I was in a far better position today than I was before my last trip to Aerie. Gregory despised me Owning souls, but not only was it a fun and enjoyable hobby, it was the quickest way to learn about a person, their history, and their culture. Through my Owned Seelie fae, I'd discovered that the current queen had gained her throne through a coup that had ended in the death of the previous royal family—all of them.

That crazy roomie I'd had in the Seelie dungeon? She'd been right. The queen was a pretender. And evidently there were some significant rebellious activities to suggest that many of the Seelie fae didn't welcome her reign.

As for who would take her place, that led me into the realm of myth and story. It was the same old shit the humans did when a kingdom was in chaos, from the princes in the tower during the War of the Roses, to Anastasia when the Tsars were toppled in Russia. A missing princess. An imposter who was killed in her place. There were tales of mythical eldritch powers granted from an ancient ancestor or because of numerology and astrology in her birthdate. Some stories told of how she was conceived from an unknown affair between the Seelie queen and the Unseelie King, and that her powers were an unbeatable combination of both rulers.

None of the fae I'd Owned had any proof of these myths being real, but for a people desperate for a hero, for a symbol of their cause, the stories were good enough.

Years had gone by and the lost princess hadn't been found, but there was unrest in the Seelie kingdom, and rebel armies had formed. The queen wasn't just dealing with my guerilla attacks through their portals and the war with the Unseelie, she was also dealing with strife within her own kingdom.

"Do you know that the other girls have the same birth-date as me?" Iselle spun the ring on her finger. "Isn't that strange? We were all born during the waxing quarter moon on the day of the autumnal equinox in the year of the hemlock."

Wait. All the girls in the towers and Iselle had the same

birthday? And Iselle remembered that the lost princess was around her age? I dug through my Owned souls' memories again and realized why all those girls had been stuck in the towers—they had the same birthdate as the lost princess. The queen was making sure the myth wouldn't come true and the heir to the Seelie throne wouldn't walk out of the forest to stir up the masses and take her throne.

Me? I would have just killed them all and made sure that no one ever found their bodies, but I'd learned that the fae were really fucking superstitious and weird. There was probably a reason why the queen didn't want two dozen young girls to die by her orders, although how that was different than all the other deaths she'd caused I didn't know.

"None of the other girls remembers being interrogated though," Iselle continued. They were just taken to the palace, then put straight away into a tower. I had days of questions. They wanted to know who you were, what your connection was with the angels and with the fae and with me, what you'd planned, when you were going to attack with an army and how big the army was. They knew you were sending the vicious creatures through their portals, and were desperate to know what else you had planned."

Lost princess. I could use this. Especially with Iselle wearing the ring, and a spy in our midst.

"I didn't know anything except that story about you and the elves and the chicken wands, but they didn't believe it. I thought they were going to kill me, but instead they put me in that tower."

"In the tower. Where all the other imprisoned girls were born on the same date—the same date as the mythical lost princess," I mused.

Iselle tilted her head. "You think one of the girls is the

lost princess? The daughter of the true Seelie queen? The one who will reclaim her throne?"

"No, not one of them." I pointed to the ring on her finger. "You."

Her eyes widened. "I can't be the lost princess! I remember my mother. She wasn't royalty."

"No one is the lost princess," I replied. "It's just a tale that grew and spread because people need hope. But you *do* have the same birthdate the original princess did, and you have the teleportation and sunlight powers that the previous queen was known for."

Another bit of information courtesy of those Owned souls. Oh, how I'd missed Owning souls!

"Surely others have those same powers," Iselle insisted. "They might be rare, but they're not exclusive to the previous queen. Do the other girls have those abilities as well?"

I shrugged. "No idea. And it doesn't matter, because I need *you* to be the lost princess, not one of them." I waited for my words to sink in. "There's a risk. We've got a spy here, and the Seelie queen will soon know that you're wearing the ring and claiming it. This could be putting a target on your back, and while we'll all protect you, I want you to know the risk."

She laughed. "I'm already being targeted by the Seelie queen. She had me taken from that encampment, questioned me about you, and put me in that tower. I'm sure she intended to hold me hostage. She'll probably try to grab me again, with or without the ring, just to get to you."

"True, but this is different," I insisted. "There are a lot of people important to me that she could take hostage, but now she'll especially want you because of the risk you pose to her crown."

She shot me a perplexed look but nodded. "I'll do it. I'll wear the ring and claim it's a family heirloom. I'll pretend to be this lost princess if you need me to. And not just because I'm indebted to you, either. The queen locked those girls up. Some of them have been alone in a tower for most of their lives. I'll do whatever I can to make sure she never does that to anyone again."

"Thank you." Patting Iselle on the shoulder I turned, and clapped my hands, telling all of the girls that I needed them to gather on the patio. For all I knew, Uriel would be here in seconds, and I really wanted to get as much information from these fairies as possible.

The girls gathered around the pool, some sitting on the lounges and others on the tiles.

"First, I want you all to tell me how old you were when you were captured and put into the tower, and what you remember of your life before that."

I went around the group and discovered that over half of them had been taken as toddlers, and most of the others had been taken at about the same age that Iselle had been turned into a deer. Two were older, the human equivalent of ten when they'd been captured.

"My family moved constantly," a flame-haired girl told me. "We had money to bribe others to look the other way when we passed through checkpoints and towns. I remember us changing our names, and that we all had to drink horrible potions to change our appearance."

"Our basic glamour is something any fae can do, but to pass magical detection requires a very powerful spell," Iselle explained.

"We did the same," the other girl chimed in. "My father tried to contact some of the rebels for assistance, and that's when I was taken. My family was all killed." Her mouth wobbled, and tears filled her eyes. "My mother had always warned me about the danger of strangers, that the queen would kill me if she or her guards found me. I don't know why, though."

"I do," Flame-hair spoke up. "She's not the queen. She's a pretender put on the throne by those who want to subjugate us all. We'll be no more powerful than human slaves if she continues to rule. There's only one who can defeat her, and that's the only remaining Seelie of royal blood—a daughter who was smuggled out of the palace as an infant and replaced with an imposter. She was hidden away in the kingdom for that day when she was old enough to rise and take her place as the rightful queen."

I held back an eyeroll.

"So the queen searches for the girl who was born on the fall equinox during the year of the Hemlock. She was born of Seelie and Unseelie royal blood from a secret affair between the Queen and the King, and the stellar alignment of her birth granted her the powers of the ancients. She'll take the throne and unite the Kingdoms in peace."

Wow, that was all the myths rolled into one. But as the girls who were old enough when they were taken to have known their birthdate confirmed, they all had been born on the same day in the same year. It might be nothing but fantasy, but clearly the queen didn't want to take any chances.

"She can't take the chance that she might spill the blood of the lost princess," Flame-hair spoke up. "If she does, then she'll lose her magic and her crown. That's probably why we're all in those towers. She can't kill us or order our deaths or be at all connected to us being hurt, or she'll risk losing everything."

But that wouldn't have been why Iselle wasn't hurt. It

was clear to me that she'd been taken prisoner to get information about me, and that she'd been put in a tower to hide her away for future ransom or leverage. The queen knew about Iselle, knew about my being responsible for the Durfts and drop bears. She knew when we had planned to cross into the Seelie kingdom. She knew that Iselle was important to me.

The Seelie queen knew far too much. And I had a good idea how she'd gotten that information.

24

Lux came back from an outing he'd been on with his Uncle Samael. While the little angel was being fussed over by two dozen fairy girls, I pulled the OG Satan aside and demanded an update from him about his duties for my wedding.

"The bachelorette party is all taken care of," he insisted. "And no, I'm not going to tell you anything. Nyalla either because that girl can't keep a secret when she gets excited. I did my fitting for the dress, found some fabulous pointy-toe pumps, and even arranged for the lions."

I blinked. "You knew I wanted lions at the reception?"

"Who *wouldn't* want lions at their wedding reception?" He smirked. "It's going to be epic."

"It *will* be epic," I agreed. At least, it would be epic if I could just manage to get Dolly Parton there.

"What's with the nubile fairy jailbait pool party?" he asked, gesturing toward the French doors.

I sighed. "They're an unexpected side-effect of my campaign to piss off the Seelie queen enough to get her to the negotiating table. As is the silver dragon panicking people in Cape May right now."

"Hmmm." Samael stroked his chin. "Fae. Tricky bastards, but very fun to annoy. Have you met with the Unseelie king yet?"

I winced. "Not officially. I kinda disrupted a Wild Hunt and I whacked some important dude's horse on the nose with the butt end of a spear."

"Black horse? Silver armor? Pale guy with long black hair?" Samael asked and I nodded. "Yeah, that was the king."

"I also kind of stole a tapestry, some bling, and a crown," I confessed. "They got caught in the stag's antlers as she was frantically teleporting around the palace, and were still attached when she ran through the portal. It wasn't my fault, but since I was riding her at the time, I'm sure I'll be blamed for that."

He laughed. "Totally. Here's what you've got to do. Take his shit back to him along with some absinthe. He likes the kind with the wormwood, and you'll need to serve it with all the ceremony. Special glasses. Cube of sugar. Everything. Make up some incantation. He loves that stuff. After he's fucked up and in a good mood, tell him that you want to partner with him just one time to put the Seelie queen's nose out of joint. He'll agree."

"And what exactly am I supposed to ask the Unseelie king to do that will frustrate the Seelie queen enough that she'll negotiate with me for peace?" I asked.

He shrugged. "That's for you to figure out. Good luck. Oh, and I'm bringing a plus one to the wedding. Make sure to seat him on the bride's side. And check him off for the vegetarian meal."

Samael left, and I texted a quick note to Nyalla, dying

with curiosity over who the Fallen's plus-one was. Uriel arrived to teleport the fairy girls to her compound after assuring them that she also had a pool, plenty of booze, and that Leethu would help them order all sorts of clothing over the internet.

Throughout the day I'd caught sight of Joe peering at us from the upstairs landing, or through one of the windows. Several times he'd come down to get stuff from the kitchen, rattling around the cabinets and obviously stalling as he eavesdropped. I wasn't a complete fool. I knew who my spy was. I didn't know why he'd decided to report on my doings to the Seelie queen. She'd probably promised him untold riches, or immortality, or some smoking-hot fairy bride, but it was clear he was the only one who'd been within hearing distance of the information the queen seemed to have magically known about.

He was a spy. And he was somehow getting his information to the fae. I was pissed, but I wasn't going to beat his ass...yet. No, I was going to make sure he had all sorts of information to send the Seelie queen—information that might scare her into surrendering, or at least negotiating.

I SPENT most of the next morning finalizing plans to step up my Seelie harassment plans. While I'd been in Aerie, Gregory had been forced to work with Ahia and Leethu to help him close the fae gates. I knew he'd expect me to go with him this evening, and I didn't expect to go empty-handed. So I was waiting impatiently, tapping my foot when a box truck pulled down my driveway followed by a black limo. Dar hopped out of the limo, sauntering his way toward the back of the truck as several humans scurried to exit the cab of the vehicle and meet him there. My foster brother looked good. His suit screamed money and power. His black hair was swept back from his face, the silver at the temples giving him a distinguished air. He looked exactly like a successful and influential politician, but I knew better. My brother was a greed demon, a rat. And no fancy suit hid the fact that he enjoyed to scrap it up just as much as I did.

"You owe me big-time," Dar said as one of his human assistants opened the back of the truck for me to inspect the contents. The trailer was filled with fifty-pound bags of seed and a bunch of cheap-ass looking drone things.

"What's with those?" I asked, ignoring Dar's drama.

"Exactly what they look like—drones. It's how you get the seed disbursed. Were you just going to dump it all in a heap inside the gateway? Because this only works if there are numerous people for Noranto to sue once their patented, genetically engineered corn turns up in the fields of non-contracted people. Or fae."

Which was why I didn't truly owe Dar shit. The corporation was thrilled at the idea of being able to sue residents of Aerie for illegal use of their seed. It was a major part of their business strategy here, and they were eager to expand it.

Find non-contracted fields with their product. Take the farmers to court. Profit financially from the damages and from the fifty-year contract their lawyer insisted the farmers sign. If the farmers couldn't afford the fine, they'd take the farm then "sell" it to one of their subsidiary factory farms. Win-win.

Dar had managed to convince them that their patent and the legal precedent of their cases here would hold up in Aerie, meaning an entire realm to profit from.

But as good as Dar was when it came to negotiation and manipulation, he wasn't all that inventive. I couldn't believe he'd thought about my delivery method of the seeds and came up with the drone idea.

"Noranto uses these drones all the time," he admitted, confirming my suspicions. "You don't need a remote to control them, they just fly a preprogramed distance and begin to scatter seed. When they're empty, they explode, leaving no trace. Even if something happened and they don't blow up, there's no way to trace them back to Noranto. No serial numbers. Cheap design. No record of purchase anywhere. It's brilliant."

Dar was downright giddy in his admiration of Noranto's deviousness. I hadn't seen him this excited since his last child was born.

I'd be lying if I didn't admit that I liked the idea of these drones, and not just for seed distribution. "Can I get thirty more of these drones?"

Dar nodded.

"What is their maximum range?"

"Two hundred miles, then the battery runs out and they crash even if they still have a full payload," he told me.

That didn't matter for what I had in mind. "Thanks. Let me know when you think the other drones will be in."

Dar left me with the truck, because that would be much easier to teleport around than individual bags of seed and drones. I parked the truck over near the barn so there would be room for any delivery vans or GrubHub, then went back inside to find Lux and Joe sitting at my dining room table. Both of them were eating cereal and drinking coffee.

"Uncle Dar?" Lux looked out the window with longing.

"Sorry buddy. He was just dropping some stuff off for me. I'll arrange a play date for you and Karrae and Maitor sometime next week, I promise."

"Truck?" Lux asked while Joe continued to eat his cereal and look at his phone.

"Full of seed," I told him. "GMO seed. I'm going to send it through the gateways to Aerie and fuck their agriculture up. They'll be eating chewy feed corn, because this shit is going to take over every field and forest they've got."

Joe coughed, tightened his grip on his phone, then continued to shovel cereal into his mouth.

"I like corn," Lux announced.

"Not this corn," I said. "It's the stuff they feed cattle. It's nasty tasteless stuff. And I'm sure it tastes even worse to the fae."

After breakfast Joe went upstairs. Lux and I changed into our swimsuits and swam in the pool. As the clock headed toward noon, I sent the little angel inside to make us breakfast, while I sat in a lounge chair, my eyes hidden by sunglasses as I kept an eye on the box truck parked over by the barn. Lux came back with sandwiches, chips, and some heart-attack caffeinated sports drink that he'd become fond of. We ate, drank, chatted, and after an hour my little guy had fallen asleep on the lounge next to me. I pretended to sleep as well. That's when I saw Joe sneaking to the box truck, carefully lifting the back and peering inside. He looked to either side then poked at a bag of seed, taking a few grains out to look at them before he stuck them in his pocket. Once more he looked around. Closing the back of the truck, he snuck soundlessly around the side of the house.

The spy. And as much as I wanted to bust him, it was in my long-term interest not to. It would be better to feed him information and let him pass that along to the fae. And this was just the start. Amber would be arriving in a few hours, and I wanted to make sure Joe heard that conversation as well.

AMBER SHUDDERED. "Why do you have this? This stuff is vile."

I rolled my eyes. "You magically genetically-engineer stuff all the time. It's totally hypocritical of you to criticize a human corporation for doing the same thing through science."

Joe was trying to hide behind a shrub by the pool. I was purposely not looking his way, and Amber was far too upset about the Noranto seed to pay attention to him.

"It's not the modifications that bother me, it's the whole mono-culture thing," she argued. "Having one particular genetic strain dominate creates a huge risk to the food supply-chain. One freak fungus or a particularly motivated pestilence demon and over half the world's food supply is wiped out in one season. Plant diversity is not only beautiful and tasty, it safeguards the planet against devastating famine."

I held back and didn't interrupt her rant because I really needed Amber to do something for me and I figured it would be easier to convince her if she got this out of her system. Plus it was good for Joe to hear all the horrible things this seed infestation would cause.

"I'm sure the fae aren't going to embrace monoculture agriculture," I assured her. Dar might have convinced Noranto with visions of Aerie becoming a planet of R2342a corn, but in reality it would never happen. The U.S. court system could issue as many subpoenas as they wanted, no one was going to force a fairy to show up to trial. Although if

I played my cards right, the threat of such a thing might keep the fae from popping over here to steal humans.

And even if I didn't play my cards right, they'd be freaked out at having their lovely, diverse vegetables being overrun by chewy, tasteless feed corn.

"Even so, what you're proposing amounts to biowarfare," Amber snapped.

Yes. Yes, it was.

"They're stealing humans. Kidnapping them and using them as servants, or for forced breeding, or to kill in gladiator-style entertainment. It's worse than even what the elves did." I'd seen the first, but not the second or third, so I was embellishing a bit. It worked. Amber paled, biting her lip. She'd spent a lot of time talking to Nyalla about the other girl's life in Hel, and felt somewhat responsible, even though she hadn't made the choice to be swapped out for a kidnapped human baby. Plus she'd spent years afraid that the elves would track her down and kill her for being a half-breed. The idea of all that on a large scale perpetrated by the fae would rock anyone's ethics, even Amber's.

"What you're asking..." She looked at the bags of seed. "It's not just instant growth, but accelerated spread. The native plants of Aerie might not be able to overcome hundreds of thousands of disease and pest resistant plants in their midst, especially because these seeds were modified to guard against blight that's typical here. Even though Aerie will have its own insects and fungi, these plants might kill out their native agriculture. And accelerated spread will allow this corn to outpace any natural defenses it encounters."

"That's the idea." I struggled for patience, knowing I needed this magic from Amber. "It's war. When we've won, we can send over a spray or something to take out the corn.

But in the meantime, we need to show them that we mean business, that we won't allow them to use this realm as an all-you-can-kidnap buffet."

Amber took a deep breath, then finally nodded. "Okay. But I'm putting a failsafe in where the accelerated spread spell will end after two seasons."

"Deal." If we hadn't won this thing in two years, I'd just have to think of something else.

25

"You're seriously going to drive that truck through the gateway into Aerie?" Gregory asked as he walked toward me.

"Not quite," I replied.

We'd met in Denmark to begin the routine of our gateway-closure, and I was excited to get started. All the drones in the truck were loaded with the magically enhanced, GMO seed. It was going to be epic, and I was already brainstorming ideas of what to do next in my Fuck Up The Fae campaign.

"I'm not sure internal combustion engines will work there," Gregory reached out a hand to rub a lock of my hair between his thumb and index finger. He smiled, caressed his spirit-self against mine, then froze, the smile turning to a frown.

"Cockroach." His voice was dark and accusatory, with a threat of violence. I shivered, totally turned on. "Cockroach, what are these fae souls doing inside you?" he demanded.

Shit. I was totally busted. Of course he'd known the moment he'd touched me with his energy. I knew that would happen, but somehow I'd forgotten with the anticipation of seeing him and all the planning and logistics I'd needed to accomplish in the last few days.

"I *had* to. There was a fight and some Seelie fucker teleported Iselle away. I needed to know where they'd taken her and how to get her back. Plus without Iselle, I had no way of communicating with them. By Owning, I could speak their language, take a convincing form that would get me through security, and know enough about their history and culture to avoid capture. I had to rescue Iselle, and Owning was the quickest and best way to do that."

He considered my words, but he'd pulled his spirit self away and I knew he was disappointed.

Well, too bad. It wasn't the first time he'd been disappointed in me and it wouldn't be the last. I was who I was.

"I understand that you may have needed to take and keep the soul of one of the Seelie fae, but you have *thirteen* of them inside you."

"The first guy was Unseelie, so he was from the wrong kingdom. The next one a Seelie scout," I told him. "But once I was inside their capital, I needed someone who could get me inside the palace. Then I went through quite a few of the higher-up Seelie trying to find anyone who knew where Iselle might be. I kept them all, because the situation was critical and I needed to be able to use any of these thirteen to rescue Iselle and get her safely home." I let him think for a few seconds, then added: "In the process I also rescued another two dozen young Seelie girls who were being imprisoned and a dragon who'd been captured and taken to Aerie against her will. That certainly should justify my torturing... I mean keeping thirteen fae souls."

He sighed, then nodded. "Okay, Cockroach. But when this conflict is resolved, you must let them go. It's not healthy for the leader of the Fallen to be collecting and torturing souls."

"Absolutely. I'll do that." I'd like to say I was lying, because keeping these souls was a fun hobby that I'd really missed, but Gregory would know if I didn't keep up my end of this bargain.

"Do any of those Owned souls know how well your previous guerrilla tactics have performed?" he asked.

I grinned. "The Durfts have terrorized the Seelie countryside. Other animals and monsters have proven mildly disruptive. The queen is furious at my ruining her gardens. It was a blow to her reputation that I managed to do such damage right in her own palace area. And my latest trip has caused even more of her subjects to doubt her strength. Finding nine dead high-ranking officials and guests in a closet after a diplomatic ball? It threw the palace into an uproar and the queen into a rage. I'm sure my releasing all the prisoners and setting her dungeon on fire two days later didn't help the situation. And then I killed her personal Security Advisor, stole the remote control to his window/portal, then set all her teenage girl prisoners free along with the dragon guard." I smiled smugly. "If she's not ready to negotiate, the GMO feed corn seed I'm going to unleash across her kingdom will force her hand."

Gregory laughed. "If you had been alive at the time of the war in Aaru, Cockroach, I have no doubt that the Angels of Chaos would have won."

My eyebrows shot up. "You can't tell me that Samael didn't pull these kinds of tricks?"

His smile fell. "I'm sure if the battles had taken place here in a physical realm that he would have. There are no plant crops or Durfts in Aaru, so my brother's tactics were different."

He so rarely spoke about the war or his youngest brother, and I knew that it was a topic full of pain and regret. It was me that reached out with my spirit-self this time, stroking him and trying to give him comfort.

"He'll be at our wedding. You've seen him twice in the last few months. It'll take time for you both to rebuild your relationship," I told him.

He shook his head. "Some wounds never heal. He'll never forget what I did."

"No, but that doesn't mean he can't forgive you for it." I stepped forward and put my arms around him.

He leaned against me, burying his face in my hair. I let his emotions wash over me, feeling his sorrow and his loss along with that glimmer of hope. Then he sighed and pulled back to smile down at me.

"Thank you, Cockroach. Now let's go fuck up some fae."

"YOU NEED TO LOOK SICKER," I told Snip. His normal appearance was at best humanish. He already appeared jaundiced and misshapen, with oversized teeth, an elongated point of a nose, and bulging eyes that were set abnormally far apart. Add in his wispy hair, his bony fingers, and his practically non-existent chin and the guy looked like he'd seriously lost the genetic lottery. But Snip's eyes were bright, his smile mischievous, and his movements quick and coordinated. That didn't lend to the terminally-ill act I needed him to perform.

Snip coughed and let some drool drip from the corner of his mouth.

"Excellent. Now make your hands shake. Not that much," I corrected as Snip flailed around. "That's better."

We'd set up in a local home that had been vacated due to foreclosure. The previous owners had left only a few pieces of their broken and cheapest furniture behind, which suited our purposes. Snip and I had ripped the eviction notes off the door and dragged one of the sagging mattresses into the living room, setting it up as a makeshift hospital bed.

I glanced at my watch, then ran over to look out the window. Dolly Parton's public relations people had called to say she would be here at two along with her staff and some media for a photo-op. I wasn't thrilled about the staff or the media, but it wasn't an insurmountable issue. All I needed to do was touch Dolly and teleport her away. We'd be gone before the others could do anything.

Yes, I'd be leaving Snip behind with a bunch of people who might decide he was at least partially responsible for Dolly's disappearance, but I knew the Low could handle himself.

We'd finalized our details, and two hours before Dolly was due to arrive, we had driven to the foreclosed house we were using. I'd sent a few Lows over earlier this week to clean the place and put some cheap, junkyard furniture in place so it didn't look so empty. I got Snip into a hospital gown and settled him on the mattress in the living room. Then I staged the scene with some flowers, magazines, and a cup of ginger ale with a bendy straw.

We waited. One hour went by. Then two. Then three.

I kept looking at my watch and peering out the window. It was two thirty and they still hadn't shown up. Maybe she'd gotten stuck in traffic. Maybe her flight had been delayed. Maybe her driver was having a hard time finding the correct house.

By the time she was an hour and a half late, I was beginning to worry. From what I'd learned about Dolly Parton, this wasn't like her to be tardy, especially with no notice.

"Can we order pizza?" Snip asked. "I'm starving. I didn't eat breakfast because I thought being hungry would make me look more sickly."

"Just wait a bit more," I told him as I dialed into my voicemail to see if the PR people had left any messages. There was nothing there, nothing in email, nothing at all.

I know it was weird for a demon to be disappointed, but I was. I'd thought better of Dolly Parton. Her people, thus her, had made a commitment to someone they'd thought was terminally ill, and they'd been a no-show. There hadn't even been the courtesy of a call to let us know they'd needed to cancel. What if Snip really had been a seriously sick child and had been excited to think that he was going to meet one of his idols this afternoon? How could someone with such a reputation for kindness and generosity let Snip and me down like this?

We ordered pizza. We waited until five o'clock, then finally went back to my house. I hadn't been so depressed in...well, in my whole life. At this point I wasn't even sure I *wanted* Dolly Parton to officiate my wedding. She'd let down a sick child. Someone who could do that didn't deserve to perform Satan's wedding.

Then I turned on the television.

"Beloved singer and songwriter Dolly Parton has vanished from her home." The news reporter stared grimly at the camera, a picture of the singer behind him. For a second I wondered if Samael or one of my Lows had grabbed her as some sort of early wedding present for me, then the announcer continued. "Witnesses saw a glowing portal open in front of the house. Six elf-like beings came through the portal, exploded the door to her home, and kidnapped the famous singer while her friends and family were rendered helpless in a magical trance."

Fae motherfuckers. They'd targeted Dolly Parton, and I knew why. The traitorous spy upstairs had heard me talking about her, knew about my plans to force her to perform my wedding. He knew she was important to me, and would be a perfect target for a pissed-off queen looking to get revenge.

Time to take off the gloves and fight like a demon. Because no one was going to kidnap Dolly Parton and get away with it. Well, no one was going to kidnap her besides me, that is.

26

"They took Dolly," I raged, pacing back and forth in front of the conference table.

The angels and non-angelic representatives of the Ruling Council were all sitting on one side of the table, as if they were in that painting of the Last Supper. Gabriel had somehow managed to score the Jesus seat. Normally I would have done anything to oust him, but I was too furious to sit so I let him have the middle chair.

"Well, what did you expect them to do?" Gabriel snapped at me. "You have made repeated attacks on their kingdom, slaughtered key individuals inside the castle, destroyed their dungeon and not only set their prisoners free, but those girls as well." Nyalla drove an elbow into his side, and the archangel winced. Uriel glared at her brother, her eyes growing dark. "I mean, you absolutely should have rescued those girls.," he amended. "That was the right thing to do, and I would have done the same."

Yes, he would have. Otherwise Nyalla would have had his balls in a vice. And who knows what Uriel would have done to him.

"Clearly there is a spy in our midst," Raphael said. "Otherwise the Seelie wouldn't have known that Sam was responsible for the attacks, nor that kidnapping Dolly Parton would be an effective counter attack."

"It's not Iselle," Nyalla hurriedly said. "She wouldn't do that. Sam saved her and released her from her deer form, and she made a binding vow to her."

"It's not Iselle," I assured her. "The Seelie knew I was responsible for the attacks if not before, then soon after she and I went to Aerie. They tracked us and when they attacked the Unseelie who'd captured us, they grabbed Iselle the first chance they could. It's not her. It's not Snip or any of my Lows. It's not you nor any of the angels, and it's got to be someone who was in my house enough to learn what I'm doing and my wedding plans. That leaves Joe."

Nyalla gasped. "No!"

"Yes. Joe's the traitor." I realized how this news hit her and toned down the anger. I'd suspected Joe was the spy before I'd come back from Aerie this last time, but hadn't done anything to confront him. Yet. Instead, I'd fed him information, hoping to use him. Maybe it was my fault Dolly Parton had been kidnapped. Although there was a good chance he'd sent that information before Iselle and I had even left for Aerie.

"You *saved* him," Nyalla raged, just as angry as I'd been. "You sheltered him in your house. You clothed and fed him. And *this* is how he repays you?"

"He was most likely sent over from Aerie specifically for this purpose," Gregory told her. "We've been closing their gateways for over a month, and had attacked the fae sent to kidnap humans. It makes sense for them to want to place a spy where they could gather information on what we planned. And what better spy than a human we rescued from pursuing shadow-fae."

"Still." Nyalla's hands gripped the edge of the table and tightened. "He's *human*. He should be loyal to us, not to those who kidnapped him."

"Humans often fall prey to those who promise to make their dreams a reality," Asta said softly. "Immortality. Riches. An honored place in fae society, elevated above the human slaves. Or perhaps they discovered someone he loved and threatened that person's life."

Nyalla's anger deflated. "I can understand the last one, but I still don't think that would be enough for me to betray my people."

"We angels won't be effective fighters inside Aerie," Gregory warned me. "But I absolutely support you and any demons or other beings you chose to take with you to rescue Ms. Parton."

I stopped pacing to mull that over. "I'll do that, but I want to plan a long-term strategy. I want an endgame. I want this shit to be over, with the fae back in Aerie and us with the upper hand."

My not-so-subtle attacks weren't going to yield the results I wanted in the timeline I now desired. The conversation with Samael tickled at the back of my memory, and I wondered if the Unseelie king could somehow be a pivotal piece in this game. The former Satan was wily and was considerably older than I was. He'd been plying the tricks of his trade before humans had even invented the wheel. If he brought up the Unseelie king to me, there was a reason for it.

One of the humans with his Marriott employee name badge walked in, an envelope in his hand. He strode to Gregory, handed him the envelope and stood with his hands joined behind his back. There was a glazed look in his eyes that I found suspicious, and I wasn't the only one who'd noticed. Gabriel had jumped up from his Jesus seat, and placed himself between Nyalla and the employee.

Gregory opened the envelope, and slid out the note. Sparks danced off the paper, and the words rearranged themselves into angelic script. A blonde lock of hair fell to the ground.

"It's addressed to the Iblis from the Seelie queen," Gregory said. "She said that she has your beloved Dolly Parton, and if you want her safely returned, you'll no longer enter Aerie and, you'll cease your attacks on their kingdom."

Bitch. That fairy was going to pay for this. And if she hurt Dolly Parton, I'd Own her soul and torture her for all eternity.

Raphael picked up the hair and frowned. "It's real hair. I thought Dolly Parton wore wigs."

"You seriously think she's going to be walking around in some cheap-ass polyester, Barbie-hair wig?'" I scoffed. "Of course it's real hair."

"There's more. She wants all of the Seelie girls returned to Aerie," Gregory read. "If you do this, she's willing to negotiate about the acquisition of humans. She also wants a hundred chicken wands for some reason."

That last demand surprised me more than any of the others. The Unseelie scouts hadn't believed my story of defeating the elves in Hel, and Iselle said the Seelie who'd questioned her at the palace hadn't believed the story either. But clearly the queen did, or figured it wouldn't hurt to demand a supply of the wands, just in case the story was true.

"We won't even consider returning the fairy girls. They have sought asylum here, and their return is off the table,"

Gregory announced. "There is no need for a vote on that matter."

It was high-handed of him, but he was right. None of us on the Ruling Council would vote to send the girls back to an eternal imprisonment, or at this point, possibly death.

"We're definitely not sending those girls back," Nyalla agreed.

"That's probably the deal-breaker of this whole thing," I told her. "

We turned to the zombie-eyed Marriott employee who'd remained standing like a statue, staring at some point a few feet above Gabe's head.

"Who gave you this note?" The blue magic of his persuasion poured from Gregory, making me want to climb into this lap and answer all his questions, even though the magic was meant for the Marriott employee.

The guy appeared unaffected, but he did reply. "A Seelie representative came into the hotel and cast a spell upon me." He pulled a chain with a polished yellow stone on it from under the collar of his shirt. "I'm to tell them of your response."

Then he'd probably explode or something, although maybe I not. Lux and I been watching too many espionage movies lately, and it had colored my expectations.

"And what should our response be?" Raphael asked.

Stall, I said telepathically to Gregory. *I've got an idea, but I need time to put it in place.*

"This sort of thing should be negotiated face-to-face," Gregory told the human. "Please tell the Seelie envoy that we will enact a cease-fire if the queen will do the same in terms of taking or injuring anyone this side of the gateways."

"We're willing to meet in a neutral area," Raphael added. "Another realm of her choosing."

The Marriott employee clutched the stone in his hand, his eyes growing even more unfocused. "The Seelie girls must be returned as a good-faith gesture. If so, the queen is willing to meet at her palace in Aerie."

I rolled my eyes. "No fucking way. That's a major negotiation point and we're not going to throw it away in some good-faith bullshit, especially when the queen isn't offering any good-faith gesture of her own."

The employee was silent for a moment. "No. The queen will only negotiate if the girls are returned. All of them. You will wish that you complied with her generous offer."

The guy's head didn't explode, but he did drop to the floor. The yellow stone turned to gray dust, and his vacant open eyes stared at the ceiling.

"No!" Nyalla kicked her chair back, scrambled over the table and knelt beside the man. "He was just a random employee at the hotel. He wasn't involved in any of this, and he didn't need to die."

"It's a show of power," I said, knowing the words wouldn't reassure her. It didn't reassure me either. The only reason Dolly Parton was probably alive was because she was an important bargaining chip in this.

But the girls. "The girls are the key," I told the angels. "She's insistent on my returning them, and I believe her rule is unstable. Iselle and the girls all have the same birthday and year. There's some prophecy or myth about a lost princess who also had that birthday. The myth is powerful enough among the Seelie that the queen went around her lands kidnapping these girls. And she imprisoned them rather than killing them and making them martyrs, or unleashing some sort of curse that she believes will come to pass. That's why she took Dolly Parton. That's why she's reached out to negotiate. The Durfts and Drop Bears and

GMO seed were bad enough, but these girls...any one of them could be used to bolster support for the rebels and topple her reign."

"So these girls *are* a major negotiating point," Gabe agreed.

"Or it could be a red herring," Uriel said. "Maybe Sam's GMO seed or the Durfts caused enough chaos that she's willing to negotiate, and getting the girls back is her saddling us with an ethical dilemma."

"Or the Unseelie king is winning the fight," Asta said. "Perhaps she doesn't have the military strength to continue with both battles. The Iblis has stepped up the attacks, and she's had her manpower divided in two."

"Or not." Gregory frowned. "The fight with the Unseelie might give her added stress, but she did seem unusually focused on the girls. They were highly secured, and guarded by a dragon. That means they're important, and their loss most likely has her panicked."

I remembered my giving Iselle the ring, how Joe's gaze snagged on it at dinner that night. "It's Iselle she really wants," I announced. "Her having the other girls would be ideal, but Iselle is the one that she really wants returned to Aerie."

"The queen wants a Seelie girl who spent her life roaming the woods after being transformed into a deer?" Gabe shook his head. "That's ridiculous. Of all the things she could bargain for, she wants a random fae commoner just because of her birthdate?"

"Iselle is important to me," I told him. "Plus I'm sure the queen no longer thinks her a commoner. I gave Iselle the queen's ring. She's wearing it. That plus the fact that I twice have been able to attack her own palace has her worried. If I can kill high level officials under her nose, ruin her gardens, set her dungeons free and on fire, then I could easily work with the rebels to put Iselle in her place."

"Your spy, Joe, has probably told the queen that Iselle remains at your home where the other girls have been sent elsewhere," Raphael commented.

"And that she's wearing the queen's ring," I added. "The ring that Lux...accidentally took. The ring has magic that supposedly ensures loyalty, but it was specifically made for the former Seelie royal family. The current queen can't use it, but the lost daughter of the former queen could."

"And Iselle is truly that daughter of the former queen?" Asta asked, confusion creasing her face.

Who knew if she was or wasn't? She could be a bastard cousin, or a child hidden away with a fake mother because of a prophecy and the threat of a coup. Either way, Iselle had been born on the right date, and did have similar powers to the previous queen.

"She *could* be the lost princess," I admitted. "Even if she'd not, the queen won't want to take any chances."

"I understand wanting to wipe your rivals from existence and secure your claim to the throne—not that I approve of those tactics," Raphael said. "But it seems odd to propose such a one-sided contract. Is her reign that tenuous that one young girl with perhaps only a drop of royal blood would depose her?"

"Legends are powerful things," Uriel said. "If the masses will follow a lost princess, then that child could definitely be a threat."

"Is this legend powerful enough that the return of two dozen fairy youth are the deal-breakers of a substantial contract?" Gregory wondered.

"Among the fae? I believe so," I told him.

"Either way, the queen has clearly flounced," Uriel said,

pointing to the dead Marriott employee. "She'll retaliate, probably by sending a team to take the girls-from-the-towers. My team and I will make sure that doesn't happen."

"And we'll protect Iselle, who will no doubt be her primary target," Nyalla added.

"Then what?" Gabe asked. "Do we just let the Seelie queen have her hissy fit?"

"Yes," I told him. "We prepare and defend, and use that time to set our plan in action."

"*Our* plan?" Raphael grinned.

"My plan," I corrected. "I need time to go back to Aerie and build some alliances. See if you all can stall her for a week or two."

"And how do we do that?" Gabriel drawled.

I shrugged. "Fuck if I know. When she proposes another negotiation, tell her that she needs to reinstate the previous contract between the Seelie and the angels, and in return we won't open a gateway, storm through with our best fighters, support the rebels, and put Iselle on the throne as the queen of the Seelie."

"We *cannot* attack Aerie," Gregory informed me. "You know that our abilities are severely hindered in Aerie. Added to that, most of our angels would question why this war is necessary when the priority should be regaining access to Aaru."

"It's a bluff," I told him. "If I can get the Unseelie king and the Seelie rebels onboard with my plan, we'll have the upper hand."

"And if that doesn't happen?" Gregory asked.

"Then we do the plan anyway," I said. "My demons and I will be the ones attacking in Aerie, while you and the angels will stay and help the humans to defend against any Seelie fae attacks. I'll have no difficulty in raising a demon army willing to go raid a new realm. Most of them are itching for some action."

"And then what?" Gregory prodded. "Cockroach, I usually applaud your unorthodox methods, but not this time. There needs to be a better plan, one where we don't end up in endless war."

This is where my plan kind of fell apart. "Iselle could be the new queen," I suggested. "Or maybe the rebels have someone they want to put on the throne. Either way, I plan to make a deal with them that we'll support their new queen as long as they reinstate the contract."

Uriel frowned. "Does Iselle *want* to rule the Seelie kingdom? She's very young, and she's spent most of her life wandering the forest in the form of a deer. I can't think that she has the knowledge or ability to be the queen, and I worry that once her deficiencies are discovered, her subjects won't support her."

"I'd favor the Seelie deciding who should lead them," Nyalla said. "And we'll negotiate with that person."

Gabriel made a choked noise, and practically sat on his hands. I knew what he was thinking. It was naive to think that the fae would support a democratic process of leadership. And there was a very real chance that whoever ended up on the throne would be worse than their current queen, at least in terms of our own interests.

Yep. It was hard to believe it, but I actually agreed with Gabriel on that.

"Let's figure this out later," Raphael spoke up. "First Sam needs to see who we can expect to support us. Then we can discuss who we should support on the Seelie throne."

"I worry that we're underestimating the fae," Gregory warned. "They are just as sneaky as demons, and far more powerful when in their own realm. The Iblis has only encountered some minor scouting parties while there, and they misjudged who and what she was. She was able to sneak into the palace and create chaos before they knew she was coming. They won't make that mistake again. They'll be waiting for you this time, Cockroach. And they'll absolutely be prepared for you to attack."

"Is anyone *ever* prepared for that Imp of yours?" Gabriel drawled. "I doubt it. We've seen what she's done to the angelic host. It's about time we used that chaos for our benefit."

I hated the dude, but I did appreciate the backhanded compliment.

"I can do this," I assured them. "Just give me a few weeks to put things in place, and in the meantime, prepare for battle."

27

Ahia and Raphael were going to be helping Gregory with the fae gateways while I was gone. Honestly, Raphael wasn't needed, but the lovesick fool wanted to go with Ahia, no doubt in case he needed to punch his older brother in the face. Gregory was grumpy, unhappy that I was going to Aerie for what he considered a fool's journey. He'd become far more tolerant of my chaos over the course of our relationship, but recent stresses had taken a toll on that tolerance. The fae attacks. And our wedding. We'd argued over a few stupid things, and I'd found myself doing the inconceivable—giving in. The chilled vodka fountain was nixed, as was my plan for lions roaming around our reception.

I didn't know what was really going on with him. I knew it didn't really involve vodka fountains and lions. But I didn't want to argue with him for once.

Dar had worked his magic and had provided me with nearly a hundred more drones, these ones loaded with sparkly confetti instead of GMO seeds. There was a chance the fae might find the confetti magical fun, but I was betting it would annoy them just as much as it annoyed everyone else. That shit got everywhere. And no matter how hard you tried, you could never seem to clean it all up.

I'd teleported the truck full of confetti-loaded drones to Alaska so Ahia and Raphael could shove them through the gates. Then I'd headed north of Juneau, deep into the Denali wilderness.

The enemy of my enemy is my...well, not my friend, but definitely someone who might be used to my advantage. That's why I stood freezing my ass off in a valley surrounded by craggy, snow-covered mountains. Behind her was a domed garden of Eden. Judging from the verdant foliage and colorful butterflies flitting about, I was willing to bet the temperature inside that dome was a lovely eighty degrees.

It was clear I wasn't about to be invited inside. There was no door to Gwylla's sanctuary, which meant I'd had to lob rocks at it and blast it with electricity to get her attention. And that was probably the reason why I wasn't going to see the inside of that paradise.

"You want to go back? To the *Unseelie* forest?" Gwylla's brow wrinkled in confusion.

"Yep. Same spot you put me in before if you can manage it," I told her.

Gregory might hate that I Owned thirteen fae souls, but it had given me a huge advantage. I knew the terrain as well as anyone could know a sentient, ever-changing, hostile forest. I knew where the capital of the Unseelie kingdom was as well as the basic layout of the royal castle. And I could waltz right in, looking like an Unseelie scout and knowing every single thing the soul I Owned knew.

The scouts that had captured us had planned to take us to the court, present us as captives and let the king know about my claims, my peculiar skills, and my tales of elves and chicken wands. None of those original scouts survived to tell that story. And since I'd seen the dead bodies being sucked under by the forest, I doubted anyone in the Unseelie kingdom even knew they were dead.

"I can send you there, but I can't bring you back," she told me. "It takes time to create a portal spell for you to carry with you, and I can't drain my power holding my own portal open for days or even weeks."

I nodded. "Yep. No problem." I'd just use one of the fae-created portals—ones that the Seelie security advisor I'd Owned knew the location of. It seemed that while the gateways moved around a mile or so here, they were fixed at the Aerie end.

"What are you planning?" Gwylla shifted her weight. "You should stay as far away as possible from the Unseelie. They are cruel and treacherous."

"And the Seelie aren't?" I laughed. "Those fuckers aren't any better than the Unseelie."

She glared at me. "Fine. Good luck, whatever you plan on doing. Even if you're not going to tell me."

"I'm hoping to convince the Unseelie king to form an alliance with Hel." It wasn't like what I was planning was any sort of secret.

Gwylla gasped. "You're not serious. He'll either kill you outright or agree to your plans then betray you."

I rolled my eyes. "The fae can't lie, and that goes for the Unseelie as well as the Seelie. Demons are no slackers when it comes to contracts, negotiations, and loopholes. And I'm not asking for one-sided support here. I can provide just as much assistance to him as he could to me."

The fae woman shook her head. "This is a fool's idea. You will destroy the balance of power in Aerie, and you'll bring forth the end here as well."

I hesitated, her pronouncement triggering my memory of the old prophecies, and of Gregory telling me of the devourer who was supposed to bring about the apocalypse. I'd seriously reined in my devouring since that near-disaster on Devil's Paw, but it still scared me. I could devour the universe. And while destruction led to creation, devouring led to nothing but an empty void.

I didn't want an empty void.

But chaos was different. Things weren't exactly stable in Aerie and hadn't been for a long time according to the souls I Owned. Me jamming a stick in their wheel might throw things in a better direction. Or wreck it all.

Honestly, I didn't give a shit. The Seelie were messing with *my* world and *my* humans. That brought about consequences, and I wasn't going to shed a tear over them reaping what they sowed. As for here...if those fae fuckers thought they could take over this world, they were out of their damned minds. I'd managed to thwart the elven invasion. I'd kept the angels in Aaru from overthrowing the archangels. And I'd diverted the Ancients, the Fallen in Hel, from their fixation on revenge to something less violent.

None of that had been planned, but it had just kind of happened. Hopefully this would just kind of happen as well. And hopefully the side effects wouldn't equal the angels banished from Aaru level of crap either.

Gwylla nodded. "Be at the fairy mound in Ireland at dawn," she told me.

I went home to find Nyalla and Iselle out by the back pasture. The horses were all gathered around the fence line, nosing Iselle for treats. The young fae had created a garden of colorful zinnias, and was petting the horses while Nyalla gathered flowers into a huge bouquet.

"Did you tell her?" I asked Nyalla as I inclined my head toward Iselle.

"No, that's your job," she replied.

"Tell me what?" Iselle gave Piper one last pat, then stepped away from the fence.

"I'm going to Aerie tomorrow morning. Well, actually tonight because I need to be in Ireland at dawn," I corrected. "I plan to see the Unseelie king and hopefully convince him to assist us. Then I want to meet with the Seelie rebels and get them on our side as well. I'd really like you to come with me."

Iselle smiled and held up her hand. The queen's ring glinted in the sunlight. "I'm to play the part of the lost princess for the Unseelie king and for the rebels?"

The girl was definitely smart. "If you'll agree to it. I'll have you remain outside the city until I've met with the Unseelie king and I'm sure it's safe to introduce you. The Seelie believe that the rebels are getting support from the Unseelie court, and I do too. I'm hoping he wants peace, where the current Seelie queen wants to rule all of Aerie. You can assure him of that peace as long as he helps put you on the throne."

Nyalla frowned. "But you're not really going to put Iselle on the throne, are you? Unless...is she really this lost princess."

"There *is* no lost princess." Fuck, I was getting tired of constantly repeating that. "But *someone* needs to rule the Seelie kingdom—someone who isn't that ass-wipe of a current queen."

"And the rebels will hopefully agree for me to continue with the charade, knowing that having the lost princess will help their cause and cost the queen some of her allies,"

Iselle said. "Once they win, they can put whoever they want on the throne."

My thoughts exactly. Two of us were in agreement, but Nyalla clearly had doubts from the scowl on her face.

Iselle remained with the horses, but Nyalla followed me inside, putting the zinnias in water and placing the vase on the dining room table before she spoke.

"I'm worried about Iselle. She'll do anything for you. The girl is young and there're so many things she doesn't know, even about her own people and kingdom. It's one thing to ask her to take the risk of posing as this princess while she's here, to send false information to the queen. But taking her to Aerie to be the symbol of the rebellion? To let everyone think she intends to take the Seelie throne? You're putting a huge target on her back."

"Both the Unseelie king and the rebel leaders will realize she's not *really* the lost princess, since it's a fucking myth and *there is no real lost princess*." I took a breath to calm down. "She's just a symbol, to help their respective causes. And because of that, they'll be very careful to ensure she stays safe. It would destroy the rebellion if the lost princess was killed, and if the rebellion dies, the Unseelie king won't get his peace. I won't be the only one in Aerie making sure she's safe."

Nyalla looked at me for a long moment. "Okay. But promise me she'll come back unharmed, Sam. Promise."

I did as she asked. And that was one promise I intended to keep.

～

I PUTTED around the house playing with Lux and killing time until Gregory came over. The three of us curled up on the couch to watch movies, then went outside so Lux could practice naming stars and planets. We swam, created water balls and water spouts, then relaxed. He fell asleep in my arms by the pool. I tucked him into bed, then went down to sit on the sofa with Gregory, knowing there was no sense going to bed since Iselle and I needed to teleport to Ireland at about midnight our time.

The sun was just sending faint golden rays along the horizon when Iselle and I arrived at the barrow. Gwylla was already there. And Gregory had woken up Lux to come with us, wanting to see me off.

"Are you ready?" Gwylla asked, extending her hands toward the barrow.

"Wait," the archangel commanded, pulling me off to the side. "I'm sorry, Cockroach. I regret arguing with you yesterday. You can have the vodka fountain at our wedding, and the lions as well."

I hugged him, breathing him in for a moment before pulling back to look up at him. "What's wrong? What's *really* wrong? Because it's not the wedding plans, and I'm pretty sure it's not me going to see the Unseelie king."

He sighed. "There is a rumor spreading among the angels that you are the reason they have been exiled from Aaru. Many believe this rumor, and think that you did this in retaliation for the Angels of Chaos being exiled after the war."

I knew that eventually this would come out, but had hoped I'd find a way to reinstate the angels to their homeland before. It would be easier to beg forgiveness once they were back in Aaru. Now...

"I've tried. I've really tried. Nothing I do reverses the banishment." I blew out a breath in frustration. "It was an accident. I never meant for you to be forever locked out of your homeland. Or the other angels either."

Even the ones I wasn't fond of. Because if they couldn't live in Aaru, they were stuck here. With me. And I *really* didn't like that at all.

"I know, but it's going to complicate things." Gregory hugged me close again. "The angels are quickly becoming used to being in a corporeal form. Those who'd rebelled against the Ruling Council will soon gather their forces and attack us again, this time here among the humans. And they won't be just trying to take over the Ruling Council, they'll be trying to kill *you*."

I smiled. "It isn't the first time someone's tried kill me, and it probably won't be the last. We'll deal with them. And I'll keep trying to figure out a way to get the angels back in Aaru."

"After our wedding." He kissed the top of my head.

"After our wedding," I agreed.

Stepping away once more, I hugged Lux and whispered to him that he should be good for his father, but not *too* good. Then Iselle and I gathered up the packs full of the shit I needed to take to the Unseelie king, and stepped through Gwylla's gateway into Aerie.

28

I knew from the one Unseelie I Owned that there were two ways to see the king: wait in a huge line once a month and hope you made it to the front before he decided he'd done enough peopling for the day, or report to an appropriate military muckety-muck, and make sure the story was amazing enough to fly up the chain of command to the king's ear.

I opted for the second choice. And I made sure my tale of attacking Seelie and the theft of our captives was intriguing and full of potential. The king wanted an advantage in this never-ending war, so my story hinted of alliances and powerful, secret magic.

Then I waited. I'd originally planned on leaving Iselle somewhere in the forest while I did my negotiations, but I was worried that it would take me weeks to get an appointment with the king, and she'd be out there in the forest eating the Aerie equivalent of acorns. It was Iselle herself who came up with a solution. I'd Owned the leader of the scouting party, Aethell, and evidently he'd made enough to afford a tiny house in the outskirts of the merchant area. He was unmarried, and had no servants, so it would be a perfect place for Iselle to hide out. It was better than her hanging around the forest where she might be caught and captured, and this way I could at least provide her with decent food.

The fairy girl held my hands and looked into my eyes, and this time it was her spirit-being that slid into me, shy and embarrassed at the intrusion. I spooled the information to her about the city layout, and the location of Aethell's house, along with images. When she felt she'd absorbed it all, she pulled back, releasing my hands with an awkward smile.

"Thank you. I wasn't sure I could do that."

"You did great," I told her, amazed that she had such an ability. None of the elves could do this. As far as I knew, no one besides the angels and demons could do this. It was an odd and powerful skill that would really come in handy if she could get over her unease with it.

"I'll teleport to the house tonight, once I'm sure you're there," she told me.

"I'll have dinner ready," I assured her. Then I'd headed into the city, thinking how quickly I'd become fond of this girl. She reminded me a lot of Nyalla.

Once she'd arrived, Iselle stayed in the house with the curtains closed while I roamed the city, exploring and reporting to the various guard and military groups that would have expected Aethell to check in. The whisper network of the Unseelie moved faster than official channels. My tale probably hadn't even reached the commanders through official channels before a bunch of guards in purple and silver showed up at Aethell's house to escort me to the castle. They hadn't wanted me to take the packs with me, but I managed to convince them I had important goods inside that would back up my claims. I think they might have pushed the issue, but there was obviously a timetable they needed to stick to, because they let me drag the two packs along without even a basic search.

The palace rooms were dimly lit and full of shadows which the Unseelie seemed to use as doorways. The fae I'd Owned had never been in the castle, so I was immediately lost. Worse, since my possession of these fairy souls hadn't transferred any fae magical abilities to me, I was pretty sure I'd never be able to get out of this place without an authorized escort.

There was that little voice inside my head that agreed with Gwylla and insisted that I'd made a terrible, fatal mistake coming here. But I was an imp, so I bitch-slapped that voice away and trusted in chaos and fate to lead me down the correct path.

My guards halted in another dimly lit room, and I stopped beside them, allowing my eyes a second to adjust. This wasn't an opulent throne room designed to awe and cower the citizens, this was a war room complete with a huge table, magical floating maps, and tiny stone pieces that looked like they belonged on a chess board. I couldn't tell what was going on here strategy-wise and neither could the Unseelie I'd Owned. Maybe if I'd managed to take the soul of someone higher up in their military, but the lowly scout I had was only perplexed and awed and the Seelie I Owned used different methods for military planning.

I wasn't awed. But I *was* smart enough to keep my mouth shut until asked a question.

The guards stood by my side as the fae with a seat at the table whispered among themselves. The king—I recognized him even from my brief encounter in the dark forest during the Wild Hunt—listened and watched with a bored expression on his face. Suddenly the fae fell silent and the king motioned for me to approach. I walked forward, my bags clanking as I moved, stopping a respectful distance, two guards at either side of me.

"Tell me what happened," the king demanded.

"Our group was scouting in the Emerald Woods when we saw a young Seelie woman dressed in strange clothing accompanied by a human woman, also dressed in strange clothing," I said, reciting the story that the fae I'd Owned would have told. "They fled when we commanded them to halt. We gave chase, and managed to capture them, but not until the human magically produced wings and took flight with the girl."

The king's eyebrows shot up. "The humans have magic now? And wings?"

I snorted, quickly covering up the noise with a cough. "Under interrogation, the woman confessed to being a demon in human form. She told us a tale of how the demons fought the elves in Hel and of a fearsome weapon called a Chicken Wand."

That got his attention. The other fae at the table whispered back and forth until the king held up his hand.

"Describe this demon," he demanded.

I gave them a basic rundown of my human form and watched the king visibly relax. He turned to the fae on his right and whispered something that sounded like, "It's not him."

Before I could ponder that, he'd turned back to me. "And that is when the Seelie attacked?"

I told him of the fight from my Unseelie Owned point of view, letting him know that after one of the Seelie scouts had teleported with the girl, the demon had revealed its wings and flew away. I made up the rest about continuing to fight and my dismay at finding that I was the only survivor of my group.

"The Seelie woman must have been important for them to have mounted a rescue attempt," the fae to the king's right whispered. "I wonder if the demon was guarding her on the queen's command, or if it kidnapped her."

"I can't imagine a demon would work with the Seelie queen," one of the other fairy males at the table said. "Last time...but that was eons ago. Things may have changed, but I think the demon probably kidnapped the girl."

"Why would a demon kidnap a young Seelie?" the woman to the king's left asked in murmured tones.

"To eat?" Right-hand fae suggested. "To torture or sexually assault, or sell? They are truly horrible creatures, motivated by base desires and greed."

Okay, that wasn't *completely* untrue. But what really shocked me wasn't their poor image of demons, but that they knew of us at all. The thirteen fae I'd Owned had never heard of demons, so this wasn't legend or fables told through the generations. I suppose the fae wandering the human realm looking to make bargains could have come across a demon or two, but from the king's reaction and what these other Unseelie said, they seemed to have more personal knowledge than what a casual encounter would suggest.

"I care not about the female demon and its lies of elven wars and magical wands." The king waved a hand. "It is the Seelie woman that I am interested in. Why was she in the Emerald Woods with only a demon to accompany her? Whether the demon was a guard or a kidnapper, both suggest the woman is a person of high value. The fact that a Seelie scouting party sacrificed their group to take her, and used strong magic to spirit her away, reinforces this. She is important to the Seelie, therefore she is important to us. Who is she, and why was she in the Emerald Woods?"

At this point, the king and his rectangular-table buddies were ignoring me. The guards didn't urge me to leave, no doubt figuring they should wait until the king dismissed me in case there were more questions coming. Not that it mattered. Neither of the fae I Owned had any idea why Iselle was important, and I personally hadn't planned on spilling any of my own theories to the Unseelie.

This whole trip was supposed to end with the Unseelie king intrigued and ready to partner with demons to win his war on the Seelie. That was the moment I'd planned to reveal my true form, bring forth the items that deer-Iselle and I had accidentally taken from the palace, and offer the absinthe as a peace offering.

Instead the king and his buddies were busy dissing my kind, and brushed us aside to conjecture about Iselle.

"I might be able to shed some light on this," I interrupted. None of the important fae paid any attention to me, and one of the guards at my side, jabbed me with an elbow, hissing, "Quiet."

"Could she be the daughter of one of the Seelie ministers or heads of state?" Left-hand fairy asked.

"Or a spy trained from birth who is being sent to the borderlands?" Right-hand fairy suggested.

"Or perhaps the lost princess," Left-hand mused.

"Bingo!" I shouted.

That got their attention. The guards nearly tackled me, freezing in place as the king pointed at me.

"What?"

"She's the lost princess. And I'm actually here to make a deal with you, your majesty. But first..." I opened the pack containing the crown, the torn tapestry, and the other bling, pulling them out as I transformed into my Samantha Martin form.

Everyone screamed. It took the two guards less than a second to stab me with their lances. Which wouldn't have been that much of a problem if the lances weren't chock full of fae magic. The king shouted, the room went dark, and I suddenly was falling through some blackened abyss of space for what felt like minutes. The falling wasn't that bad, but the landing was. I'd bled out by that time, so a dozen broken bones didn't really make me any more dead.

But not-dead-dead.

The joy of living in a dead body was that it didn't hurt. The not-joy was that I couldn't tell the extent of my physical injuries, nor could I tell if the other pack, the one that held the absinthe and bribery items had fallen with me, or if it had survived the landing intact.

At least I could see, which was quite a feat with dead eyes. I was in a room that wasn't shitty enough to be a dungeon, but wasn't nice enough to be guest accommodations. I lay there as a corpse, surveying what little I could see from my wide-open, unmoving eyes. Dark grey stone ceiling mosaiced in a carefully randomized pattern. Stone walls of the same color and texture, visible because a round blob close to the ceiling gave off a cool blue light. I was pretty sure the floor was identical to the walls from the amount of damage I'd suffered when I'd hit the ground. I couldn't see if there was even a bare-bones chair or bed or table in here with me, but I was willing to bet not.

That done, I counted the ceiling stones until the magic from the lances wore off enough for me to slowly fix my body. I kept to my Sam form this time, and was very careful not to damage the clothing beyond what the king's guards had already done.

When I was once more among the living in terms of a corporeal form, I sat up and better surveyed my surroundings. The room was definitely not a dungeon. The stone everything was a bit cold and inhospitable, but I'd never seen a dungeon with a sofa, a desk and chair, and a selection of books on an end table. The desk had a decanter with a brownish liquid, a glass, and a plate with some nuts, dried fruit, and what looked like biscotti on it.

Best of all, the second pack was there by my side. Crossing my fingers, I opened it and was happy to find the bottle of absinthe still unbroken inside its several layers of bubble wrap. One of the glasses was chipped, but still looked usable. Not that I'd probably have a chance to offer any of this to the king.

I wasn't sure where I'd gone wrong. Had it been my changing form? But surely transforming into a human wasn't a threatening move? And returning the king's goods should have shown that I was there in good faith. But the fae were a skittish bunch, and either my being in possession of royal property or being able to transform my shape must have sent them over the edge into panic.

And here I was, trapped in a window-and-doorless room of stone with minimal comforts. How long would I be kept here? Would they continue to feed me? I guess I could always just drink the absinthe if I got bored, but what would happen to Iselle? After a certain amount of time, she'd get tired of staying hidden in the house, and most likely risk discovery to come find me.

Oh fuck. She might already be a prisoner. The guards had collected me at Aethell's house, and would likely go back to search it. Hopefully Iselle heard them and managed to get out before she was captured. Although the length of time a Seelie fairy girl could remain undiscovered in the capital of the Unseelie kingdom was probably a matter of days if not hours.

I reached through that thread of a bond that our latest connect had left behind, reassured to find it still intact. She might already be a prisoner, but at least she was still alive. If I pulled on the bond then she said she could teleport to me, using the bond as a sort of locater beacon. It was a tempting idea, as Iselle might be able to teleport the both of us out of here and to safety. Or not. I didn't know much about fae magic, or the wards in this palace. There was a good chance she couldn't reach me, or if she did, neither of us could get out. And while I'd enjoy the company, it wouldn't do to have her trapped in here as well.

My stomach growled, interrupting my thoughts.

I'd been paranoid about eating or drinking anything in Aerie, but this time around I'd come here with a total "fuck-it" attitude. And I decided that attitude was going to extend to food and beverages. I doubted any of their enchantments would work on me, and if the stuff was poisoned, then I'd just hang out as a corpse for a while longer until I could fix myself. Or wander around like a zombie.

That last idea really appealed.

No one was technically offering the food or drink to me. It was just sitting here on the desk. As far as I was concerned, I was stealing it, which wouldn't obligate me in any way toward whatever fae had placed it here.

The biscotti, nuts, and dried fruit were awesome, and the brownish liquid turned out to be something that tasted like brandy. After I'd eaten and drank, I explored my room in detail, having a bit of deja vu from when I'd been in the Seelie dungeon. Not that this was anywhere near as unpleasant as that dungeon. It wasn't damp. There was furniture and palatable snacks and drink. No phosphorous stuff grew on the walls and ceiling, although that was a bit of a bummer. Of course, I didn't have the means to ignite it since I'd given the ring to Iselle. And given how that crazy fire had burned through stone, I wasn't sure I wanted to attempt that trick again anyway.

There was no way out of this room that I could find. I'd just about reached the point where I was ready to break into the absinthe when two fairies appeared in the room, each of them surrounded by a bluish force field.

It was Left-hand and Right-hand from the war room.

"The king would like to ask you some questions," Left-hand guy said.

"About your presence in Aerie and about what happened to the alleged lost princess once the Seelie took her from our scouting party," Right-hand woman added.

"I'll answer the first question, but the second one I'll only answer directly to the king." I held up my hand as Left-hand began to protest. "Let me finish, and I'm sure once you relay all this to the king, he'll agree to see me."

I wasn't sure, but I'd trusted in fate and in Samael so far. Might as well continue to do so.

"An infant angel inadvertently gated into Aerie and the Seelie kingdom," I explained. "He's a newborn with no knowledge of contracts or even where he was wandering. I'll admit fault in not watching him as carefully as I should have, but I'm a demon and we aren't exactly known for our helicopter style of parenting. The Seelie queen took this as a violation of the contract and began incursions in the human realm, kidnapping the residents as she saw fit. As the Iblis, the head of the demons and the representative of the Angels of Chaos on the Ruling Council, I am responsible for a large portion of the human population, and their theft is something I consider to be a direct attack."

Right-hand sucked in a breath. "The Unseelie have nothing to do with these attacks on those you consider under your protection."

"I know. That's why I'm here. The Seelie queen not only wants to use the human world as her personal slave-buffet, but she wants to destroy the Unseelie kingdom and rule all of Aerie. That means the Unseelie king and I have a common enemy. Plus..." I pulled the bubble-wrapped bottle of absinthe from the pack. "My friend Samael told me that the king was particularly fond of this ritual drink. I'd like to share this with him and tell him about the lost princess and how she can assist his cause."

Left-hand narrowed his eyes. "But I thought you said the Seelie captured the lost princess."

My smile was very, very smug. "And I rescued her. In the process I killed several high-level Seelie fae in their palace, set their dungeon on fire after I released all the prisoners, and also freed two dozen of the queen's captives that she'd been keeping in a remote location under dragon guard. Not only do I have the lost princess, but she's willing to bargain with the Unseelie King, and I'm willing to join forces with the him to bring peace to Aerie and to the human world as well."

"How do we know you have the real lost princess?" Right-hand asked. "The Seelie queen has imprisoned many girls over the centuries. Just because she hunted down and captured this girl, doesn't mean she's the true heir to the throne."

Here's where I exercised my natural ability to lie.

I glared at them. "Seriously? I'm a demon, the Iblis, the Ha-Satan. I don't make it a habit of rescuing random fairy girls. I wouldn't have bothered going after her or even escorting her around Aerie if she wasn't the true lost princess."

They exchanged skeptical glances and I held up the bottle of absinthe again. "Did I mention I have the special booze-from-Hel that the king likes? And the implements for the drinking ritual? And that I'm friends with Samael?"

"How did you come to have the king's tapestry and crown?" Left-hand demanded. "They were stolen during a rather...chaotic event."

I winced. One option was to lie and say I'd discovered them, or bought them from the thief to return as a gift to the king, but I was worried upon closer scrutiny the Unseelie ruler would recognize me from the night of the Wild Hunt. It certainly wouldn't take much brainpower to put together a winged demon with their deer-prey, and a pair of the same description tearing through the palace on the same evening.

"That's something I'd rather explain to his majesty in person," I finally said. Even Samael had known this would be a hard sell. Hopefully the king would be more willing to forgive and forget when he was half bagged on absinthe.

The pair vanished without a word, leaving me once more in the stone cell. This time it was only a few hours until they appeared again with two guards that motioned for me to rise.

"The king has agreed to grant you an audience," Left-hand informed me.

Right-hand's lips twitched. "And his majesty said to be sure you bring your gift of liqueur."

Hell-yeah! I owed Samael for this one big-time.

The guards put a set of magical restraints on my hands that were a more powerful version of what their scouts had. Then they looped a silver chain over the restraints, and I felt instantly drained and exhausted. I had limited powers here in Aerie, but I got a feeling my ability to heal, change form, or even reveal my wings had now been temporarily removed.

Dark fog rose around us, and suddenly we were before the king in an opulent sitting room the size of my entire house. The fog cleared and everyone bowed. I hesitated a second, then inclined my head, not sure where the line between respect and acknowledgement of equals lay.

"Leave us," the king commanded. "And remove her restraints."

Left-hand sucked in a breath. "Your Majesty... We don't recommend—"

The king waved his hand. "If I can't defend myself against a demon in my own realm, then I'm not much of a king. Take off the restraints, and leave."

The guards did as they were told, and in seconds the fog cleared again, leaving the king and me alone.

"Well," he pointed toward the pack I'd slung over one shoulder. "Break out your offering and let's start the ritual. And tell me how you know Samael. It's been over a thousand years since I've seen that rascal. How is he?"

29

"I apologize for the reaction of my advisors," the king said once I'd updated him on Samael's latest shenanigans. "Few among the populace know of demons, but there are those who have encountered them. Not many of those encounters turned out to be positive ones, so we tend to take fast preventative measures when facing one of your kind. But if you're a friend of Samael's then I'll give you a chance to prove yourself, especially since you've brought that magical elixir."

I'd removed all my items from the pack and set them up. Samael had said the whole ceremony of the drink was important, so I'd gone all out, bringing an absinthe fountain, as well as ornate spoons and the heavy, hand-blown glasses.

"It's all good," I told him as I opened the bottled water and poured it into the fountain. "I seem to die pretty regularly these days, and I appreciated the food and brandy."

Reaching my energy into the water, I mumbled a made-up incantation and froze small globes into chunks of ice.

The king nodded, clearly impressed. "My advisors wanted to lock you in the dungeon, but I had you sent to the room where we put potentially hostile emissaries. There was no sense in offending a possible ally, after all."

Right. Because stabbing me with a poisoned spear and dropping me a few hundred feet onto a stone floor wasn't at all offensive.

But I wasn't going to quibble. Instead I poured the absinthe, and centered the ornate spoons over the top of the two glasses.

"As I'd mentioned before you put me in the potentially-hostile-emissary holding room, I'm here on a diplomatic mission." I put a sugar cube on each slotted spoon. "The lost princess of the Seelie kingdom has agreed to work with me. If she takes the throne, she vows to restore the former contract between her people and the angels. She is also willing to broker a peace treaty between your two kingdoms once she is on the throne."

"It isn't the first time I've heard that promise of peace. It would need to be a binding agreement in blood before I'd agree to help her," he replied.

"The current queen intends to conquer the Unseelie kingdom," I told him as I centered the glasses under the fountain spigots. "It's not just a war over the borderlands like before. She's planning on genocide."

With a wave of my hand I opened the spigots and the first drop of icy water fell on the sugar cubes. The king watched eagerly as the sugar slowly dissolved with each drop.

"She might plan on that, but her ability to actually enact that plan is lacking," he countered. "The tide turns in this war with regularity, but even when the queen is in a favorable position, she doesn't gain much more than a portion of the borderlands."

I changed my tactics. "The endless war must be exhausting for both you and your subjects. How many sons and daughters have died? How many houses and crops burned? How many towns razed? Those in the borderlands have probably given up hope. And your treasury must be strained from all this military cost, and the lost products, productivity, as well as the need to assist citizens who've lost family or homes."

The king flinched when I mentioned sons and daughters, but quickly returned his attention to the melting cubes of sugar and the swirl of opaque white lightening the green absinthe to a lime-yellow shade. "I will not openly support a Seelie rebellion or a contender to their throne, but I *will* assure you that as far as I am concerned, the bargain that was struck between the Unseelie and the angels remains in place. We Unseelie only take humans who have willingly entered into bargains."

"I'm glad to hear that." I noticed he said "openly support" and took heart that he might be willing to do some less-than-open support.

I slid him the not-chipped glass, and waited until we'd taken the first sip and smiled in appreciation before bringing up the topic that might end any alliance before it even began.

"I have a bit of a confession to make, and find that I must beg your forgiveness." The king took another sip of his drink, so I continued. "On the night of your last Wild Hunt, I found myself protecting your prey, and I think I *might* have accidentally bopped your horse on the nose with the end of a spear."

The king snarled, dark fog rising from the floor.

"Wait! Wait!" I squealed. "The deer your were hunting wasn't a convict. It was a young Seelie girl who'd been turned into a hart by her mother to protect her as soldiers approached. I don't know how she ended up with the ruby necklace on, but she was not a condemned convict, she's the lost princess."

The fog melted away. "*She's* the lost princess?"

I explained Iselle's history, embellishing quite a bit with a wild tale of how the former queen had swapped her own foretold heir for another, hiding Iselle in the outer reaches of the kingdom with her nursemaid posing as her mother. The king listened, fascinated.

"Those necklaces aren't readily available," he mused. "Only the huntsman has access to them. If a prisoner accepts that punishment, the head warden contacts the Office of the Hunt, and one of the necklaces is delivered to be installed on the prisoner the day he is set free for the hunt."

"And the huntsman is the only one who touches the necklaces?" I asked.

The king sipped the final bit of absinthe from his glass. "I don't know the exact procedure. I'm sure he has trusted assistants who perform the majority of the administrative work, but putting the necklace on the convict at his release has always been the duty of the huntsman himself."

"But there are records?" I asked, finishing off my absinthe. "Records of which prisoners accept the deal and when they are released to be part of the hunt?"

The king frowned thoughtfully. "Yes. And any swapping of prisoner would need to involve either the huntsman or the warden. The convict is turned into the deer, escorted to the woods via a specialized cart, then the necklace is placed on them before they are set free."

"That's a bit of travel before the necklace goes on," I pointed out. "Maybe the deer could have been swapped out of the cart during that travel?"

"It makes more sense than smuggling a deer into the city and having it exchanged for the convict in the prison, or having the warden or huntsman, both trusted subjects I've known for most of my life involved." He pushed his empty glass toward me. "I'll look into this. In the meantime, rest assured that I will honor the contract with the angels, and will continue to fight against the Seelie. And I wish your princess and her rebels luck."

I squirmed, because I had no knowledge of the rebels and no way to contact them. And yet, my whole plan hinged on their support.

The king raised an eyebrow. "You haven't allied with the rebels yet?"

"We plan to do so. As soon as I know who to contact, and how to contact them," I confessed.

He laughed, waving at me to pour another round of absinthe. "Did these plans involve wandering the forests for months? Approaching random Seelie fae to ask if they are with the rebellion?"

I began the sugar-cube-and-booze ritual again. "Actually I was hoping you knew how to contact them. I'm sure you and your advisors at least know who the main players are in this rebellion."

"I would be very displeased if my spies had *not* kept me informed about this significant threat to the Seelie queen." He leaned back with a smile. "I'd be willing to send you with someone who could make the appropriate introductions. But, of course, I would need something in return."

These fuckers were worse than the demons. "I would

think that ending this stupid war and giving your kingdom peace would be enough."

"The question you should be contemplating is which of us has the luxury of time?" He picked up his glass and toasted me. "Yes, this war is onerous and I long for peace, but I can continue to fight and to wait. You, though, have the lost princess you need to keep alive, and a potential alliance with rebels who may be wiped out before the winter's snows melt. *And* you have humans clamoring for relief as well as angels who might not be so willing to support you once they all learn what you did."

My mouth nearly dropped open. Wow, this guy really did have one hell of an intelligence network.

"I will offer you a similar deal to what I offered the previous Iblis," he continued. "I will provide you with credentials and introductions to the Seelie rebels, and in return you will allow me to ride the Wild Hunt in the human realm one time during each of their years for the next thousand years."

"Only if this hunt is BYOS," I countered.

He tilted his head. "BYOS?"

"Bring Your Own Stag," I explained. "No hunting humans or any other creature besides the convict fae who has agreed to be transformed and part of the hunt. And if you have not caught the deer before the sun begins to rise, they will be given their freedom in the human realm and no longer pursued in future hunts."

His lips twitched. "The white stag will not be transformed back at the end of the hunt. If they earn their freedom, they will continue to live in their animal form."

I shrugged. "Fine with me. It's not like I want some fairy murderer or rapist running around among the humans on two legs with his magic abilities. Even if they escape the hunt, I'm willing to bet their head will be mounted on some dude's wall within the year."

The king held out his hand. "Then we have a deal."

I shook his hand, thinking that this was an oddly human gesture for a fairy. "We have a deal."

30

Iselle and I trudged through that horrible sentient, movable forest in the borderlands for days. Our guide refused to tell us where we were going or even the names of the rebels we'd be meeting with, and I was beginning to lose patience.

"You know, I can just kill you and Own your soul, then I'll be in possession of all your memories and knowledge. Plus I can torture you for all eternity. That idea is definitely appealing to me right now."

The Unseelie held up her fist, then extended her middle finger. A ray of dappled sunlight caught on a band of silvery-black metal around the digit. "You might kill me, but you'll not take my soul. And the king won't send someone else to guide you. Plus you'll still owe him whatever you bargained for this introduction."

I kinda hated this fucking woman. Admired her, but hated her.

"Oh let her be, Sam." Iselle huffed. "We'll get there when we get there. I'm sure Sidia is taking the shortest route. She probably doesn't want to spend any more time with us than absolutely necessary."

Iselle was still pissed at me for all the time she'd paced Aethell's floorboards, scared that I was dead or in a dungeon, or being tortured. My drunken explanations and even introducing her to the Unseelie king hadn't helped her mood, and she'd been irritated with me the whole journey.

Which, to be honest, hadn't really been that long. Sidia, our guide, used a teleportation scroll to take us to the edge of the borderlands. I wasn't sure if we were going to have to walk over the mountains and halfway through the Seelie kingdom, or if the rebels had set up shop somewhere in the woods. As much as I hated these stupid trees, I really didn't like the idea of hiking all over Aerie.

That night we made camp. Sidia gathered firewood while Iselle and I ate our bread-and-dried-fruit dinner. Then we started a fire while Sidia ate. The Unseelie and I continued to sit staring into the flames while Iselle dozed on her bedroll. When the moon had crested the tree line, Sidia made a fist, then opened her fingers, blowing across them into the fire.

The flames turned green and surged ten feet high before reverting to orange and dropping back down. Green sparks drifted above the canopy, and I hoped they didn't set the whole fucking forest on fire.

I scooted over closer to Iselle and waited, because that was a message if I'd ever seen one. By the time the moon was overhead, I felt the trees stiffen, then shift, their branches rustling as if they were talking. Sidia tensed, and a fairy walked out of the woods towards us.

I doubted that this dude was one of the rebel leaders. He wasn't much older than Iselle with a shock of white hair, golden brown skin, and dark eyes. His gaze roamed over the pair of us and fixed on me.

"Who is this human?" he asked.

Sidia stood. "On behalf of his majesty, the Unseelie king, I introduce to you the Iblis, the Ha-Satan of Hel, the demons, and the Fallen Angels of Chaos. She has a proposal, an alliance that you will find interesting. One that will aid your cause."

The rebel continued to stare at me. "I thought the Iblis was a male demon. Although, I've been told they are fond of changing their appearance and their genders."

"The former guy retired." I stood up, dusting the dirt from my ass. "I'm the new Iblis. You can call me Sam."

"I'm Lynst," he said. "So you are proposing an alliance?"

"I am. I'm willing to escalate the attacks I'm currently making on the Seelie and also provide a team of demons that will mount a more conventional attack in conjunction with your own. The queen is kidnapping humans without any bargain or agreement on their part. I intend to either see her dead or force her to honor the contract between the Seelie fae and the angels once more."

"What if the queen agrees to your terms? Can we no longer count on your support then?" he asked.

"You can still count on my support, but it will be different. I will only target the queen and her court as opposed to generally attacking the Seelie kingdom."

"I'm pretty sure she'll insist on contract terms that prevent you from doing that," he drawled.

I shrugged. "Then I won't sign. I'd prefer her dead, but my goal isn't just the bargain involving the humans, it's getting her off the throne and the rightful heir reinstated."

He snorted. "And which of those girls you freed from the tower is the lost princess? Did you just randomly pick one of them? Yes, the Seelie will rally behind the true heir, but only if she's the real thing. And I refuse to support a fraud just to give our cause a symbol. Our people have been taken advantage of for too long and by too many. I refuse to be one more that lies to them."

Now I felt like shit. I was all prepared to lie and say Iselle was the lost princess, but this kid's stupid ethics were totally in the way of my plan.

But Lynst wasn't done with his lecture. He waved a hand toward the sleeping fae girl. "And this is who you choose as your fraud? A child who sleeps so soundly our conversation doesn't even wake her? That's no one fit to wear the crown."

With a blur of motion, he pulled a knife from his belt and threw it at Iselle. I dove for her, but was too late. The knife flew past me and clear through Iselle to thunk into hard ground.

The illusion of the Seelie girl shimmered and fell, leaving us to look at a blade half buried in the dirt.

"I'm not a child, you pig's behind," Iselle snapped as she walked from the shadows. "A Seelie fae who can't recognize an illusion when he sees one? That's not a leader I'd want to help me regain my throne." She waved her hand and the forest lit up with light, revealing half a dozen Seelie who all held bows and knives at the ready. "And these fools are just as bad. I walked behind every one of them unnoticed. Some rebellion. I'd be better off going into battle with a broom and a herd of sheep."

Yikes. Where had my teenage fairy girl gone, and who had replaced her with this...this *queen*?

"Child's tricks," Lynst sneered.

Iselle lifted her chin. "Tricks that fooled your fighters, the people are supposed to reclaim the Seelie kingdom from the pretender who sits on the throne? It's not conventional warfare that will bring our kingdom peace and prosperity, it's tricks like these, it's the alliance of the Iblis and her demon army, it's the alliance between us and the Unseelie king, as well as the support of the humans. This uprising needs to be swift and unconventional if we are to succeed."

I stared at her with my mouth open. Lynst stared at her as well, his eyes narrowed.

"What proof do you have that you're the real lost princess?" he demanded.

"Her date and year of birth are those of the lost princess," I told him.

He laughed. "And so were the other two dozen girls locked in those towers and guarded by a dragon."

"She can teleport," Sidia spoke up. "She has the power of illusion, of light and of weather. And that is in addition to her affinity with plants."

I knew from my Owned souls that few fae had more than two magical abilities, and that some of those abilities were very rare. That Iselle had so many meant she was at a minimum very powerful. And it made her the perfect girl to play the lost princess.

"Also, I wear this." Iselle held up her hand and showed him the ring. Light sparked from it, and a ball of fire appeared in the girl's hand.

I blinked, taking a step back away from the sudden heat. Well. That was new.

Lynst frowned at the ring a few seconds. I could practically hear him thinking.

"I still have my doubts that you are the lost princess, but I'm willing to have you join our rebellion. You can call yourself whatever you want, but I won't support your claim to the throne until I'm convinced you're fit to rule, and I won't call you the princess until I know that to be true without a doubt."

Iselle shrugged. "Fine. But I won't be shoved into some menial position in the rebellion. I will be afforded the same level of respect and allowed to give equal input to your top leaders. Otherwise my demon army, my allies, and I will take the kingdom without you. And then you will be nothing but pig-herders and beggars while those who have proved their loyalty take top positions in my court."

Yikes. I'd created a monster. Or Nyalla had created a monster. Probably both of us had created this monster.

In spite of her speech, Lynst seemed unimpressed. "We will need to assess your fighting ability. And while we will allow you to have a voice, we will not risk the lives of our soldiers on the whims of a girl with no military experience."

Iselle sucked in a breath, and I eyed the ball of fire she held, worried she was going to lob it at the young Seelie fae. Then she clenched her hand and the fire vanished.

"I'll agree to that. But we only have a week to prepare. After a week, we go to war."

LYNST and his troop had stayed with us through the night, leaving in the morning. We broke camp, and said our thanks and goodbyes to Sidia who was returning to the Unseelie kingdom. Then Iselle and I began to walk. She assured me that once we were out of the woods and onto the mountain pass, she could teleport us to where my Owned security advisor knew a fae portal to be.

"What the hell was all that about?" I asked Iselle as soon as we were a good three miles away from Sidia. "You were a total teenage badass last night—a stealthy, fireball-wielding badass."

She giggled, absolutely ruining the badass image. "Nyalla and I watched Wakanda Forever before we left for Aerie. Basically I tried to think of what Queen Ramonda would do in that situation."

"Well, I think you need to channel your inner Queen Ramonda more often," I told her. "And the Dora Milaje warriors as well. But when did you learn to do that fire-in-the-hand trick?"

The fairy girl shrugged. "It just happened when I went to show that jerk the ring, so I pretended I did it on purpose."

"You totally had me fooled." I was all admiration.

"I was scared," she admitted. "When the trees grumbled about the intruders, I just about wet my bedroll. Then suddenly I was ten feet away, hiding in the woods and looking at an illusion of myself as Lynst was talking to you. I don't know why the soldiers didn't hear or see me when I walked around behind them."

"Guess we'll just add that to the fire-in-the-hand thing. Unexpected magical ability when you're so scared you almost piss yourself," I replied.

She nodded, then shot me a nervous glance. "I'm not sure about this 'assess my fighting skills' stuff. Lynst and the others are going to expect me to be somewhat proficient, and I'm going to fail terribly. I've been a deer most of my life. I don't know how to use a sword or a knife, or shoot a bow."

"But you can run fast and silently," I pointed out.

"So can every other fairy," she scoffed.

"You can manipulate weather and plants."

She rolled her eyes. "I can only do certain weather and

plant magic. A gentle rain and blooming roses aren't going to send my enemies running in terror."

"You can teleport, sneak around unseen, create illusions, and if none of that works, you can throw those balls of fire at them."

"You're right. Those *might* be useful skills in a fight." She gnawed on her lower lip. "But that Lynst won't think so. He'll think I'm weak and useless because I don't know how to fight."

"No he won't," I lied. "Just be sneaky and trust your instincts."

"Still, I wish I'd handled more than a butter knife in my life," she said.

"I don't know how to use a sword," I confessed. "And my sentient Iblis sword is pretty fucking pissed about that. Did I tell you I used it to chop tomatoes once? And split firewood?"

She gasped, then giggled again. "You split firewood with your magical sword! And it didn't abandon you? Or kill you?"

"I get the idea that being the official sword of Satan, the weapon is fairly used to that sort of mistreatment."

The fairy sighed. "I wish *I* had a magical sword. The only attack magic I have is that fireball thing, and I don't even know if I can summon it at will or what kind of damage it will do. It didn't burn my hand at all."

"Of course it didn't burn your hand. You're the mage...I mean the fairy that summoned the element. And I'm sure it will be a terrifying weapon in battle," I said, trying to boost her confidence.

"Still, I'd feel a whole lot more confident if I knew some basics." She eyed me. "Maybe I shouldn't ask you try to teach me to use a sword, though. How are your archery skills?"

I laughed. "Shitty. You'd need an elf if you wanted to learn archery. I might be able to convince Gregory to teach you to use a sword. It's been his primary weapon for billions of years, so I'm pretty sure he can out-sword even the best fairy."

Her face lit up at that. "Would you? I'd really appreciate it."

"We only have a week though," I warned her.

A week for Iselle to practice using weapons. A week to plan both an attack and a defense. A week to gather demons and a whole lot of supplies.

A week before we went to war.

31

I went into the fae portal first and knocked Ahia flat on her ass when I came through. Iselle was so close behind me that she fell over the two of us and right into Raphael's arms.

"Whoa there." He set her aside and gave her one of his devastatingly gorgeous smiles.

"Thhhank you," the fairy stuttered, flustered by the smoking hot archangel.

"Hey babe." I gave Ahia a hand up, then jumped into my beloved asshole's arms. "We did it. The Seelie rebels are on board with my plan. They'll gain additional support from the populace by claiming to have the rightful Seelie heir on their side. I'll bring over a force of demons, and we'll attack in one week."

"And the Unseelie?" He asked as he kissed the top of my head.

"They can't openly support a Seelie rebellion, but they're doing it on the sly. And they're willing to coordinate a huge attack at the same time as ours. We'll be hitting the queen on three sides."

"And what did you have to promise him in return for this stealth assistance?" Gregory asked dryly.

"Just one Wild Hunt per year here among the humans for the next thousand years." I held up a hand at his protest. "They're bringing their own prey and will not hurt any of the indigenous life here. It's going to rock. We can totally monetize the shit out of a fae Wild Hunt. We'll sell tickets for people to be at the portal and they'll be able to watch exclusive live-stream footage of the fight." I just had to find a way to convince the Unseelie to wear Go-Pro cameras, and have drones to video from the air. Hell, *I'd* pay to see that.

"We'll discuss this later." Gregory's voice sounded ominous.

"Nothing to discuss," I told him. "It's a bargain sealed with our vows and over several rounds of absinthe. He's a cool dude. Maybe he'll let me ride along on one of the hunts. Diablo would love it."

Actually Diablo would get a demonic hair up his hybrid equine butt and start biting the other horses. He'd probably run right past the stag because the prick thought everything was a race.

"One week," Gregory mused. "I'll need to call an emergency Ruling Council meeting, and prepare forms 629334 and T6 so that you can attack a foreign entity without reprisal."

Right. I was going to have thousands of angels trying to kill me soon, but it was important to request formal permission to attack Aerie first. I just didn't understand angels at all sometimes.

"I also need you to give Iselle some sword lessons." I glanced over at the girl who was chatting with Ahia and Raphael. "There's a lot of moving pieces, and the pair of us need to be back in Aerie in seven days."

"Tight timeline," Gregory agreed.

It was. But there was one thing that had moved to the top of my to-do list, and sadly it wasn't the fitting for my wedding dress or rescuing Dolly Parton.

"Is Lux at home?" I asked Gregory.

He shook his head. "I didn't want to leave him with that spy, so he's at the Baltimore aquarium with Gabriel and Nyalla."

Then he'd be gone all day. Gabe and Nyalla were downright obsessive when it came to oceanic life, and Lux would probably end up in the tank with the starfish much to the staff's dismay. Heck, for all I knew all three of them would end up in a tank swimming with sharks or petting eels or something. And then there would be lunch at an Inner Harbor restaurant, and possibly a paddle-boat jaunt on the Patapsco River. I honestly didn't expect Lux home until dinnertime, or after.

Which meant I could confront Joe without any witnesses.

"There have already been attacks from the Seelie queen," Gregory said, interrupting my violent plans for Joe. "They wiped out an entire town in Vermont. Killed everyone and burned all the buildings. They also put a curse on the area where no one can live there or cross into the town limits. Same thing with a city in Portugal. The humans are furious. We've informed them that this is not the elves, but fae, and that we are working on the situation."

"Let me guess: the humans don't think you're working fast enough and are planning to handle any future attacks on their own, just in case the angels need to discuss various defense plans for the next few decades."

"Yes." Gregory smiled and shook his head. "I'm not sad about that, Cockroach. I think it's time for the humans to fight back and show the fae that they're not stupid and inept. And for once, thanks to your insanely abbreviated timetable, the Ruling Council won't be able to take centuries or decades to act."

"Good." I turned to glance at Iselle. "Do you mind keeping her busy for a few hours, then bringing her home? I've got something I need to address and I don't want her to see it."

He nodded. "Absolutely. We'll do some sword practice, and I'll have her home for dinner."

RATHER THAN GIVE Joe warning about my arrival, I just teleported right into his bedroom, catching him in his underwear, and holding a glowing stone. He yelped and jumped up, dropping the stone and knocking a plate with a sandwich and chips onto the floor.

"Ever heard of knocking?" he snapped. "I know it's your house and all, but I should be entitled to privacy in my room."

"Spies are entitled to nothing," I told him.

He paled, and backed up as I walked toward him.

"The Seelie fae knew I was responsible for sending Durfts and other vicious animals through their portals. They knew when I was coming to Aerie and all about Iselle. They knew to specifically target Dolly Parton." I kept my voice calm—scarily calm.

"I don't know what you're talking about." Joe swallowed hard. His eyes darted toward the bed, then back to me.

I bent down to pick up the plate and the sandwich. As I sat them back on the bed, I lifted the stone he'd been holding when I appeared. It was no longer glowing. In fact, right now it didn't emit any sort of magical energy signature at all. It was just a stone—until I sent my personal energy into it and realized it wasn't any sort of rock found here.

"Souvenir from Aerie?" I asked Joe.

He stared at the rock for a second. "I found it in my old clothes when I was balling them up to throw them away. I don't know how it got there."

I had no time for this bullshit.

"Okay Joe." I kept walking forward until he was against the wall, between the headboard and the closet door. "You can either tell me why you're giving information to the fae, or I'll kill you and Own your soul and find out everything I want to know that way."

He sucked in a breath. "I can't...I didn't. They kidnapped me. I escaped. I hate them."

The last rang true. He'd practically spit the words out, and his mouth was twisted in a scowl. He did hate the fae. They did kidnap him. But the escape? That was a lie.

They'd let him go. And the only reason they'd do that is to gain information. Gregory and I had been closing their portals. Angels had been attacking the fae who were kidnapping humans. It would have been easy for them to send Joe through right when my fingers had brushed the gateway. And those shadow creatures that were supposedly hunting him had focused their attacks completely on us, not on Joe.

He was clearly their spy, but I was beginning to doubt that he was a willing one. Had they cursed him in some way that he'd die if he didn't deliver the information they required? Did they have a loved one of his held hostage to ensure his compliance. The guy looked like he was going to either keel over from a heart attack or puke, and his eyes kept going to the stone in my hand.

I could crush it, or burn it, or abandon it on the surface of Mars, but there was only one real way to destroy something for good. I held it up for Joe to see, then raised my eyebrows in a silent question. He stared at the rock, not nodding his approval, but not shaking his head with a terrified "no" either. So I devoured the thing.

It took less than a second, but while matter can be devoured, spells cannot, so I shoved the magical energy into my spirit-being. It took about three seconds before I felt the fragmented magic rise up inside me. Breaking a spell usually results in a sizable explosion, but I'd never actually devoured one before, especially a fae spell. All sorts of terrible outcomes ran through my brain. Would I explode? Could I survive that? The magic felt like sharp chips of glass in my chest and throat. The pressure and pain built, making me worry that my exploding would take out the house, the barn, maybe everyone within a hundred mile radius. I tried to hold it down, but there was no stopping it. I opened my mouth to scream and instead burped.

I'm not talking some little polite burp or even one of those rippers that tears out of your throat when you've been chugging beer all afternoon. This was the belch of champions. I was sure it shook the house. It definitely shook Joe who might have peed a little when the sound hit him.

"Now will you tell me how you came to spy for the Seelie, or am I going to have to do the same thing to you," I threatened.

Not that I'd devour him, because then I wouldn't get any information at all. No, I'd just kill him and Own his soul, adding Joe to the thirteen fae I already Owned.

"The rock always listens." He squeezed his eyes shut.

"Well it's not listening anymore." I burped again, this one not as loud.

He opened his eyes and slumped against the wall. "Then instead of dying now, I have forty-eight hours before they don't get their next set of information and they kill me. If I were to tell anyone about the rock, or that I was relaying information to the fae, or any details on what they had me do, I would have instantly died. If I would have thrown the rock away or go more than twenty feet from it, I would have died. If I fail to send information via the rock every forty-eight hours, I'll die."

"You've got more than forty-eight hours," I assured him. "The rock can't kill you, so when they don't get their transmission, they'll have to send someone from Aerie to do the job, and trust me, they're going to be way too busy in a week to do that."

"A week?" Joe grimaced. "That gives them five days to kill me. They'll find me. They probably have some magical tracking device inside me. They'll find me, and I'll be dead. But I'll tell you everything I know before then."

I moved the plate with the sandwich and sat on the bed, motioning Joe to do the same. "Did you make a bargain? Did they give you immortality or something in exchange for your information?"

He sat up near the pillows, folding his legs crisscross in front of him. "I hate those fairies. There's nothing they could give me that would make me help them. Not that they ever offered. They picked me out, stopped whatever enchantment I'd been under since I'd been kidnapped, then told me what I was going to do, or I'd die painfully and horribly. They'd send me through the portal, and I was to befriend whoever was on the other side, making sure I remained with them so I could gather information."

"And we were the suckers helping a scared escapee," I said, a little bitter at how easily Gregory and I had been taken in. Although I did remember I had some doubts about Joe in the beginning, so maybe I wasn't such a sucker after all.

"I really *was* scared. I still am." He clenched his hands as they began to tremble. "And I felt bad about betraying you, especially after Nyalla was so nice to me. But you're Satan, and that angel is an *archangel*. As powerful and terrifying as the fae are, I couldn't believe they'd be a match for the two of you. And I could tell they were unnerved by the things I was telling them—mostly about Iselle."

I was more than a little annoyed that the Seelie were more upset about a teenage fairy girl than Satan coming for them, but that was kinda the story of my life.

"I'm so sorry about Dolly Parton." He looked down at his hands. "I'm a big fan of hers, and I never thought they'd kidnap or harm her. I was trying to think of things to tell them that didn't have to do with your plans or strategy, so I told them about your wedding."

Some of my anger subsided with that. He'd been doing his best to misdirect the fae while still trying to keep alive.

"They're attacking a few cities and then they plan to put forth another demand," Joe said. "They're asking for all those tower-captive girls back, but they really want Iselle. And you. No matter what you and the angels end up agreeing to, they won't rest until you're dead."

"I'm really hard to kill." I smiled. "And if they think they're getting Iselle or any of those girls, they better think again."

Joe's frown deepened. "But they've got Ms. Parton. They'll kill her if you don't meet their terms. And they'll keep attacking cities and killing humans too."

"I'm bringing the fight to them, and they can't fight three

wars at the same time plus attack human cities. Trust me. I'm pissed, and that means I'm going to fuck their shit up."

There was a brief smile at that, then Joe went back to his worried frown.

"Then I'll rest easy knowing you've delivered justice." He sighed. "It feels weird that I'm expecting righteous justice from Satan."

"That's what the position historically entailed," I told him. "The adversary. The one who tests people's faith. The one who punishes the unrepentant and the wicked. Although, to be honest, that's a huge job. I'm only one demon/angel. I do the best I can, but it's a drop in the bucket as far as justice is concerned."

He nodded. "Cool job though. Mucking everything up, and scaring the crap out of people? Plus all the partying? I mean, you were going to kidnap Dolly Parton to perform your wedding ceremony. That's some wicked stuff right there."

I sat a little straighter on the bed, thinking that maybe Joe would be my first human admirer. Nyalla didn't count, and my human friends tended to be on the fence when it came to a lot of my actions. Was this what it was like to have a worshiper? If so, then I could understand how it could go to a demon's, or angel's, head.

"I wish I wasn't going to die in the next few days," Joe added. "I would have liked to get to know you better."

It was blatant flattery for an obvious goal, but I loved flattery as much as I loved presents.

"You must have known that they would have ended up killing you anyway," I commented, thinking of the poor nameless Marriott employee.

He nodded, looking up at me. "Yeah, but there was always that irrational sliver of hope, you know? And each day was one more day I got to live, so I kept trying. And now...well, at least I'll have two more days."

I sighed. Once again I was a total sucker, but it was so nice being admired and appreciated. "You'll live for more than two days, but you're going to have to do as I say."

Joe sat up, eyeing me eagerly. "I will. I'll do anything. Just say the word, and I'm totally onboard."

I needed to make sure he was somewhere he couldn't communicate with the Seelie fae if this was all a lie and he was still helping them. And in case he wasn't, I needed a place where he could be safe from the fae, and safe from whoever the fae might convince to come kill him. There was only one place that met both those criteria.

"Then pack up your belongings Joe," I told him. "Because you're going to Hel."

32

"How is this going to make me any less dead?" Joe asked as he stared at the bone-embellished house I'd inherited when I'd killed Ahriman.

"The fae would never come to Hel," I explained. "The only fairy who's ever been here is Gwylla and that's because she was exiled and forced to take refuge with the elves. Even then, she never left the elf lands. None of the demons knew she was in Hel. You'll be totally safe from the Seelie hitmen here."

"Totally safe?" Joe pointed at a demon oozing his way up the street who'd opened up a gaping circular maw of sharp teeth and slimy drool.

"That's just Ellen. She's cool." I waved at the demon who snarled back at me. "She lives two houses down in that dirt-covered cave-looking place."

Joe shuffled closer to me until our shoulders practically touched. "Your house has locks on the doors, right? And maybe a shotgun?"

Silly man. As if locks and a shotgun could keep Ellen out. Luckily the steps to the porch *did* keep Ellen out. She'd make it up three, and slide back down. Good thing since she was known for constantly borrowing small appliances and not returning them.

Joe's fears clearly weren't alleviated once we'd gotten inside the house.

"The décor is a little extreme," I admitted, "but the place came pre-furnished. And my household seems to like it."

"Is that human skin on those chairs?" Joe reached out a shaky hand to point at the furniture.

I eyed the cushions because Ahriman had used a variety of beings in creating his furniture and artwork.

"Yep. Human skin. Nice work on the tanning process too." Ahriman had been a psychotic monster, and he'd taken his hobbies as seriously as he'd taken everything in his long, murderous life.

"You...?" Joe took a step away from me.

"Oh no," I waved a dismissive hand. "The previous owner did these." I knew better than to try tanning or taxidermy myself. I didn't have the skill or the patience. It was better to take my kills to a skilled professional when I felt like preserving a trophy.

Joe let out a relieved breath, but gave the chairs a wide berth as he strolled around the room. He'd only made it as far as the carved Ent coffee table when three of my Lows burst into the room. All three of them squealed, then rushed Joe, surrounding him and stroking his clothing and skin. Fingers, who was about seven feet tall and less than ten inches wide petted the man's hair, as if he were a cute doggy I'd brought on a visit.

"Okay everyone, hands off Joe." I clapped my hands for attention. "Give the dude a little space here. He bites when he's afraid."

Fingers stepped back a few feet and tilted his head. "He

has very dull teeth. I don't think his bite would be dangerous."

"Blunt teeth crush and tear big chunks of flesh off, rather than the stabby-stabby of pointed teeth," I reminded him. If he'd ever been bitten by a horse, he'd know the incredible pain blunt teeth could cause coupled with a strong jaw. Although Fingers, like most demons, appreciated pain, so that probably wasn't a deterrent.

"I can't stay here," Joe told me. "I'll take my chances with the Seelie."

"Nonsense." I waved Snoots, Fingers, and Brow closer. "I'm going to leave Joe here for a week or two. Maybe three. He's not part of my household, but you should still treat him as a respected guest. He gets the human food and bottled water in the pantry—nothing else or he'll have the shits for days. That may sound like fun times to you all, but upsets to his delicate digestive system can cause lasting damage. He also has sensitive skin and hair, so gentle touches with his permission only."

Fingers eyed Joe's hair. "How often should we groom him?"

"Never. He'll self-groom. And he doesn't need to go on walkies, so put that leash away, Brow."

Brow sighed and tied the leash back around his waist.

"Should we set up the litter box for him?" Snoots asked.

I glanced over at Joe with raised eyebrows.

At first he grimaced and shook his head, then he paused. "Are there toilets here? An outhouse? A chamber pot?"

"Use the big litterbox," I instructed Snoots. "Put it in a private place, because humans generally don't like to pee or shit with an audience." Unless the audience was canine or feline, although I don't think the humans had much of a choice about that.

"Which bedroom, Mistress?" Fingers asked.

The Lows usually slept wherever they wanted, but they knew that some of my guests wanted a specific room for that activity.

"Let him have the one Dar uses when he's here," I told the Low. There were clean sheets on that bed. There were clean sheets on the bed in Leethu's room too, but there were also other things on that bed that Joe might not appreciate. Plus, the S&M equipment lining the walls would probably terrify the guy.

The Lows all nodded, promising that they would keep this human safe and pampered until my return.

I reached out and patted Joe on the shoulder. "Well, good luck. I mean, have fun. I've got to go raise a demon army, so I'll let you get settled in."

"Wait." He made a quick movement to grab my arm, but I teleported away.

Bringing Joe to Hel wasn't just an attempt to keep him alive, it was also a way to keep him from communicating anything else to the fae. If he'd lied and he was still planning to convey information to them somehow, he'd find himself absolutely unable to do so. I was pretty sure he'd be too scared to leave the house. He'd probably be too scared to leave his room.

Walking through the streets of Dis, I stapled fliers to houses, posts, and even the random demon. I'd already spread the word throughout my household that any demon interested in killing fairies was to meet in front of my house on Wednesday at two o'clock eastern standard time. I probably would have been more convenient to have them all meet at the barrow mound Gwylla used as the basis of her portal to Aerie, but I didn't have a searchable GPS address for that location, so I'd just need to teleport my army there when they arrived.

Any stragglers arriving after two were warned that they would be left behind and miss all of the fun and spoils of war.

❦

"I WILL OPEN the gateway to Aerie for you and the demons," Gregory offered that night as we sat on the couch, a sleeping Lux between us.

I turned my head to look at him in surprise. "Won't that be another violation of the contract we're trying to restore? I thought no angels were allowed in Aerie."

He smirked. "No angels are going to Aerie. There's nothing in the five hundred pages of that contract that stipulates we can't open passageways there. Even if there were, what else could the queen do? She's already been kidnapping humans and now she's attacked two cities here. Lux's five minute visit to steal a ring is nothing compared to what she's done."

I smiled and scooted against him, leaning my head on his shoulder. "Thanks. I trust your navigation far more than I do Gwylla's. And I think she's getting a little nervous about all the portals I've asked her to open for me. She might be exiled, but I know she still has dreams of maybe one day being able to go home for a visit, and pissing off the Seelie queen isn't going to get her pardoned."

"No, but I'm sure the new queen will be in more of a pardoning mood." He grinned and tugged a lock of my hair.

But would Iselle be queen? Was that a role she really wanted to take? It's not like she could wear the crown for a trial period, then decide ruling a fae kingdom wasn't for her.

If she became the queen, she'd have to stay the queen. And I wasn't sure that was the sort of lifetime decision a teenage fairy girl should be making.

"How large of an army have you assembled?" Gregory asked.

I shrugged. "I'll see who all shows up Wednesday. Could be ten demons, could be ten thousand demons. I'm thinking I'll get a good turnout. No one wants to miss bloodshed and pillage."

He nodded. "I can imagine this will be viewed as the event of the century."

"Absolutely. It's going to be the demon equivalent of Woodstock, only without the music. And with a whole lot more violence." I shifted the sleeping Lux so I could cuddle the two of them better. "How are things going for you at this end?"

He moved his arm to my waist. "We were able to quickly establish an emergency alert system using something the humans already had in place for severe weather warnings and missing children. Key officials in each city are able to activate the alert which goes out to all their citizens as well as a select group of angels. The humans take shelter. We teleport to the location and defend them against the attacking fae."

"That's a great idea," I said. "Were there any more attacks when I was in Hel?"

"Just one false alarm," he told me. "A man was illegally burning trash outside of Sparks Nevada, and residents thought it was a fae attack because a dozen aerosol paint cans exploded."

"Sparks." I chuckled. "Because that's the perfect town to be set on fire."

"No, Cockroach, it isn't." Gregory scowled. "The man

died, and there was significant property loss. Thankfully the emergency system worked, and we were able to immediately extinguish the blaze."

"Did you manage to get those forms approved for my attack?" I asked. Not that I gave a rat's ass if the angels signed off on my actions or not.

"I did." He lifted an eyebrow. "And speaking of forms, I'm assuming there will be a four-nine-five report coming our way at the next Ruling Council meeting? For Joe," he added at my confused expression.

"Oh, I haven't killed him. He's not dead...at least he's not dead yet." I told Gregory about Joe and the fae and that he was currently in Hel, at my house in Dis. "I might leave him there a few additional weeks, or maybe a month. I figure he deserves some punishment."

"True." Gregory pulled Lux onto his lap.

I scooted so I was pressed against him, and he adjusted the baby angel so he was laying across both our sets of legs. I sighed, again putting my head on his shoulder. Lux began softly snoring and I closed my eyes, hoping everything went well next week, so we could have more nights just like this.

———

33

I selle and I stood in front of my house Wednesday at two o'clock, waiting for my army to appear. The Seelie queen had made another set of demands on Monday, this one with the addition of my banishment to Hel. We'd rebuffed her deal, which this time cost a private courier his life. Tuesday, the angels had thwarted two fae attacks with minimal property loss and no additional loss of human lives. Gregory expected another attempt this evening, most likely on two cities at once in an attempt to divide the angelic response, so it was important for us to act as soon as we arrived in Aerie and show that we intended to retaliate.

Which is why there were eight crates of Durfts, drop bears, and crocodiles next to us.

I'd been releasing animals through the fae portals, but these ones I intended to send directly into the capital city, and possibly the palace. We were going to hit them right after we arrived and be out, hopefully before any of their wards sounded the alarm.

Then we'd journey to meet the rebels, get the plans for tomorrow's attack, and prepare.

But this would all fall apart if no demons showed up to my party.

Gregory strolled out of my house, Lux beside him. He looked around my driveway and road, then frowned.

"They'll be here." I couldn't hide the note of desperation in my voice. We'd still have the rebels and the Unseelie, but my inability to raise even the tiniest of armies would ruin my cred among the fae and seriously hinder our attempt to overthrow the Seelie queen.

"It's two o'clock," Gregory commented.

I winced. "You can't expect demons to be on time. Give them another fifteen minutes."

In reality, demons were unusually prompt when it came to things like battles, orgies, and parties. The fact that no one had arrived seriously worried me. Had I printed the wrong date and time on the fliers? Was my army as directionally challenged as I was and waiting at some random house hundreds of miles away, wondering where the fuck I was?

Fifteen minutes past. I was getting ready to tell Gregory to go ahead and open the gateway when a line of tour buses came down the street and turned into my driveway. I stared as demons of all shape and size poured from the buses, organized by the warmonger, Harkel.

He trotted over to me, grinning. "Amber told me that you were attacking the fae. I was kind of in the middle of something else, but there's no way I was going to miss something this epic, so we loaded up the buses and headed east."

I shook my head, bemused that he'd used these luxury tour buses rather than teleporting his army here. Human-style transportation aside, I was glad to see him. Harkel was skilled when it came to strategy, and absolutely ruthless in achieving his military goals. I could safely leave the army under his command while I focused on the queen.

"Mal! You bitch! How come I didn't get a personal invite to this shindig?"

I grinned to see Dar stepping off the bus. This day was getting better and better.

"I didn't think the ball-and-chain would let you come along," I replied, knowing that Asta generally frowned on this sort of thing.

"I got a hall pass." He trotted over to me. "She said I needed a vacation, a demons'-night-out, and I wasn't going to argue."

I slapped him on the shoulder, glad that Asta had let him come, although the angel probably had some trip she'd want to go on in exchange.

"So what's the plan?" Dar asked, rubbing his hands together.

"Harkel and the army are going to the rebel encampment, or as near to it as they can get," I announced. "If a fairy greets you and asks for the password, it's 'string cheese.' Otherwise just wait for me to return and I'll get you all past the wards and illusions hiding the camp. Iselle and I and now Dar will be teleporting immediately upon arrival in Aerie to the palace where we will let all these animals loose and fuck some shit up before Iselle teleports us out again. Consider it a little pregame before the actual war."

"Good." Harkel did a fist-pump. "That will enrage the queen and her army and make for a gloriously fun battle tomorrow."

Hopefully it would also unsettle her that I'd once again been able to launch an attack directly inside her palace. I doubt she'd roll over and give up, but the Durfts, drop bears, and crocodiles would hopefully upset her enough that she'd make some serious mistakes.

"Are we ready?" Gregory asked. "I need to be available in case we get an emergency alert."

"Let's get this show on the road." I pointed as Gregory formed the gateway. "Dar, Iselle, and I go first, then Harkel follows with the army."

It took some assistance to get all the crates through the gateway, but as soon as we were in Aerie, Iselle took Dar's and my hands, and the forest vanished, replaced by a long corridor filled with windows, paintings...and fae.

The Seelie screamed as we appeared, then continued screaming as the boxes crashed to the floor, some of them opening and spilling out their contents. Durfts and crocodiles raced after the fae while the drop bears dug their claws into the walls, climbing upward and running along the ceiling to pounce down on the fleeing fairies. Dar and I opened the crates that hadn't broken during transport, then fought off the animals who were just as willing to bite and claw us as they were the fae. As soon as the last box was open, we raced back to Iselle and grabbed her hands. Suddenly we were back in the forest again.

Harkel eyed us, taking in the torn, bloody clothing that Dar and I wore before nodding. "A successful attack?"

"We won't know until tomorrow, but I believe we've made our intentions clear." Dar grinned. "It was the most fun I've had in weeks."

An arrow shot past my ear. Harkel snatched it out of midair and snarled.

"String cheese!" I shouted. "String cheese!"

Someone whistled and three Seelie I didn't recognize materialized at the edge of the clearing.

"You are the Iblis?" One asked me.

"I am. And this is my army," I gestured broadly, then waved a hand at the warmonger.

"Which will be led by General Harkel."

The fairy who'd spoken nodded politely to Harkel, but the other two were staring at Iselle, whispering so softly I couldn't make out what they were saying. Instead of scolding them, their leader turned looked at Iselle as well, then bowed deeply.

"Your Highness."

His voice held a note of reverence, and I was surprised at the sincerity. I'd expected them to be as skeptical about Iselle's fake claim as Lynst had been, but either these fae desperately wanted a symbol, or Lynst had swallowed his doubts and enthusiastically supported the girl as the Lost Princess.

Or Iselle was just that convincing. She was wearing sturdy cargo pants and a T-shirt with her long hair pulled back into a simple braid. It made her look like a very young hiker, not royalty. My gaze snagged on the ring she still wore, and I wondered if the loyalty magic had played a factor in her reception. Although that would mean Iselle truly *was* related to the former queen.

Nah. It was probably just superstition and belief in the myth.

The three fae led us a short distance through the forest, then through an illusion of trees and rocks into a huge encampment. Dar took charge of getting the demon army settled somewhere they wouldn't be tempted to start killing our allies, while Iselle, Harkel, and I were led to a small yellow tent.

Inside, the tent was big enough to hold fifty people with rooms sectioned off. The walls appeared to be glossy wood instead of fabric. I touched one to see if it was an illusion, and my fingers met a smooth hard surface.

"Greetings!" Lynst stood behind a table where eight other Seelie fae were seated. "Join us, allies. Let us begin with introductions."

I promptly forgot who the eight other fae were, but I did note that they kept glancing over at Iselle in surprise and wonder. Lynst did not seem as enchanted as his advisors. He ignored the girl, instead focusing on Harkel and me as he outlined the battle plan for tomorrow. I let Harkel field most of the questions, since he and the demons would need to coordinate closely with Lynst's forces. Once I could manage it, I'd be charging ahead on my own to the palace and to the queen.

Kill the queen. Rescue Dolly Parton. Everyone else could take care of the actual battle outside.

"I can't teleport an entire army," Iselle interrupted in a voice so furious I wondered that the tent didn't spontaneously combust. "I can only transport two living beings and six or seven objects. There's no way I can get your elite force inside the palace."

Lynst sighed as if she were a small child having a tantrum over eating her vegetables. "You *should* be able to transport a small group. It's one of the important tactical magical abilities of the true royal family."

Iselle bristled and I reached out to put a hand on her arm. "Your elite force will need to fight their way through to the palace, as I intend to do. Unless you don't think they're capable of that?"

Lynst glared at me, then let out a long breath. "Fine. We'll do that. Does anyone else have any last-minute changes to our plan?"

I noticed he didn't address Iselle as "highness" or

"princess" as others had done. And he truly seemed to be making it his mission to piss her off.

Probably because he wanted in her pants. I know that was my go-to method of persuasion when *I* wanted in someone's pants.

No one had changes to the plans, nor they were all too intimidated by our young rebel leader to speak up. The meeting ended, and Iselle stomped back to where the demons were setting up camp, obviously fuming.

I wasn't about to get in the middle of this, so I left her and found Dar to tell him about the plans for tomorrow morning. We'd all packed food, wary of accepting anything from the fae even if they were our allies, and it was best to keep the adrenaline-fueled, excited-for-battle demons away from the Seelie, so we ate in our camp. Most of the demons were too amped up to sleep, but I convinced them to keep the noise to a minimum, informing them that if the fae didn't get enough sleep, they might "accidentally" shoot a demon instead. I couldn't sleep either, and wasn't in the mood for the demon games or tales of bravado, so I walked around the camp, noticing that many of the Seelie were also suffering from insomnia the night before the big battle. As I neared the yellow tent I heard hushed voices arguing. Coming around the corner, I recognized Iselle and Lynst and quickly backed up.

Peeking around the edge of the tent, I watched the pair. They were too quiet for me to hear what they were saying, but the wild gestures and fingers poking each other's chest as well as their rapid-fire back and forth let me know that they were absolutely furious with each other.

With a smirk, I turned and went back to the demon encampment.

34

Those who actually slept were up before dawn. The rest of us were weaponed-up and ready to go. Lynst had secured a portal spell that would put all of us within fifty yards of the city gates, so we assembled in the formation that would give us the ability to launch an immediate attack. I was up front with Dar and Iselle, where Harkel had placed himself closer to the demons. Dar was in his giant-rat demon form with a bandolier of knives across his chest. He was holding a knife in one hand, and a kusari-fundo in the other.

"Hey Splinter, are the turtles coming too, or are you going to fight this one alone?" I asked.

He bared his teeth at me then grinned, swinging the kusari-fundo. I ducked, deciding it might be wise for me to space myself accordingly. I'd never seen Dar use that weapon before and he was just as likely to hit me by accident as on purpose.

Iselle was at my other side clutching a delicate-looking sword. From the expression on her face, I guessed she was daydreaming of sinking the blade into Lynst. Which probably meant there had been no angry-sex last night.

Lynst walked from the encampment to a spot in front of both armies. He wore lightweight leather-looking armor, and carried an ornate sword. With his free hand, he held a glowing red stone. Throwing it to the ground about ten feet away, he raised his hand and shouted *ymlleana*.

A portal the size of a parking lot opened in front of us. The fae roared and rushed toward it. Not wanting to lag behind, the demons also roared and ran. For a second I worried that everyone was going to get stuck trying to go through the portal at the same time, but the fighters managed to sort themselves out, and with some sidesteps and fancy-dance moves, they entered and exited the portal without incident.

Lynst and Harkel had gone in ahead of their charging armies, but Dar, Iselle, and I waited and brought up the rear. By the time we cleared the portal, the fight was well underway with city guards and militias pouring from the gates and engaging with our fighters.

"Now," I told Iselle. That elite fighting squad of Lynst's would need to fight their way through, but I'd lied about my doing so. We were going to teleport into the palace like civilized people, and hopefully have the queen dead before the Seelie rebels made it through the gates.

Iselle took Dar's and my hand. And nothing happened.

I looked over at the Seelie girl and saw her eyes widen as she turned to me.

"Somethings blocking me. I can't teleport inside." She frowned and squinted. "There's a shield around the city. It's like a magical dome."

"We can't get in?" This was going to really suck. If our

epic battle turned into an endless siege, then my demons were going to get bored and go home.

"Physically, yes." Iselle made a frustrated noise. "I mean, we can enter on foot, but I can't teleport past the city gates."

"Clearly our little retaliation yesterday had unintended consequences," Dar drawled.

"Then we need to fight our way to the palace." Just like those fucking elite guards, damn it all.

"Last one to the palace is a Low," Dar said right before he took off at a run.

I let him go, because the only thing better than a shield was a giant-rat-shield whacking fae left and right with a staff and a kusari-fundo. As Iselle and I slowly advanced through the battle, I saw that we were making very slow progress toward the city gates. A nine-foot-tall demon with the head of a snake and the body of a lion broke through the front line of the queen's guard, creating a wedge-shaped opening that nearby rebels and demons quickly took advantage of. Iselle darted for an open space, slashing out at one of the city guards with a move that looked fairly proficient to my untrained eye. The fae fell and I jumped over his body, trying to keep up with Iselle.

So far I hadn't killed anything. Which was okay. I was saving my killing for the queen, and I was focused on keeping Iselle alive so she could take the throne when this was all over. If she wanted it, that is.

Shadows shifted along the city walls and the ground, extending and widening. Iselle kept running forward, heading for the gate and right toward one of the shadows. I put on a burst of speed and tackled her as the shadow fae wound its narrow arms around her legs. The girl screamed. Grabbing the dark limbs with my personal energy I did the only thing I knew that worked on these fuckers—I devoured.

Iselle and I bounced onto a sunlit section of ground. I helped her up, noting the long burn-marks on her pants and the smell of blistered skin. Spinning around, I tried to summon my sword, cursing when once more it didn't appear.

Aerie. I hated this damned place.

Four of the shades detached from the shadows and came toward us. I'd managed to devour one, and thought I might be able to take out a second one before I started puking. That would leave two—more than enough to kill both Iselle and me. And the additional shades rising from the ground and separating from the walls were probably enough to kill most of the demons and fae fighting on our side.

I moved to grab the closest shadow fae, and jumped aside just in time to avoid getting hit by a ball of white fire. It missed me and hit the shade, which died in a burst of onyx smoke. Turning I saw Iselle, lobbing balls of fire at the shadow fae with surprising accuracy.

"I've got these," she shouted to me. "Get to the palace. I'll catch up."

I hesitated, then saw her take out four more shades— one of which had just grabbed Lynst by the arm. He spun around, eyeing her with astonishment. I bit back a grin, and ran for the city gates, realizing that the teenager who'd spent most of her life as a deer had matured significantly in the past few weeks.

Groups of rebels and demons had managed to make it inside the city before me and were steadily pushing the guards backward down the main street with their attacks.

Frightened faces looked out of windows, but no one ran from their houses or businesses to assist either side. Instead I saw doors being shut and bolted, and curtains being drawn. A colorful haze flashed up around several buildings as fae set their wards and hunkered down to wait for the outcome of what must have seemed to be a lifetime of endless battle. The Unseelie had never made it this far into the Seelie kingdom, but a good number of these people must have remembered a similar fight when the previous queen and her family lost their lives, and a new queen took the throne.

Hopefully this would be the last time they saw this bloodshed. I liked a good fight as well as any demon, and I wasn't particularly fond of Aerie, but these fae deserved to live the rest of their lives in peace. And hopefully prosperity.

Since I didn't care about fighting city guards, I darted down an alleyway, through a backyard, and then into a house, trying to placate the screaming residents as I raced out a side door. I kept on trespassing and invading various homes and businesses until I was far enough inside the city to reach the palace unaccosted.

Okay, so "unaccosted" was an exaggeration. I had to do a lot of sneaking around, and Own five Seelie guards before I managed to make my way into the delivery door of the palace.

The kitchen and other servants' areas were eerily vacant. I resisted the urge to make a detour to the wine room, and instead accessed the memories of that dude who'd been screwing one of the queen's ladies-in-waiting, so I could figure out how to get to her private chambers. I doubt she realized exactly how I knew the layout of the palace, but clearly she must have known I was working off a map or something, because the place had changed since I'd been here last. The ballroom wasn't where it was before, and after the sixth time seeing a statue of a naked fairy mid-dance step, I realized that I'd been circling around the same set of hallways. Three more times and I realized that it didn't matter whether I turned right or left or went through any number of doors, I still ended up in the same place. None of the fae I Owned had any information to assist me out of this magical maze, so I went on impulse and began breaking shit —starting with that stupid fucking statue. Furniture and artwork I smashed into the walls. Doors were ripped from their flimsy-ass hinges. I flung the head of statue guy at a window, shattering the glass. Then I watched it nearly brain a palace guard before digging a divot out of the blue and green grass.

This time when I destroyed my way down the hall, the ballroom was where it was supposed to be, and the hallways were different. I looked behind me at the mess, and in front of me at the intact furnishings, and headed for the queen.

I'd assumed she would be in her private quarters, but no one was there, so I went to the room where she had a golden throne set up on a dais to greet supplicants and guests. There she was, crown on her head, jewels around her throat, completely unguarded on the huge, ornate chair. Deciding this was a little too convenient, I took a knife out of my belt and threw it at her. The illusion vanished, and the air filled with arrows and darts.

I waited for all the weaponry to hit the ground, then walked toward the throne.

"Sam!"

I ducked at Iselle's voice, an axe whistling right across where my head had just been. Kicking out, I nailed the guard in the thigh, then grabbed his soul and spooled it in. The axe fell as I Owned him, the fae's body following.

"Don't move."

Looking up at the unfamiliar voice I saw the Seelie queen. She was wearing loose pants and a long tunic of red with gold-embroidered thread in a leafy pattern. And she held Iselle with the girl's arm twisted behind her back and a knife to her throat.

I slowly stood, my hands held out to either side. "Let her go. Take me instead. I'm the one who's been a pain in your ass for the last few weeks. Trade her for me."

The queen laughed. "Why would I let the lost princess go when her life threatens my throne? Murdering her would cause an uprising, but for her to die at the hands of some demon? Or for her to commit suicide because her rebels were losing their battle? Those sad things happen all too often."

"She's just one of the random girls from the towers. There is no lost princess. She's an herbalist's daughter."

"An herbalist who used to work in the palace." The queen sneered. "An herbalist who transformed her 'daughter' into a deer using a spell crafted by one of the city's finest. An herbalist who was living in a house in the borderlands purchased with money that traced back to the former queen. Why do you think I bribed the Unseelie prison warden to tag her for the Wild Hunt instead of the convict who'd agreed to that sentence?"

But all those girls in the towers.... There was a reason she hadn't killed them and claimed a terrible accident, or suicide, or had them vanish with their bodies never found.

"Kill her and you'll be cursed," I told the queen. "The former queen spent all her magic on that curse before you killed her. You know what will happen if you end the life of the lost princess. You'll lose your kingdom, and your life."

"I'm going to lose my kingdom and my life if she lives." The queen laughed. "I'll take the risk. And if I die, at least I'll know that her line died along with me."

She sliced into Iselle's throat. I screamed and dove for them as the knife flashed. But just like with Lynst's knife in the forest, the queen's knife met an illusion that quivered and vanished.

I slammed into the queen, knocking her to the ground. As I wrestled for her soul, she stabbed me repeatedly with the knife. The pain took my breath away, and my grip on her soul slipped. Rolling, I tried to pin her arm or trap the knife with her body or her clothes, but she twisted, and ended on top of me, now stabbing my chest instead of my back.

The poison from the knife was spreading through me. Organs were shutting down. My limbs felt like cement. The only weapon I had was my ability to Own, and my ability to devour. Again and again, her soul slipped through my hands, oily and dark. I saw the sharp flash of teeth, the horror of her true form and ripped at her glamour, desperately trying to win this fight.

Fragments of the queen's memories flashed like a movie highlight reel before my eyes. My body was dead, and while I was as alive as ever inside this corpse, I could no longer keep my grip on the fairy's soul. I saw her stand, saw her true form clothed in the tatters of her beautiful glamour. I saw her lift the knife, beginning a spell that would end my life for good. I wanted to close my eyes, but I could do nothing in this dead body but watch the knife come towards me.

A ball of white flame hit the queen. And then another. And then another. She screamed, the glamour melting like wax. One more blast of Iselle's fairy fire took the queen's true form and shattered it into onyx fragments that disintegrated into dust before they hit the ground.

I wanted to shout with joy and relief. I wanted to praise Iselle, to thank her, to tell her that her timing and her magical ability were fucking awesome. But I couldn't do any of those things because I was currently in a dead body—a dead body that I couldn't even manage to animate right now.

"Sam! Oh, Sam!" Iselle bent over me. I could see the top of her head as she held me. I could hear her sobs. Damn it, if only I could talk, or moan or even wiggle a pinky finger to tell her I was okay in here. She'd seen me dead before when the Unseelie scouts had attacked us in the Emerald Forest, but she probably thought that the queen was powerful enough to kill me for real.

And she *would* have killed me if Iselle hadn't gotten to her first.

My dead ears heard the sounds of a ruckus. There was a rush of footsteps, and the clang of metal. Iselle lifted her head and looked over at someone.

"She's dead," the girl sobbed.

Dar's face came into view. Then he smacked my cheek. "She's not dead. Her body's dead, but she's just fine in there. Give her some time to figure it out and she'll be shambling around like a horror movie monster."

"Fuck you," I told him, except it sounded more like "Uhhh, uhmh."

Iselle squealed and hugged me, but Dar just laughed.

"We've won. The Unseelie attacked the north gate, and with that divided the queen's forces enough for us to get the upper hand. The city is under control of the rebels, and the remaining queen's guard are surrendering as fast as they can."

"Uh muh dummas?" I moaned.

Dar shrugged. "The demons are shopping. War's over. Time to grab some souvenirs before they go home."

Shopping. That meant looting.

"Ell tem to ech."

Dar nodded. "Two souvenirs each. Got it. Now get up so we can go home. I'm starving, and there's no way I'm eating any of this fae food. Asta will kill me if I end up a fairy's sex slave because I couldn't resist a sandwich."

"Caaant nee two rskooo dly." I struggled to sit up, slowly recreating muscles, tissue, and organs into living, functioning ones.

"Then meet me at the city gates when you're done," Dar said. "I'm going to go make sure your demon army doesn't strip the town bare."

Iselle helped me to my feet, steadying me as I purged what remained of the poison and once again clad myself in a living body.

Tilting my head from side to side, I cracked my neck. "You go check on the rebels and let them know that the wicked queen is dead. I've got a country music singer I need to rescue."

THANKFULLY THE MEMORIES I'd managed to grab from the queen as I wrestled with her included where she'd imprisoned Dolly Parton. Instead of a dungeon or another windowless and doorless tower, I found the woman pacing the floor of a luxurious suite.

She took one look at me and picked up a rather solid

looking candlestick. I remembered how kickass she'd been with a broom and that frying pan, so I held up my hands and kept my distance.

"Ms. Parton, ma'am. I'm here to rescue you." I placed a hand on my heart. "I'm Samantha Martin. The Iblis. The Ha-Satan. I'm a huge fan. Huge, huge fan."

Ugh, I sounded like a groupie. Which, I guess I was.

"Satan has come to save me?" She gave me some serious side-eye. "I think maybe I'll wait around a bit for someone else."

"Seriously. I know the former Satan and I don't have the best of reputations, but all I want to do is to escort you out of the palace, through a portal, and back to your home. I swear it on all the souls I Own."

She waved the candlestick at me. "You're not going to trick me or harm me? You're going to take me home, and that's it?"

"I'll admit I did originally have plans to kidnap you and hold you prisoner in my house so you could officiate my wedding to the archangel Michael, but when the fae grabbed you, all I thought of was rescuing you from them. The Seelie queen knew what a huge fan of yours I am, and was holding you hostage. I felt guilty that it was my fault you'd gotten taken, so I had to do something." I was babbling, a little starstruck and not sure what to do or say. I really did want her to perform our wedding vows, but after all this, there was no way I could kidnap her or make her do something against her will. I'd return her home, and then she'd be safe from both the fae and me.

Hopefully that Elvis impersonator was still available.

Dolly lowered the candlestick, then placed it back on the table. "Okay. I believe you. Which sounds crazy, but I really want to get out of here and back home. Evidently I want that so bad that I'm willing to leave with Satan."

"Are you okay?" I asked, still keeping a respectful distance. "The Seelie queen didn't hurt you did she?"

"Physically I'm okay, but look what that woman did." Dolly gestured at the shorn locks. "I'm pretty sure that's against the Geneva convention right there."

"Don't worry. We killed her," I replied.

Dolly's eyebrows shot up. "I think that might have been a little extreme, but I'm not gonna complain."

I stood aside and gestured toward the doorway. "Then allow me to return you home, Ms. Parton. After you."

She eyed me again. "Why don't you go first, that way I don't need to worry about having Satan at my back."

I MET DAR, Harkel, the demon army, and Iselle at the city gates. That's when I realized there was a flaw in my grand plan. Gregory had opened a gateway for us to arrive in Aerie, but I hadn't made any arrangements to get myself or this demon army back home, and trooping the entire army through the forest to one of the fae portals probably wasn't a good idea.

Luckily Lynst hadn't forgotten, no doubt because he wanted us all to leave Aerie as soon as we'd helped him win this war. The Seelie fae approached us from outside the city, accompanied by the Unseelie king.

"I hear you all could use a portal back to the human world," the king said, his voice cheerful.

I groaned, thinking that there would be another bargain I'd need to make for this favor.

"Free of charge." He smiled. "Well, almost free of charge.

In return for this transportation, I would like you to accompany me on our next Wild Hunt."

Hot damn. I'd been hoping to sneak along, but now I was getting an official invite.

"And there is an invitation I would also like to receive." His smile broadened. "To your wedding, which I believe is in a month or so?"

I could absolutely squeeze in another guest. Or two, or twenty.

"For transportation to the human realm via a portal of my army, my associates, myself, and Ms. Parton, I will accompany you on the next Wild Hunt and issue you and a guest of your choice an invitation to my wedding."

That weird chiming sound happened again. I looked around but didn't see any smoke detectors to malfunction. Maybe it was a bird?

Iselle reached out to grab my hand. "If you don't mind, I think I might stay for a while."

I bit back a smile. "To wear the crown?"

She wrinkled her nose. "To help stabilize the kingdom. I...I don't know about the crown. Even if I am the lost princess, I don't think I have the experience or the ability to rule a kingdom."

I hugged her. "Then stay. But you need to make sure you're back for my wedding. You and maybe a guest?" I purposely didn't look at Lynst.

"I'll be there," she replied, also not looking at Lynst.

The Unseelie king stepped forward, and with a slashing motion and a few words, the air was rent with a shimmer of light. The demons began to make their way through the portal. Once they'd all left Aerie, I stepped up.

"So I hear there's a wedding everyone's going to?" Dolly Parton asked.

I paused before the gateway. "There is. It's in Vegas and there will be angels and demons and lions and one or two dragons. There's an iced vodka fountain. Did I mention angels?"

"Sounds fun." I saw her nod out of the corner of my eye. "I hope I get an invitation. And I might be convinced to officiate if someone were to ask very nicely."

EPILOGUE

My wedding reception was in full swing. The iced vodka fountain was a huge hit, and so were the twelve Elvis impersonators that had mistakenly been booked. Each one of them sang a few songs, then hit the dance floor with my guests. Elvis was in great demand.

Dolly Parton had pronounced Gregory and I Angel husband and Satan wife, and was promptly whisked off by Gabriel and Raphael to talk about vibration patterns, the virtues of kale, and pancake recipes. My bridesmaids were looking fabulous in their gowns, especially Samael who'd gone completely Lady Gaga with his makeup and hair. He and the Unseelie king, whose name I still hadn't asked, were off in a corner, drinking shots of tequila.

Iselle hadn't brought Lynst as her plus one, but was far from lonely. She, Uriel, Leethu, and the two dozen other fairy girls had formed a conga line around the dance floor and were laughing as they moved in time to the music.

Austin and Karrae had been adorable as ring bearer and

flower girl, and my heart had swelled with pride to see Lux standing beside his father as we exchanged vows. The little angel had totally charmed everyone and was now making his way over to Uncle Gabe and Uncle Rafi, determined to see if Dolly Parton would agree to dance with him.

And Maitor. I adored Dar's newest baby, the first Angel of Chaos born since Ahia's parents had hidden her away in Alaska. The world had changed so much since then, and this little guy would grow up doted on by a whole host of angels and demons; free to be a little agent of destruction.

Life was good. Life was really good.

"Sam," Nyalla slipped up beside me and leaned close. "I'm not sure if you're aware of it, but one of the dragons ate a lion."

It was Prue, the silver dragon who'd been kidnapped by the fae and forced to guard the girls in the towers. She'd had plenty of fresh beef since her jail break, but clearly had come to the wedding hungry.

"She didn't realize lions weren't on the menu," I told Nyalla. "She promised it won't happen again."

Yes, it was a good life. And my honeymoon? Well, that was going to be the best two weeks of my very good life.

YES, there will be an Imp 13! No, I don't have a release date for it yet.

But you'll be the first to find out if you join my demon household and sign up to receive my newsletters at https://debradunbar.com/subscribe-to-release-announcements/

In addition to new release alerts, sales, and general mayhem, I plan on sending out some microfiction including

Sam's bachelorette party, Gregory's bachelorette party, Samael's reception playlist, the honeymoon, and the first Wild Hunt.

And I might just have to write Iselle and Lynst's story. Maybe.

ACKNOWLEDGMENTS

Thanks to my copyeditor Kimberly Cannon whose eagle eyes catch all the typos and keep my comma problem in line, and to Cover Villain for cover design.

ABOUT THE AUTHOR

Debra lives in a little house in the woods of Maryland with her sons and two slobbery bloodhounds. On a good day, she jogs and horseback rides, hopefully managing to keep the horse between herself and the ground. Her only known super power is 'Identify Roadkill'.

For more information:
www.debradunbar.com

ALSO BY DEBRA DUNBAR

IMP WORLD NOVELS

The Imp Series

A Demon Bound

Satan's Sword

Elven Blood

Devil's Paw

Imp Forsaken

Angel of Chaos

Kingdom of Lies

Exodus

Queen of the Damned

The Morning Star

With This Ring

A Crown of Imp and Bone

∼

California Demon Series

California Demon

Sinners on Sunset

Ventura Hellway

The Devil Went Down to Glendale

Route 666

City of Angels (TBD)

~

Half-breed Series
Demons of Desire
Sins of the Flesh
Cornucopia
Unholy Pleasures
City of Lust

~

Imp World Novels
No Man's Land
Stolen Souls
Three Wishes
Northern Lights
Far From Center
Penance

~

Northern Wolves
Juneau to Kenai
Rogue
Winter Fae
Bad Seed

~

The Templar Series

Dead Rising

Last Breath

Bare Bones

Famine's Feast

Royal Blood

Dark Crossroads

∼

∼

the USA
formation can be obtained
ICGtesting.com
041255151023
21LV00001BB/135